Herbert Kastle was born and brought up in Brooklyn. He has been an English teacher, an editor and an advertising copywriter, but he now devotes his time to writing. Mr Kastle is the author of many successful novels including *The Movie Maker*, *Cross-Country*, *Hit Squad*, *Dirty Movies* and *Sunset People*.

By the same author

HERBERT KASTLE

Bachelor Summer

WILDSIDE PRESS

To my mother

I am not resigned to the shutting away
of loving hearts in the hard ground.
So it is, and so it will be, for so it has
been, time out of mind:
Into the darkness they go, the wise and
the lovely. Crowned
With lilies and with laurel they go; . . .

From *Dirge Without Music*
Edna St Vincent Millay

1

I woke up and heard music. The radio was playing. I didn't know the time, but the sun was still in the windows so it wasn't noon yet. I felt a hundred and five instead of thirty-five.

I rolled over, closed my eyes and waited for sleep. It wouldn't come. I knew it wouldn't come. But I didn't want to get up. The thought of getting up made my stomach twist. And it wasn't the first day I'd felt like spending in bed. It was only one of many that suddenly appeared a few years ago – or was it just a year ago, or maybe six years ago when I got married? Or had it really started in the army, or before that when I was a kid? No, it couldn't have been when I was sixteen or seventeen. I'd been alive then, moving then, excited about things, excited about my future.

'Someday I'll be an artist,' I used to tell Dad. 'I'll paint beautiful things, and they'll be exhibited in galleries.'

Hell, that was ambition, faith.

So when had it started – the not wanting to get up, the not wanting to do much except sit around and watch television and wait for night to come and hope for night to come fast so I could have the excuse of mixing a few drinks without Ellie making worried faces? When?

The baby's voice came from the living room. She was asking what had happened to her aluminum dishes. I hoped Ellie wouldn't find where I'd hidden them, on top of the closet. I wanted to get through the morning without that racket pounding into my brain.

I turned over on my left side, listening to the beat of my heart. I didn't like it and turned back. I couldn't forget death and defecation with life pounding away in my ears. Heart pounding, pounding, and some day it stops. Sure it does.

Just like it was. And the briar pipe fell from his hand, and they gave it to me.

The radio blasted me out of my thoughts with a strident commercial.

'Ladies! Are you tired of that old vacuum cleaner? Do you dream of owning a new one? But new ones cost eighty, ninety, even a *hundred* dollars! You can't afford that kind of money, can you? But hey, listen here! The Trylon Reconditioning Company has a limited amount of fully guaranteed – '

I sat up and rubbed my eyes. 'Turn it down, will ya?' I yelled.

No answer. Water was running in the kitchen.

'Ellie! Turn the damn radio down.'

The baby came running to the door, pushed it open and looked in. She held a red wooden disk in her right hand and a yellow one in her left, and she smiled.

'Daddy, you're up?'

I answered the smile. 'Yes. C'mere and give Daddy a kiss.'

'No. I wanna play with my dishes.'

I sat there and looked at her. She looked back at me, her wide, gray eyes clear.

'You put my dishes away, Daddy?'

I wondered where she'd picked up that delivery, that intonation. From my mother, probably.

'You put them away, Daddy?'

Smart little sonuvagun. Two years old and knew everything. Twenty-five months old, to be exact. I understood every word she said. So did Ellie and Mom. Some people didn't.

'Where they are?' Debbie said.

'Where are they,' I corrected.

Her face twisted suddenly and the tears jumped from her eyes, literally jumped. Her voice rose in a shrill wail.

'Okay,' I said. 'Daddy'll get your dishes. See? Daddy's getting out of bed. Don't cry. See?'

She stopped crying. But I didn't want to get out of bed. I'd suddenly thought of Louise Gorden, Stan Henrich's secretary. I wanted to lie back and develop the thought. Stan was art director for all publications except the picture mag. He'd had three secretaries in the four years I'd been with Lobert Publications, and each one had been a pip. This one was the best, even though she wasn't really pretty. She made me squirm every time she walked by. She had a swing and sway, a hip movement, a shake of the breasts. She didn't seem to know she had it, but that made no difference. When Ellie and the baby went up to the lake this Friday, I'd have the apartment all to myself. A whole ten weeks, and all to myself. Maybe I'd be able to talk Louise into visiting me.

'Ellie!' I yelled. 'Ellie, c'mere for a minute!'

'Well, don't shout,' she said, appearing behind the baby.

'The radio,' I said.

'I turned it off. Anything else, master?'

'Yes, stop being clever long enough to get the kid's dish set from the closet. Top shelf.'

'So that's what happened to it. You hid it in the closet. And she was crying her heart out.'

'I'm a cruel and heartless father. I'm a monster. I admit it. Give her the dishes and close the door.'

'It's five to twelve. You promised we'd visit my mother.'

I looked at her. Her face was round and chubby, but still pretty. She was wearing a skimpy summer housedress that would make the delivery boys sweat – it showed everything. I'd had everything for six years. It didn't affect me at all.

'I'd still like to sleep.'

'You make me sick! Always laying around – '

'Lying around.'

'Pardon me, oh great brain.'

'Quite all right. Always willing to help out a high-school graduate.'

The baby caught the anger and irritation entering our voices. 'What Daddy said?' she asked Ellie.

Ellie waved her hand. She sang, 'If you're so smart, how come you ain't rich?'

'Because I married young and got myself a drag.'

'Because you're a natural eighty-dollar-a-week failure.'

I lay down and rolled over on my stomach. 'You'll whistle in hell for that trip to your mother's.'

'I'll drive over without you.'

'Good deal.'

'What Mommy said?' Debbie asked.

'I'll be glad to get away from you for ten weeks,' Ellie said.

'Okay,' I said placatingly. I knew she wasn't half as glad as I was. 'Okay, I'll get up in a few minutes.'

She didn't answer, and I rolled over to look at her. Her eyes had that thick, damp look. Then she said, 'We used to be so happy, Harry.'

'All people used to be happy,' I said. 'Time and tide wash happiness away. Enough time washes life away.'

She came to the bed, sat down on the edge and touched my face. 'It's your father. You were terribly hurt.'

'Yeah,' I said quickly.

10

'Twelve weeks ago last Tuesday,' she said. 'Almost thirteen –'

'Let's go somewhere tonight,' I said. 'A funny movie.'

'You haven't forgotten that Mort and Laura are coming?'

I looked at her. 'Hey, that's right.' I felt good. 'Hope we've got some liquor in the house. Stores are closed on Sundays.'

'You've got that fifth of rye.'

I nodded. 'Yeah. How come I forget these things?' I smiled.

She answered my smile. 'You get excited when Mort and Laura come over. You like them, don't you? It's nice to see you like someone.'

'I like everyone.'

She shrugged. 'You don't show it. But you show it with Mort and Laura.'

I nodded. Mort was a buddy. He was a photographer, and we had a solid friendship. A rare thing in my life.

'Want my dishes!' Debbie wailed. 'Want them!' She threw the colored wooden disks on the floor.

Ellie got up and walked around the bed. She picked up the wooden disks and took Debbie's hand. 'All right. Mommy's going to get them.' They left the room, and a second later those damned aluminum dishes began to clang all over the place.

I closed my eyes and tried to recapture the picture I'd had of Louise Gorden, but it was gone. I finally got up . . .

We visited Ellie's mother. It was a drag. I killed some time watching the Yanks lose the first game of a double-header with Cleveland, and it made me feel even lousier than before.

We got home at six-thirty, and Ellie went into the

bedroom to put the baby to sleep. I turned on TV. The second game was still going. I watched the last inning and a half, and the Yanks won two-to-nothing. It made me feel good for the first time that day. I loved those Bombers.

Later, after the baby fell asleep, Ellie made chicken sandwiches and we ate. By eight-thirty we were sitting on the couch, watching a variety show on TV, sipping highballs. We didn't say three words to each other.

Mort and Laura were coming at nine, which made it a nice Sunday. Better than most. Better than sitting in a lousy office, working on lousy illustrations for lousy magazines. But then again, the office had pretty secretaries, Ellie would be going away for the summer next Friday and maybe things would happen.

Hell, for a corpse I had prospects.

2

Mort and Laura came at nine-twenty. By ten-thirty, I knew the evening was a bust. Mort had a good time, but I didn't. I drank enough, but it didn't have the usual effect. Things had changed; I was forcing the laughs.

They left at two. Ellie fell asleep as soon as we got into bed, but I tossed around. I started to think of Dad, but managed to cut it short by bringing up Louise Gorden's image in my mind. Nice image. Very nice. Admirably suited for procreating the species, or going through the motions. Nice motions. Pleasurable. Only thing that made sense to me. That and baseball . . .

I left the house at eight-twenty the next morning, which meant I'd get to the office at nine-ten or nine-fifteen, which wasn't bad. I was supposed to be there at nine, but editors and art-department help drifted in between nine and nine-thirty. Of course, consistent lateness might eventually get me canned. I didn't give a damn.

I caught the West End Express on the elevated platform, entering the last car and moving to the very end. It was the least crowded section of the train, especially this late in the morning. Despite every seat being taken and the many standees, there was some elbow room, and it was a hell of a lot better than the rush hour.

I held on to the last pole, and a tall kid in blue jeans and gray work-shirt ran into the car just as the doors slid shut. He walked right up to me, turned his back and leaned against the pole. I had to move my hand because he was pressing it. I stared at the back of his neck and

13

wondered why his mother, or someone else in his family, didn't make him wash more often. Also, they could've taught him some manners. I had to move my hand again as he settled himself more comfortably against the pole.

We stopped at 50th Street, 45th Street, 9th Avenue and then went underground. I closed my eyes and thought of last night. I had no desire to see Mort any more. Buddies one minute, nothing the next. And he was the last real friend I had. There were people I spoke to in the apartment house, and my old-neighborhood friends Irv, Joe and Warren still phoned occasionally. But I didn't go places with any of them. Also, my brother-in-law was around once in a while, and I saw him at Ellie's mother's house, but that wasn't anything. And my sister lived in Philly. So I had no friends, and didn't seem to want any.

I just wanted to go my way, somehow, and be left alone. Except for women. New women. Strange, exciting women. Like Louise Gorden. Exciting woman – or girl. Just twenty and not really pretty, but she had a terrific figure and dressed beautifully. Her father was well off and she didn't really have to work, but she'd tried two years of college and found it wasn't for her. She couldn't be called intellectual, but neither was she stupid. Just a healthy kid with men on her mind, with marriage on her mind. But maybe I could make her forget marriage for a while, though her manner was distinctly reserved whenever I tried to get personal. Still, she was lonely because the type of men she went for hadn't been coming her way.

Taking her features one by one, only her eyes held definite beauty – large, thick-lashed, light brown eyes, golden eyes. Her nose was thin and long; her face small and narrow with high cheekbones; her hair black and cut short; her lips small but with a certain sensuous fullness.

14

Yes, only her eyes were beautiful, but I liked her hair and lips too. She was five-four or five, full-breasted, narrow-waisted, with flaring hips, swelling buttocks and slender legs. Excellent legs.

The more I thought of her the more I felt she was the most attractive woman I'd seen in years. And yet I knew she wasn't beautiful and knew I wouldn't have gone for her when I was dating in college. Maybe that's why she was having trouble roping her kind of man; maybe kids couldn't see the unique quality of her face.

I made up my mind to ask her to lunch the first chance I got.

My heart began to pound; and then the kid leaning against the pole moved down, slouching, and mashed my hand. I drew away, annoyed. He slouched even more, and I began to wonder, and then he slid to the right of the pole and fell straight back, full length upon the floor of the car, head hitting the shoes of a girl sitting near the window. The girl cried out. I looked at the kid and wanted to move, and wondered why one of the other passengers didn't help him. His eyes were closed, his cheeks pale, and his facial muscles worked spasmodically. Epileptic, I thought, but then a great jet of vomit shot from his mouth and he choked and raised his head. He kept vomiting, splattering two people sitting near the doors, then fell back. The two people, a young man and young woman, jumped from their seats and brushed at their clothing and made faces. The other passengers, including myself, had stepped away quickly to avoid being soiled. At least twenty people stared at the boy lying on the floor, and no one did a thing. Of course, it had all taken place in under half a minute, but I was ashamed of myself when a short, elderly man reached out, helped the boy up and said in a loud voice, 'You all right now?'

15

The boy was white-faced, trembling. He nodded, cleared his throat and looked down at his filthy shirt and pants. 'Blacked out,' he said. 'Blacked out.' He staggered, and the short, elderly man shoved him into the seat vacated by the young couple. They were still trying to clean themselves with handkerchiefs, muttering to each other, not looking at the boy. I didn't blame them, but I blamed myself. Why hadn't I moved to help him?

The boy was sitting with head in hands when the train pulled into Canal Street. He got up and said, 'Got to get cleaned.' He stood near the doors, and no one looked at him except the short man. The short man said nothing more. The boy got out, and the short man and four other passengers followed.

I walked to the front end of the car, found a seat and sat down. No one here seemed aware of what had happened in the back.

That kid had been cocky and strong and ill-mannered in his taking exclusive possession of the hand-pole for his back. He'd been sure and aggressive one second, and a sick animal the next. Just like that – a snap of the fingers – and he was a prostrate, puking, helpless, disgusting animal. And that man I'd seen lying in front of the grocery store a few weeks ago – well dressed, shiny black shoes pointing up at the sky and sagging slightly outward. Dead. Dropped dead as he was on his way home from the station. Shoes pointing up and arms outflung, and a funny little smirk on his face. And as I watched, a cop covered him with sheets of the *Daily News* and he was a shapeless mound. Dead. Family waiting but he wouldn't come home.

And Dad.

I stood up, changed seats and waited for the image to pass. I looked around, read the placard ads and tried to push away the thoughts as I had for three months. But this time they wouldn't go. This time they stuck.

And Dad. Mom calling me to ask if I'd heard from him. He was late, so she'd called the store where he worked as a salesman and they said he'd left for home an hour ago. She was worried. And then the store calling me, saying Dad had been taken sick and the police had called them because of the number on his business cards and asked them to get in touch with his family. How sick? I asked. The worst, the manager answered, voice shaking. And I stood there and listened to the voice telling me where he was, and I thanked the voice, hung up and called the police station. Yes, he was there. Yes, Louis Admer. Yes, there could be no mistake. Would I come as soon as possible to identify him? It was raining, but I drove like a maniac, and Ellie was with me. We came into the station, and the desk sergeant pointed at a door leading to a center yard and driveway. Someone was lying on a stretcher elevated between two wooden blocks. Someone was covered with a sheet and I told myself it wouldn't be Dad, and a cop walked ahead of me and Ellie held my arm. He never had heart trouble, I said. Took a cardiogram two months ago, and it showed he was perfect. Sixty-two, but sound as a dollar. The cop sighed and reached for the sheet, but I didn't have to look. I saw the hat lying on the ground, gray, rain-splattered, bent out of shape. It was Dad's. The tears rushed to my eyes and the sickness struck at my chest, and I saw him as he'd come into the house for Debbie's birthday party just three days before. I heard myself arguing with him about some triviality, and I remembered how tired he'd seemed. The sheet was down and I looked at his face. There was a smudge on the forehead, and the skin was unnaturally pale, but otherwise he was my Dad.

17

So he was dead and a cop gave me his old pipe. I took it home, and that was just about all I had of him.

It taught me something. It taught me something even the war hadn't. I'd seen death during my stretch in Northington General Hospital. I'd been sick enough, with my twisted spine and broken disks after that training plane crashed, to fear for my own life. But at twenty-one death was unreal. At thirty-five death was quite real. And, after seeing Dad in that driveway, everything changed.

Full awareness of mortality, I called it.

But maybe it wasn't that. Maybe it was just that I'd reached maturity. Maybe my education and practical experience and intelligence had finally combined to create a purely adult outlook.

Maybe I was nuts.

The train stopped at 42nd Street, and a conductor on the platform yelled, 'Last stop!' I got out and walked up the stairs onto 40th Street. I hurried toward Fifth Avenue. I wanted to see Louise Gorden. I wanted to do something exciting.

It was nine-fifteen when I pushed open one of the double glass doors and walked into the waiting room. Audrey, the middle-aged switchboard girl, glanced up and smiled. I said good morning. She stopped me with a wave of the hand. 'Telephone message, Harry.'

I picked up the pink slip she shoved through the arch in the glass and said, 'Mean to say I got this call *today?*'

She smiled again. 'Some people get up on time.'

I laughed at her joke. It was my first laugh of the day, but it wouldn't be my last. I'd laugh a lot. I'd laugh at almost everything. It wasn't free, uninhibited laughter, but neither was it entirely forced. It was my way of staying sane, of maintaining normal relationships, of keeping my job. It was a habit I'd developed four years

18

ago on first coming to Lobert Publications, after doing free-lance art work for almost three years. Some people shriveled and grew morose under the daily pressures. I laughed. I was well liked in the office.

Only now I was beginning to wonder if it made any difference whether I was liked or not. Who the hell cared?

I read the pink slip. Mort Brenner had called. He would call back later in the day. I tossed the slip into a stand ashtray, went through the back door and into the hallway. I took two steps and opened the door on the right leading to the bullpen.

'Welcome, thrice welcome, poor man's Picasso.'

I laughed. Mary Braken sat beside the door. Her greeting was the same each morning. She thought it was the ultimate in humor. Mary was proofreader for the mystery and western magazines. Approaching fifty, she was fighting hard to appear younger and doing a pretty good job of it. She was married to a screwball who called himself a composer, though he'd never had anything put before the public.

I walked across the small section we shared, sat down at my desk, put on the fluorescent lamp. I took pipes, tobacco pouch and charcoal pencils out of the top drawer. I loaded a corncob, lit up, looked at the drawing board to my left. Work was waiting. I had to do some retouching of sex photographs for the men's magazines. Eleven shots in all, and they'd keep me busy until three or four.

I flipped through the glossy prints, turning them over to read the notes I'd penciled on them when Stan Henrich had given me his instructions Friday. The one of a big-busted Italian starlet made me grin.

'Too much nipple showing – fog it out.'

I puffed at my pipe, yawned and turned away from the

19

board. I looked through the glass partition separating Mary and me from the big room of the editorial department where four people worked – two facing the glass partition, two facing the opposite wall. Because of my centrally located position, I could usually see everyone's face.

Francine, to my right and facing the opposite wall, had her head turned and noticed me first. She was young, a proofreader who handled the science fiction, love and men's magazines. She nodded, smiled and said, 'Happy, happy Monday.' Her voice carried clearly over the glass partition. I laughed. She looked tired.

Moe Crown, the senior editor who handled our mystery and science-fiction books on the side, sat to my left, facing the opposite wall. He wasn't at his desk.

Curt Sawyer, editor of *Raw*, our men's mag, and our western mags, sat with his back to Moe, facing the glass partition on my left. He was small and pale, and he dressed in dark suits and bright vests. He fancied himself a connoisseur of wine and women, and was always bragging about the 'little doll' he'd dated the other night. He was fifty; a tired, lonely man who'd never stopped regretting his broken marriage. His wife had remarried and now lived in Los Angeles. Except for business, I rarely said more than good morning and good night to him.

Ramona, our short, thin, dark-haired typist, sat facing the glass partition on my right. She came around to my desk and said, 'Mr Sawyer wants to know if you'll have those photographs ready for him today.'

I puffed at my pipe. 'He could raise his voice and ask me himself.' I glanced at him. He had his head bent over a sheaf of papers.

'Yeah,' Ramona said. 'Anyway, he wants to know.'

'Sure, he'll get them. Only they'll come through Stan

Henrich, art department head. Stan has to check them first. What's he worried about, anyway? Doesn't he always get them on time?'

Ramona glanced through the glass, saw that Sawyer was still reading, shrugged. 'Miss Kearny came up from the ninth floor before you got in. She said something about your doing two sketches for the crossword-puzzle magazines. Mr Sawyer wants his work done first.'

'My, aren't I the important one,' I said, and relit my pipe.

'Mr Bottleneck,' Ramona said, and looked pleased with herself.

I gave her a big laugh; she was happy and scurried back to her desk.

I got to work. I retouched busts and buttocks. I was starting on the fourth photo when the door behind me opened and Moe came in. I didn't have to turn to know who it was; he walked like a triphammer – click, click, click, click! Fast. Aggressive. Always rushing. And nervous as they come. He had good reason to be nervous. He was sixty, the last of the old-timers, drew about fourteen thousand a year and knew his salary was no longer commensurate with his position. He was overpaid. He'd run out of magazines to direct and put together. At one time he'd helped turn out almost forty. Now he had a grand total of eight.

He came to my desk, slapped my back and said in a throaty whisper, 'How's it going? We need good illustrations. You get any good illustrations?'

'Good morning,' I said.

He was a short, thin, bald-headed man who wore double-breasted suits that invariably hung on him. He smoked cigarettes all day long, and coughed his guts out. He stared at me. 'Huh?' he said. And then, 'You think I was sleeping up to now? I was in Seldon's office. I was sweating, but good!'

Mr Seldon was our vice-president. He was a portly, stupid, self-important man who understood nothing about the history or traditions of magazine publishing. He'd started as an accountant, was still an accountant, would have liked to close out the fiction magazines entirely because they didn't show enough profit on his books. The fifth floor – the pocket books, movie magazines, confessions and crossword puzzles – were his babies. But the big boss, Walter Lobert, had made his fortune on pulp fiction and had a soft spot in his heart for it.

'We still in business?' I asked.

'Huh? Oh, you and your funny sense of humor.' He slapped my back again, dug out a cigarette and lit up. He coughed for a full minute and then gasped for breath.

'Why don't you give them up?' I said, as I'd said a hundred times. But then I wondered if my advice was any good. I'd given up cigarettes over a year ago, and I'd talked my father into doing the same.

He died alone on a subway platform and fell, and the pipe dropped from his hand and chipped, and they gave it to me. His favorite pipe. I gave it to him for Father's Day and he liked it best, always, even after getting the meerschaums and the two Wally Franks. I smoke it all the time, even though Ellie thinks it's something psychological. She's wrong. It's just a good pipe. But he could've kept on smoking cigarettes. His heart stopped, not his lungs. Maybe the change –

I shook my head and looked at Moe, and he was staring at me. 'You listening to me, Harry?' he said.

'Sure. You were in to see Seldon.'

'Yeah, Seldon. Stupid jerk. He ought've been around when I first started here. We'd have stuffed his ass full of

22

type and dropped him out a window. Damned accountant. A lot he knows. When Street and Smith was making millions, when we were almost as big as them, he was sucking his thumb. Stupid jerk. The women I loved were better men than him.'

I laughed, and almost meant it. 'How's that girl friend of yours?'

'Wanda?' He jetted smoke through mouth and nose. His words were wreathed in smoke. 'Hell, Seldon's a better woman than she is. I wish my wife were alive.'

'And when she was alive – '

'I wished she was dead.' He laughed, really hauled off and slugged my back. 'Harry, you'd have been okay in the old days. You think like we used to.' He turned, rushed around the partition and dropped into his chair. He was working before his fluorescent lamp flickered on. But he got up a minute later and came rushing back around the partition to my desk. 'Hey, you feeling all right? You don't look good to me. Stan Henrich and I are splurging on lunch. We're going to the restaurant-bar on Lexington. Martinis – two of them before we eat. Martinis represent the highest achievement of Western civilization. Want to come along?'

'I have a tentative appointment, Moe. If it falls through, I'm your man.'

'Okay.' His hand came down on my shoulder, but very gently. 'So that's the way it goes. You lose a father. Everyone loses a father. Everyone loses parents and wives and husbands.'

'Comforting,' I said, and grinned to show him I was kidding.

'Yeah,' he said. 'What I mean is, no use crying. No use whatsoever.'

'I agree. No use whatsoever.'

He blinked his watery blue eyes at me. 'No. I don't mean that. Life is good. Life is wonderful. You mustn't write it off because you've been hurt.'

'Who's writing it off?' I said, and wondered at his perceptiveness. 'I intend to stick around long enough to get a ten-dollar raise out of Seldon.'

He nodded. 'Sure.' He hesitated. 'I seen men and women go down the drain because they gave it too much thought.'

'Gave what too much thought?'

'Death. Don't give it a chance to work on you. Don't become one of those fools who support psychiatrists. Fight it out. You've got no God, okay. But fight it out. It's summer. The sun is bright. There's swimming and boating and fishing and all kinds of playing. There's your wife and kid. You're young. You've got plenty to live for.'

I laughed. 'What's got into you? You don't see me drinking iodine, do you?'

'There's other ways of dying,' he said, and he refused to stop being serious. 'Each man has his own way. You can die right here at this desk, and no one will know it. You can go on working for years – ' He stopped and shrugged. 'Hell, boy, you know what I mean.'

I raised my eyebrows, as if to say he'd baffled me. He went back to his desk. I looked at the sex photos and thought of what he'd said and wondered if I hadn't already died.

I retouched another half-nude Italian, and then the door opened and high heels clicked across the floor. I turned in my chair. It was Louise Gorden. She was wearing an outfit I hadn't seen before. Simple, really, but it made my pulse pick up speed. A pale blue dress with some kind of white trim, cut low and square, tight at the waist and flaring from the hips. It made her look like sweet sixteen, and yet she radiated sex – to me, at least. I said, 'Louise, may I see you a moment?'

She swung around and came over to me, body undulating naturally, suggestively. She was my candidate for Girl I'd Most Like To Walk Behind. And it was just as good watching her head-on. For the first time, I allowed my eyes to move down her body, letting her see me examining her breasts and hips and legs. She stopped close to my chair, looked at me and smiled nervously. 'I've got to deliver these cover sketches to Moe.' She shook the sheaf of heavy drawing paper in her right hand. 'It's for the science-fiction book.'

'This will only take a minute.' I lowered my voice so that Mary wouldn't hear. 'I'd like to speak to you about something important. How about lunching with me this afternoon?'

She paled. Her tongue came out and flickered over her lips. Her eyes fell away and traveled to Mary, then through the glass partition to the main room. 'But can't you tell me now?' she said, and her voice was husky. 'I mean – '

'No. Not here. There's a nice place on 40th, just a block away.'

She was breathing heavily, and then she smiled, still very nervous, and said, 'Why, Harry, what would your wife think about it?'

I shrugged, answered her smile and looked deep into those golden eyes. 'I don't know,' I said. 'I don't really care.'

She flushed. 'Maybe I should give her a ring?'

I lifted my phone. 'My number – '

She giggled, shook her head, stood there.

'Well?' I said, and I was excited and pleased at my

excitement. But, at the same time, I knew there was a difference in the way I was reacting to this situation now and the way I'd have reacted to it a few years ago. I wasn't worried about what would happen if Ellie found out. I wasn't worried about what anyone in the office would think. I wasn't worried about having Louise scream blue murder when I eventually made my play. I just wasn't worried about anything. I knew it wasn't safe to feel that way – like having your nerves go dead so that your body can suffer damage without the warning of pain. I knew it was what Moe had been talking about. I knew lots of things, but I didn't give a damn.

'Well, how about it, honey?' I said. I used the word 'honey' softly, with meaning.

'I really don't think – '

'Twelve?' I said. 'Would you like us to meet outside the office?'

She rustled the roughs and nodded weakly.

'You know the Turtle Club on 40th?'

She nodded again, eyes flying around to see if anyone were watching us. And someone was. Moe had turned in his seat. He turned away as I glanced at him.

'Harry,' Louise said, 'I'm not the type to – ' She didn't finish.

'Sure, honey.' I picked up a pencil. 'See you at twelve.'

'It'll take me ten minutes to get there.'

'Yes. Twelve-ten.' I smiled, reached out and squeezed her left hand. Then I let go, and she went around the glass partition and gave Moe the roughs. I saw him talk, saw her answer and give out with that high giggle of hers. Then she walked back around the partition, swinging along beautifully. I looked at her and smiled. She answered my smile, and there was something intimate about it. She went out, and the door closed.

I got back to work. I did two more photos, and then Moe was slapping my back. He looked at me, puffed at his cigarette and jetted words and smoke at the same time. 'That tentative appointment definite now?'

'Yes,' I said.

'Aha. Well, take it easy.'

'Sure,' I said, and went back to my drawing board. He stood behind me a full minute, but I ignored him. When he went away I took off my jacket and hung it on the back of my chair. It was getting warm, even with the air-conditioning. Next Friday was the 24th of June. July and August were the hot months. Ellie and the baby would be up at Sylvan Lake until Labor Day. I'd come up on week ends. I'd be alone in the apartment from Monday to Friday, ten full weeks.

I loosened my tie and worked fast.

3

My mother called at eleven-thirty. She sounded tired, very tired. She'd sounded that way since Dad had died. She said, 'I finally rented out the room. A young couple. They both work, Harry, so they won't be around too much. Thirty-five dollars a month. That means my rent is only twenty dollars.'

'Fine,' I said, and wondered what it would be like having strangers in my house. That's the way I thought of it – my house. I'd lived in the five-room apartment ever since I was six. But I hadn't been there since the funeral. I just didn't want to go there. It made me feel uncomfortable. I didn't have to go there and feel uncomfortable. I didn't give a damn what the neighbors thought about my not visiting Mom. She came to our apartment twice a week, and Ellie always drove her home. 'That's fine, Mom. How're you feeling?'

'I'm all right, Harry. And you?'

'Great.' I had nothing to say to her. 'Guess I'd better get back to work.' But then I was ashamed of cutting her short. 'Well, next Friday Ellie and the baby move up to the lake. Remember, you're going to spend some week ends with us.'

'I'll love it,' she said. 'But not until the middle of July. I got to get the boarders settled. Which reminds me – you're not really going to stay alone in your apartment? I know you said so, but now that it's been three months – ' She cleared her throat. 'I can cook your favorite dishes, Harry.'

'I know, Mom. I'll be over a few times a week for supper. But it's better if I stay at my own place.'

'Why?' She sounded anxious, pained. 'You ought to forget, Harry. Memories shouldn't stand in the way – '

'It's not that, Mom. I have work to do most evenings. I take home sketches and stuff. I need quiet.' It was a lie. 'But we'll talk about it again. Maybe after the first week or two – ' I let it hang there.

'All right. Whatever will make you happy.'

'Good-by, Mom.'

'Wait. I got a letter from Helen today. She says she's three weeks over her period. She thinks maybe this time it's the real thing.'

'Oh?' I hadn't seen Helen since the funeral, and I hadn't seen her before that for two years. Philadelphia was just three or four hours from New York, but neither of us cared to make the trip. Helen was a year and a half younger than me. We'd never gotten along. She'd always been boy-crazy, stupid, under-educated. She married a loud-mouthed insurance agent a year before I married Ellie. Ellie disliked them both. I didn't feel as if I had a sister. 'Sounds good. If it'll make you happy I hope she has triplets.'

Mom laughed. 'One healthy child will be good enough. How's Debbie? How's my *shaineh maidelleh?*'

'Your beautiful girl is fine.'

'She eat her breakfast?'

'Yes. Say, Mom, I got some work to do.'

'All right, Harry. And please think about what I said. It would be nice having you with me this summer.'

'Okay. I'll think about it.'

We hung up. I looked at the drawing board, and the phone rang again. It was Mort Brenner. 'Hey,' he said, 'you weren't with it last night. Got the blues?'

'Sort of,' I said. 'Look, Mort, could I call you back later? I've got an early luncheon date.'

'Sure. But what I've got to say won't take long. Ran into a little gal I used to know. We got to talking, and she mentioned that she loves science fiction – reads it all the time, even tries to write it.'

'Ah me,' I said.

He laughed. 'Wait'll you see her. She used to model. Works as a secretary in a TV studio now. And when I told her I had a friend who knew a science-fiction editor, she flipped. So I halfway promised I'd give you a ring and set her up. Her name's Terry Drego. Tall, blonde, terrific. She'll call sometime this week. See the pretty baby, won't you, Harry? You won't be sorry.'

'How come you didn't mention her last night?'

'Are you kidding? With the balls-and-chains present?'

'Okay, okay. I suppose she'll bring some of her writing along?'

'Sure. Has typewriter, will you-know-what.' He laughed. 'Just promise to give her stories a boost and you're in.'

'You expect to collect an agent's fee, Mort? In trade?'

'No, nothing like that. Just a favor for an old chum.'

'Okay, good-by.'

'So long.'

I got up, put on my jacket and walked out. I went down the hall and turned left, glancing at Stan Henrich's door to see if Louise was around. The door was open, as always, and Louise was typing away, back to me. Stan wasn't at his desk.

I moved softly, came up behind Louise and said, 'It's almost twelve, honey. Just a reminder.'

She turned, her eyes startled. I reached down and rubbed the back of my hand across her cheek. It made my heart pound. She drew back, face growing pink. 'Harry, I've been thinking – '

'No,' I said. 'It goes this way. Ruben, Ruben I been thinking, what a sad world this would be, with no blanking and no drinking – '

She laughed. I got out fast before she could start thinking again. I went down the hall, past the stockroom. Gil and Vince were lounging around, talking and smoking cigarettes. Gil was a tough kid of nineteen, short and broad and muscular. Vince was taller, two years older, just as tough. They came from the New Lots section of Brooklyn, and New Lots had changed for the worse in the last ten years. I got along with both of them, and with Sol who was senior man in the stockroom. Sol was thirty, ran the room on this floor and the one on the fifth also, though he rarely came up here.

'Wha hoppen to the pool?' I said, stopping near the open door.

'Nothin' happened,' Vince said. 'I was around early this morning. You wasn't at your desk. Wanna pick now?'

'Yes.' I walked into the room and leaned against the battered table. Vince took an envelope from his shirt pocket and held it out to me.

'Three left,' he said, his broad, swarthy face set in its perpetual sneer. 'If you'd get up on time maybe you'd – '

He stopped as I grinned at him. My grin wasn't friendly; it was a warning. 'Don't annoy the executives,' I said, still grinning.

He shrugged and said, 'Pick.'

I picked a folded slip of paper, opened it, said, 'Cleveland. Not bad.' I searched my pockets for fifty cents, but couldn't make it in silver. 'Change a buck?'

'Sure.' He took my dollar and gave me two quarters.

He turned to Gil, who'd been leaning against the shelf-wall, watching us. He said, 'You should've been at the party, Gil. Man, I got looped on Sneaky Pete. It was some shindig.'

Gil shrugged and glanced at me, as if to say he didn't like talking while I was around. I said, 'Cellar club?'

Vince turned. 'Yeah. Happy Warriors.'

Gil said, 'My old man made me stay in. I had a fever, he said.'

'Fever?' Vince asked.

Gil shrugged again, contemptuously. 'I sneezed twice. Ah, I know he don't want me down at the Happy Warriors. He thinks it's something bad. He's been seeing too much of them movies about juvenile delinquents.' He snickered. 'Juvenile delinquents. That's you, Vince.'

Vince kept looking at me. 'Didn't I hear you was from Brooklyn, Harry?'

I nodded. 'Boro Park.'

'Oh. Nice section, ain't it?'

'Very. Before I was married I lived on East 93rd Street. Not too far from New Lots.'

Vince smiled. 'That so? I know a girl lives on 91st, near Kings Highway. Hey, you did all right, didn't you? I mean, college and all that.'

'The GI Bill. I gave the army four years of my life; they gave me four years of education.'

'Good deal,' Vince said, but he didn't seem to mean it.

I waved my hand, went out the back door and walked to the elevators. When I got downstairs I crossed Fifth and walked west half a block.

The blue canopy had *Turtle Club* stenciled in white letters across its sides. I stepped into a doorway to light a cigarillo. As I blew out the match Louise Gorden walked past me. I took two long strides and was beside her. 'Hi, sugar,' I said.

Her head jerked around and she said, 'Oh, Harry, you frightened me!'

'Why? Don't men ever speak to you on the street?'

'Well, yes – but not nice men.' She smiled, but she wasn't at ease. 'I mean, I'm not used to having them come up to me like – ' She didn't complete her statement. She left sentences hanging in mid-air quite often. It seemed to indicate lack of confidence, nervousness, general unease with people.

I put my right hand on her arm, my fingers pressing the soft, smooth flesh. Her arm tightened, and she managed to pull it away as we turned under the blue canopy. She glanced around nervously.

'We're just having lunch,' I said, wondering why I wasn't annoyed, why I wasn't wearied by her juvenile approach. 'It's not as if we were sneaking into a hotel.'

She turned startled eyes on me, giggled once, said, 'It's just that people talk. Not that there's anything to talk about – '

'Yet,' I said.

She giggled again. I pushed open the glass door, and she moved past me. I watched the way her bottom managed to shape itself against that full lower part of her dress. I kept watching as I followed her down a passageway to the entrance of a small, square room jammed with tables. The headwaiter met us and said, 'Two?'

I said, 'Yes. Upstairs.'

He nodded and motioned us to follow him, and Louise dropped back. 'It's very expensive here,' she whispered. 'I was here once before, with a boy, and he paid twenty dollars just for dinner and a few drinks. I don't want you to spend – ' Another hanging sentence.

'It's all right,' I murmured, and understood perfectly. She was refusing my mink coat, ermine wrap, diamond tiara. I couldn't buy her with expensive presents.

I wondered even more at my acceptance of her childish personality. Hell, it made me feel positively evil to be out with this kid. And I liked the feeling. It cut through the beating of my heart and the dull despair and the memories of death. I wanted to reach out and pat her bottom and see what would happen. I contented myself with putting my arm around her shoulders as we moved past the bar and up a spiral flight of stairs. I squeezed hard and put my face close to her black hair. She said, 'Harry, please – '

I squeezed again and let her go as we reached the second floor and the oval, candle-lit dining room. There weren't more than ten tables, and only four were occupied. The headwaiter led us to the north wall and a tiny table set near the huge fireplace. During winter, the fireplace was kept in use throughout serving hours. Now, air-conditioning hummed, and the room was cool and pleasant.

'It's nice here,' Louise whispered. 'I didn't know they had an upstairs room.'

'Few people do. That's why it's nice.'

The headwaiter pulled out the table and Louise slid onto the wall-bench; he moved the table back into place and I took the chair facing her. The headwaiter stepped away, and a white-coated bus boy placed water and silver and napkins before us. I moved my chair and shifted weight, and my right knee found Louise's knees. She didn't move. I puffed on my cigarillo, and a waiter walked up and said, 'Order, sir?'

'Two Martinis,' I said.

Louise looked as if she wanted to correct me, but the waiter moved away.

'I drink Pink Ladies,' she said, and smiled apologetically. 'I don't think I like Martinis.'

'Well, try it this once.'

'All right.' She began examining the other people.

I looked at her hands, lying still and flat on the tablecloth. They were large hands, as large as my own, but smooth and white and evenly proportioned. They couldn't be called beautiful hands, and yet they excited me. They looked strong, and I could visualize them moving over my body. Gently, softly, exploring me and exciting me. I thought of them reaching down to take hold of me. Stroking and squeezing.

My mouth went dry. I reached out and took her left hand in both of mine. 'Louise,' I said, 'I've wanted to speak to you for a long time. I've wanted to tell you how much I liked you, how attractive you are – ' I stopped. I was amazed at myself. I was floundering, almost stammering, excited as a teen-ager. 'For six months I've watched you in the office, wanted to touch you, wanted to put my arms around you. Honey, I know you like me a little. I want you to like me a lot.' And I meant it. The hunger was overwhelming now. 'You're so damned pretty – '

'No, I'm not pretty.'

It stopped me. She'd stepped out of character. 'Of course you are,' I said. 'Why do you think I've wanted to be with you?'

Her face was pink, her breath coming fast. She moved her hand, but didn't struggle when I held onto it. 'I know I'm not pretty. You just like me.'

I tried to think of an answer to that but couldn't. The waiter brought our Martinis. I raised my glass and said, 'To a pretty girl.'

She didn't smile. She looked at me out of those big, thick-lashed, golden eyes. 'You just like me, Harry.'

'Yes. And I want to see you more often.'

She gulped half her Martini and said, 'I won't go out with a married man. Definitely.'

She meant it. I was trying for the wrong girl. But that was why I wanted her. 'Please,' I said, and put my glass down because my hands were trembling. 'Please, honey. Have dinner with me sometime next week. Just dinner.'

She finished her Martini, looked at the table and shook her head. Her voice changed, became cold and hard. 'No. Why should I? What's in it for me? I mean, you're already married, so what can happen?'

I picked up my glass, drank the Martini and told myself it was a dead issue. When a girl asks a question like that there's no answer. If she hasn't the answer in her own mind, if her feelings haven't told her why she's with a non-marriageable male, then there's nothing to work on. But the drive was still there, and I had to fight.

'Then you go out with a man only because he's a prospective husband?'

She thought that over. 'Yes. What else is there? I know the type of man I like – the good-looking ones. When one of them falls for me, I'll get married.' She licked her lips, looked at me. 'That drink was strong,' she said. 'I feel numb. My cheeks, my nose.' She touched her face. 'I'm not pretty. I hate my face. If I had a nicer face – '

'You have a wonderful face. Don't think that tooth-paste ads and Hollywood movies define beauty. You have a *different* face, and that's beauty hard to find.'

She smiled. 'You're not really my type, Harry. I like them shorter and broader. I like guys who're almost

36

chubby, but good-looking. And you don't laugh enough. Still, if you were single – ' She giggled. 'I'm hungry.'

'I'll order in a minute. First I'd like to know if you ever dated a man you didn't want to marry.'

'Sure. Plenty of times. Just dates. Just to kill a Saturday night.' Her speech was slightly blurred; the Martini had hit hard. 'Every girl does that.'

'And haven't you ever kissed them, petted with them, grown excited – '

'Ask a foolish question and you get a foolish answer.' She giggled and put her hand over mine. 'Sure, Harry.' She giggled again. 'You should see the look that came into your eyes – your face, too. You're jealous?'

I was puzzled by the change in her. The Martini had done its work, but she was showing a side I hadn't known existed. 'Definitely jealous,' I said. 'Because you turned me down, and went out with them. Why not go out with me, Louise? I'm just another noneligible male, just another guy you won't marry.'

'A guy I *can't* marry.'

I shifted my legs and her knees were there, and she didn't move them. I rubbed knees with her, leaned across the table and said, 'How do you know you can't?'

She laughed. 'Now you're getting a divorce.'

I laughed too. In some ways, she was quite a gal. She was a baby; she was also a shrewd, calculating woman.

'I didn't say that.'

'You bet you didn't.' She looked around, shook her head and said, 'Harry, I think we should eat and get back. Isn't it getting late?'

'Okay. But before I call the waiter, promise that I can take you to dinner next week.'

'Your wife is leaving for the country, isn't she? Next week?'

'Yes. I told you about it some time ago.'

'Yes. And so you want some fun.' She was still smiling, but her eyes were down and I suddenly wished I could see them.

'Okay, so I want some fun. But not just with anyone. With you. And dinner and dancing would be enough, if you wanted it that way.' It was a lie, but a small one.

She kept looking down. I held her hand and stroked the smooth flesh and waited. 'All right,' she said. 'Next week. Dinner. Just once.'

I raised her hand and kissed it. Her lips parted, and she looked at me and said, 'You're sweet, Harry.'

The waiter came to the table without my calling him. Louise mumbled over her menu, saying something about a sandwich. I knew I'd pay out more than I could afford, but I told her the brisket of beef *au jus* was terrific. We both ordered it, and ate quickly and silently. When we stood up to leave I pulled the table away, and she had to squeeze by me. I leaned forward; her breasts and stomach and thighs brushed my body. I gripped her arms, bent my mouth to her hair. 'Honey,' I whispered, the fire rising in me.

She stopped for a second, then pushed me away. 'Don't, Harry.' It was said thoughtfully. 'Please.'

We came into the street, and after the air-conditioned dimness it was hot and glaring-bright. We walked to the building and rode the elevator to the nineteenth floor and got off. She said, 'Good-by,' and moved toward the back door.

I said, 'When, Louise?'

She stopped and turned her head. She smiled in a strange way, as if she were thinking of something that had happened a long time ago. 'I'll let you know.'

'I'll be going up to the country Friday nights and coming back Monday mornings.'

She nodded. 'I know. Monday to Thursday are my visiting hours.'

'Listen, I can always take a week end – '

'Only kidding,' she said, and laughed and walked around the corner. I heard the door open and close. I went through the waiting room to the bullpen and got to work. I was excited. I stayed that way until Moe Crown called me to his desk for a conference on a new science-fiction cover. Then I argued with him, saying that shrieking nudes and bug-eyed monsters weren't going to sell magazines to today's science-fiction fans. We needed covers with a touch of artistic and symbolic integrity. Moe's answer was that our magazines had sold 300,000 copies per month ten years ago with the shrieking nudes and BEM's. Now our circulation was below 50,000.

We went through some rough sketches and finally agreed on one. Moe took the sketch, stood up and said, 'I'll bring it into Stan Henrich.'

'Let me do it,' I said. 'I want to discuss the colors – '

He grinned. 'You want to look at Louise.'

'You're right,' I said, and took the sketch from him and walked away. I went to Henrich's office and gave him the sketch and talked about using pastels for a change. He nodded and said he'd try it, taking into consideration the way pale green and blue reproduced. All the time he talked I looked at Louise. She never stopped typing for a minute; she didn't glance at me once.

When I got back to my desk I was thinking of her. I was thinking of her face and figure and healthy coloring. I kept thinking of her while finishing the retouching and while doing the two sketches for the crossword-puzzle book. Then it was five o'clock, and I cleared my desk and went into the hall. Curt Sawyer was waiting near the elevators, and he nodded at me. I answered the nod, walked up to him and looked around. Mary Braken was there, talking to someone from the movie magazines, a tired-looking woman of forty or so.

The down-lights flashed red five or six times, but no car stopped at our floor. Then Louise Gorden walked into the hall, and I smiled at her. She barely answered the smile. She walked to Mary Braken and the tired-looking woman and joined their conversation.

The snub hurt me. I wanted that girl to show some interest. And yet I knew it was her very lack of apparent interest that made me want her so much.

On impulse, I turned to Curt Sawyer and murmured, 'What do you think of Stan Henrich's secretary?'

Curt glanced at me, surprised, and then turned to Louise. He shrugged and said, 'Not bad, but too semitic-looking for my tastes.' He showed his teeth in what was supposed to be a smile. 'Kidding, Harry, kidding.'

Like hell he was. I could see the cold glint in his little pig eyes, and I wanted to dig right back at him. But I'd asked for it, so I pushed away the anger.

'Sure,' I said. 'But for an old semite like me she should be fine.'

He bared his teeth again. 'I didn't think you indulged.'

'Who said I indulged?'

He shrugged again. 'Well, a bachelor like me has to indulge. You should've seen the little redhead I met at La Vie en Rose two weeks ago. She was with some puerile Joe College, and when he went to the john I made my pitch. It worked like a charm, and she wound up with me an hour later. Don't know how she ditched the rah-rah boy, but she sure appreciated a mature man.'

40

He pursed his lips in a silent whistle. 'She filled an evening gown like a frankfurter fills its skin.' He looked at me expectantly.

I did what was expected. I laughed and said, 'Like a frankfurter fills its skin. That's good.'

He showed his capped teeth again. 'And was she friendly! We lay – if you'll pardon the expression – around my apartment until – '

An elevator stopped at our floor and I moved toward it, thankful that I wouldn't have to take any more of his humor. I stepped inside the car, edging away from him, and Louise was somewhere behind me. Just as the doors were about to close Moe came dashing down the hall. 'Hey!' he yelled. 'Hey, hold it!' He squeezed in beside me, and we started down. 'Ellie leaving for the country on schedule?' he asked.

I nodded.

'We'll have to throw a little beer and poker party at your place some night.'

'Sure thing,' I said.

The elevator stopped, and we got out. I glanced back. Louise Gordon was walking slowly with Mary Braken. Moe said, 'You getting a lech for that kid, Harry?'

I grinned. 'Don't be silly.'

'Uh-huh. How's your mother these days?'

'Okay. Recovering slowly but surely.'

'That's the ticket. You should follow the same – '

I didn't want any lectures, and he would walk me down 40th Street right to the Broadway entrance of the downtown BMT. He used the uptown IRT, 7th Avenue line, a block past Broadway. And he looked like he was going to probe and pound me all the way.

'Hey,' I said, 'I just remembered a damned good

joke. You hear the one about the showgirl who dated Superman?'

He gave me a hard glance, then shook his head. 'No,' he said. 'And it better be good.'

I launched into the story. I stretched it, adding my own pornography, and I didn't give him the punch line until we reached the BMT. 'So long,' I said, not waiting to see if he got a laugh out of it. I went down the stairs fast.

A West End train was waiting. I pushed through the mob on the platform, got inside and found a seat. I leaned back and closed my eyes and tried to think of Louise Gorden. But now I couldn't. Now I couldn't think of anything. The train began to move, and I dozed.

I woke up as we were going over the bridge. I looked out at the river – the gray water and ships and tugs. I looked at the skyline we were leaving behind. Great city. People coming from all over the country, from all over the world, thinking to conquer it. I'll conquer you, imperial city! The young artists, the young writers, the young singers and musicians and doctors and lawyers; the young people walking the streets and thinking, I'll conquer you, New York!

Big deal. Make a few bucks and live in an expensive apartment and think that's a conquest. Walk into a restaurant and have someone recognize you and think that's a conquest.

Big deal. One chicken heading for the pot says to another chicken heading for the pot, 'Say, aren't you Joe Blow, the great chicken from Des Moines?'

Or a conquest of true love, like in the movies. The boy gets the girl after much trial and tribulation, and they live happily ever after. Until she develops cancer of the intestinal tract and he has a stroke.

We left the bridge and went down into darkness.

Down, with the roaring and shrieking and grinding of metal. And that was nothing compared to what a sound it would be if they put all the human groans and cries and shrieks –

I couldn't take it. I had to stop thinking. Or think of Louise Gorden. But she wasn't anything now.

Death was everywhere. And death was all-triumphant. And wasn't it stupid to put off the inevitable – once you realized it *was* inevitable?

We came up out of the ground, onto the elevated, and it was bright and hot. People turned to the windows, like flowers to the sun, and smiled more and talked more and shut their books and papers.

I wondered why they couldn't see the corpses, smell the rotting flesh, hear the screams.

My station came along, and I got off and walked down the stairs to the street. I stopped at a candy store for a lemon coke. It tasted wonderful. I went home.

The baby ran down the foyer when I entered the apartment. She held out her arms and yelled, 'Daddy's home! Daddy's home!' I picked her up and kissed her, and she smelled sweet and clean. 'Had a bath,' she said. 'See how nice Debbie is? See, Daddy?'

I said yes and hugged her. I put her down, and Ellie came out of the kitchen, kissed me and said, 'I made pot roast and potatoes.' She kissed me again and we hugged, and then I went into the bedroom and took off my jacket, shirt and shoes. I had a wife and child who loved me; I had a job that paid for pot roast and potatoes; I was healthy.

Like Moe had said, a man could die without anyone knowing it; a man could be dead and work at a desk for years. I went into the bathroom to wash up for supper.

4

The week passed. I went to the office and worked at sketches and layouts and retouchings. Louise Gorden came to my desk on Friday and said she'd have dinner with me the following Tuesday. I said fine and tried to take her hand, but she moved away and never looked back. I hadn't been able to get a smile or any other sign of warmth out of her since we'd lunched together. She puzzled me, and interested me, when I could forget certain harsh truths.

Later on, at four o'clock, Ellie called and said she was ready to leave the house. She'd drive by way of the Belt Parkway and Brooklyn Battery Tunnel, and would be in front of the office building at about ten to five. I asked if I'd forgotten to pack anything in the car the night before. She said I'd left out a few odds and ends, but they hadn't been anything she couldn't pack herself. I told her I'd be standing in front of the building at a quarter to five so she wouldn't have to wait.

At four-thirty I went into the washroom and cleaned up. I came back, stopping in at the stockroom to check the scoreboard the boys had set up. Vince was there, working the stamping machine. He said, 'If Cleveland keeps up the way they been going you got a chance for low this week, Harry.'

'Two bucks are better than none,' I said.

'Sure. You should buy me a beer if you win.'

'Okay. I'll buy you a beer, and you take me down to one of those cellar-club shindigs.' I'd said it just to make talk, but when I saw him nodding I suddenly felt it might be fun. 'That a deal, Vince?'

He stopped nodding and said, 'You really want to go? It's nothing much – just drinking and dancing and, well, you know. Nothing much. Sometimes it gets pretty rough – fights and all. Sometimes strange guys crash in, and then it gets real bad.'

'Sounds like a ball,' I said.

'Well, your wife won't like it.'

'My wife won't be there. I'll come alone and have a few drinks and dance a little. Or am I too old?'

'No, sometimes older guys come down. My cousin, he's twenty-eight and he comes down lots of times. No, you're not too old. How old are you anyway?'

'About your cousin's age,' I said, and grinned.

'Yeah? Cheez, I figured you for thirty-five, maybe.'

'When's the next party?'

'We don't have it planned yet. The Saturday after this looks good, but it ain't set for sure. We got to chip in about four or five bucks apiece, you know.'

'Is it always on a weekend?'

'Yeah. Sure. When else?'

I nodded. I'd have to stay in town one week end when they had their party. Maybe it would be exciting.

'I don't know if I can get you in without paying the tab, Harry.'

I nodded. 'I was only kidding about trading a beer for an invitation. If there's a party I'll chip in like anyone else.'

'Well, okay.' He grinned, an unusual thing for him. 'Be your luck if we have a brawl. How would it look for the art man to come to work with a black eye?'

I grinned back at him. 'Or the stockroom boy with no teeth?'

He shrugged. 'Aw, you're touchy. Can't you tell I was kidding?'

'Sure. And so was I.' I moved to the door. 'Don't forget to let me know.'

He said okay, and I went back to the bullpen, put on my jacket and cleaned up my desk and drawing board. I walked around the glass partition and told Moe I was leaving a few minutes early. He nodded and went right on pasting up a western mag. I said so long to everyone and went into the hall. I walked out the back way, hoping to catch Louise Gorden alone, but she was typing and Stan Henrich was working at his desk. I went down in the elevator and walked into the street. It was a hot day – more like mid-August than late June. About five minutes later I spotted the green Dodge coming down the street. Ellie pulled up and waved and slid over. I got behind the wheel and looked at Debbie sitting between us and then looked in back. We were loaded to the scuppers.

'How'd she drive?' I said.

'Fine. I took it very easy. We'd better get going; there'll be plenty of traffic on the Henry Hudson Parkway and Taconic.'

She was right. But we moved along anyway, averaging about thirty miles an hour. Two hours and fifteen minutes after leaving the office I pulled off the Taconic and headed for Sylvan Lake raising dust on the dry dirt road. Ten minutes later we were turning onto a narrower dirt road, and then driving through the gate leading to Sylvan Lake Cabin Community, Inc.

We parked, got out and walked to our cabin which stood about a hundred feet from the lake front, on a hill. It was nice. We'd cleaned it up during a few visits in May. We'd brought up an old crib Ellie's mother had given us, some old dishes my mother had given us, and sheets and towels and other stuff. We were all set, as soon as I moved the stuff from the car. But I wanted to get into that lake first.

I asked Ellie to come with me, but she said she had to start getting things ready for supper. She asked me to move the cardboard carton of food inside the cabin before taking my dip. I did so, then changed into shorts and walked down to the lake. There were about forty cabins scattered over twenty acres of land; roomy enough for a summer colony. But not many people had come up this first week end of the contract season. I saw only four – an elderly couple sitting outside a cabin west of ours, a young woman in a red sun-suit rocking a carriage on the grassy decline leading from the hill to the lake, and a boy of fifteen or sixteen walking along the lake front. The teen-aged boy was wearing wet bathing trunks.

'How's the water?' I asked as he glanced at me.

'Oh, it's okay. Little cold, but it's okay.'

'Been up here long?' I asked, putting down my towel and moving into the water.

'Oh, just today. This morning. They don't allow you to come up sooner – not and sleep over. Today's the first day. Most people won't be up for a week yet. I been here three summers – ' He stopped as a girl of thirteen or fourteen came running along the shore. She wore blue jeans and a tight sweater, and she jiggled appealingly. The boy said, 'Hey, Arlene! Hey! I almost didn't recognize you!'

The girl slowed down, smiled and said, 'I grew two inches. I'm five-three now.'

'Yeah,' the boy said, but his eyes were more interested in her jeans and sweater than her height. 'Yeah. What cabin you got?'

47

They walked off, and then the boy remembered me and yelled back, 'So long.'

'So long,' I said, and felt the sting of icy water on my calves. I took a deep breath, lunged forward and dove in. The shock was something, and I began to swim hard to get warmth back into my body. After a few minutes the water didn't seem quite as cold, and I turned over and floated. I looked up at the sky, breathed deeply and wondered what I was going to do tomorrow and Sunday. Swim and play with the baby, and maybe play a little handball and tennis. That's right. What else did people do on summer vacations? What else was there to do?

Maybe listen to the ball game on the portable. Which reminded me that I didn't know how the Yanks had made out today. Which reminded me that they hadn't played today – they were playing Boston in a night game at the Stadium.

That was something. If I couldn't be with Louise Gorden Yankee baseball was next best.

I swam to shore, dried myself with the towel and headed for the car. I took an armful of clothing and went up to the cabin. Ellie said she'd be serving supper at eight – just twenty minutes from now. I made three trips from the car and brought everything to the cabin. Then I put on slacks and a polo shirt, stepped outside and watched the sky turn deep red and purple. Years back, a sunset brought me distinct pleasure. Years back, just being where the air was clean and there was a lake for swimming and a court for handball was enough to make me happy. Now I was worried about how time would pass up here.

I missed the office. Or I missed the activity that made time pass at the office.

I went inside the cabin. I got out the bottle of rye and

had myself two shots despite Ellie's, 'Must you, Harry?' Debbie was put to bed, and Ellie and I had supper. We finished at eight-forty and I helped her with the dishes, and then we took the two beach chairs outside, placed them under the low, leafy sycamore tree and sat in the warm darkness.

'Isn't this wonderful?' Ellie said, sighing. 'I wish we could live in the country all year long.'

I grunted. I'd once felt the same way – was it two years ago, or three, or before I'd gone into the army? Hell, I couldn't remember. But I'd stopped feeling that way. The country wouldn't make any difference. Nothing would make any difference. There was nothing to do, nothing to be happy about, nothing to make one forget the heart measuring out life in quick, deep strokes.

But the Yanks were playing.

Somehow, I didn't think it would be interesting tonight.

Was I losing taste for that, too?

Maybe making love . . .

I got up, went over to Ellie and bent to her. I kissed her cheek and lips and neck. She said, 'Harry, wait – '

I caressed her, my hands sliding over the front of her thin summer blouse. Her breath picked up speed, and I felt her nipples, freed of a brassiere now, become hard. She said, 'Harry, people will see – ' We went inside the cabin.

Ellie was getting excited now. She made a little moaning noise when I grabbed her and kissed her again, pressing against me. She had a nice body, this wife of mine. It had not lost its shape after the baby and now I could feel her breasts against my chest, the firm curve of her hips and buttocks as I stroked them. I pushed my tongue deep into her mouth, trying to arouse the kind of excitement I felt when I imagined doing this with Louise

49

Gorden. I couldn't. It just wouldn't come, not in the same way. I felt a kind of production line desire, the familiarity of this body producing a more or less automatic response. I was afraid Ellie would sense it, so I renewed my attentions, nuzzling her neck and fumbling with the buttons of her blouse. She moaned some more, pushing me away as she glanced towards Debbie's cot. Then she smiled seductively and backed into our bedroom, tugging the buttons loose herself. I eased the door shut, and when I turned back to my wife she was standing in nothing but her panties. I dragged the polo shirt over my head and kicked out of my pants. It was still light outside, but the trees dappled the small room with shadow, Ellie's pale skin patterned as she stretched on the bed.

I lay down beside her and put my arms around her. She kissed me eagerly now, her hands stroking my shoulders and waist and hips. I hooked a thumb in her panties and slid them down her slender legs. I was still feeling that automatic response. It wasn't Ellie I wanted, it was Louise Gorden. It was excitement, difference. I knew this body too well, had known it too often. I did my best to keep that feeling from my wife as I touched her with my hands and my mouth, feeling her respond. She was moaning louder now, becoming more aroused as I sucked on a nipple, my hand moving between her legs. I could feel her wetness, and I rolled on top of her before the automatic response was overcome by disgust or boredom or whatever the hell it was I was feeling.

Ellie's legs parted and she reached down to guide me into her. She was very wet, and she gasped as I entered her. She put her arms around me, holding me tight against her as she drove her hips up to meet my thrusts. I buried my face in her neck, faking passion, not wanting

50

to look at her. I kept my eyes closed tight, conjuring up an image of Louise Gorden.

It wasn't very successful – not for me. It might be the same way with Louise Gorden.

No, not the first time; not the first three or four times. That would be exciting. That would be living for a few sharp moments.

I showered and went outside and sat in a beach chair. It became quite cool, and Ellie brought out a sweater for me. We sat there until after eleven. Then Ellie said good night and went inside. I sat looking up at the stars and wondered if some extra-terrestrial race would ever come down and change our lives. I hoped it happened in my lifetime. No matter what they did, it would be interesting.

Hell, even being back in the army would be better than this. Anything would be better than this!

I sat there and fought a mounting panic, a mounting sense of utter helplessness and despair.

It was such a senseless existence.

The week end passed slowly. More people came up to the lake, and by Sunday afternoon Debbie had found a little boy friend and they were chasing each other over the grass. I played with them a while, and then a short, hairy guy in yellow bathing trunks swaggered over and said, 'My name's Leo Brun. That's my kid.' He nodded at Debbie's playmate, stuck out his hand and smiled.

I shook hands and gave him my name, and we stood there and looked at the kids. I'd been thinking of taking another swim, but Leo Brun seemed good for a game of ball. I felt like knocking myself out.

'Care for a few sets of tennis?' I asked. 'Courts are empty.'

He wrinkled his brow thoughtfully. 'Haven't got a racket up here.'

'You can use my wife's. It's a solid weight.'

'Well, to tell the truth, I'm not very good at tennis.'

'Handball?'

'Well, to tell the truth, it's a little early in the season for me. I don't want to get stiff and sore. Maybe next week end.'

I nodded, said so long, and went back to the cabin. Ellie came out of the bedroom and said, 'Where's Debbie?'

'Left her at the bottom of the hill with another kid. The other kid's father is watching them.'

'But they're strangers! They could walk off and leave her! How could you – ' She ran out.

I got into my trunks and walked down the hill. Ellie and the short, hairy man, Leo Brun, were chatting away while the kids fought over the ball. I waved my hand, gave them a wide berth and reached the lake. There were three women bathing near shore as I plunged into the cold water. One of them, a blonde with a year-old boy, really filled out her bathing suit. Every time she bent over I changed my mind about going back to the cabin. After half an hour she finally left and I did too.

Ellie and Leo Brun were still talking. I smiled and walked over to them. Ellie looked pleased; Leo dropped his eyes and looked guilty. He'd probably had a few naughty thoughts in relation to Ellie's well-packed shorts and halter. I spoke about the water being cold; Ellie spoke about how well Debbie and Leo's son got along together; Leo cleared his throat and raised his eyes and spoke to me about the weather without once looking at Ellie. It was obvious he'd been impressed with her, and just as obvious that she'd spotted it and was flattered. I asked him about his wife, thinking it would really be a laugh if he were married to that sexy blonde. He said, 'She's back at the cabin. We got up here just a few hours ago, and she's cleaning.'

I excused myself, saying I wanted to get out of my wet trunks. Ellie grabbed Debbie, said good-by to Leo and followed me. When we got to the top of the hill, I said, 'You've made a conquest.'

She flushed and told me not to be silly.

At eight-thirty, we'd eaten and the baby was asleep. We sat outside, listened to the portable and looked up at the stars.

Later in the season there'd be dancing at the recreation hall every Saturday and Sunday night. But right now I was bored. I was restless. I wished there was something doing. I thought of mixing myself a stiff drink, but then decided against it.

We went to bed at eleven, and the baby woke up four times, crying, belatedly reacting to the new surroundings. I was tired and irritable when I got up at six Monday morning. I ate quickly and was on the Taconic by six-thirty. Traffic was heavy. It was nine-twenty before I reached the parking lot on 39th Street, and nine-thirty before I got to the office.

'Hey,' Mary Braken said, looking up as I came through the door. 'You've lost your beautiful green complexion, Picasso. You look almost human now.' She grinned to show she was complimenting me. I grinned back and went to my desk.

As soon as I was settled Moe Crown came around the glass partition, jetted smoke and said, 'Got to rush out three black-and-white sketches for the mystery book. Artist we were counting on sent in such lousy stuff I'll swear he was plastered when he did them. You got to help out, Harry.'

I nodded. 'Sure. But I won't have time to read the crap. You'll have to give me a description of the characters and situations you want illustrated. And you'll have to go in and tell Stan Henrich. I don't want him thinking I'm goofing off on the layout work he gave me.'

Moe nodded, puffed his cigarette and began to cough. He coughed for at least thirty seconds, and his face was beet red by the time he managed to catch his breath. He made a disgusted sound, then pressed his hand to his chest. But he took another drag, went into another fit of coughing, and finally walked out the door on his way to Stan Henrich's office, still coughing and still smoking.

'He's killing himself,' Mary Braken said. 'He just can't smoke cigarettes – not with that terrible cough.'

I didn't turn. 'Yeah. But he smokes three packs a day.'

'God! Three packs – ' She'd have said more, but we both heard Moe's quick, nervous steps, and then he was back. He came to my desk, grabbed a pencil and pad, bent over and began to write.

I read as he wrote. He was outlining three black and whites he wanted. His outlines were clear, simple, precise. As soon as he finished, I said, 'I'll try to have them for you by quitting time tomorrow.'

'The latest, Harry.' He coughed briefly. 'The very latest. I'd really like them today – ' He choked, coughed and shook his head. He leaned against the desk, his thin body shaking, his face redder than any face had a right to be.

'It's about time you cut down to fifty-nine cigarettes a day, Moe. That sixtieth one is murdering you.'

He nodded, stopped coughing and caught his breath. 'Yeah.' He put his cigarette back in his mouth. 'At my age, what difference does it make? Get those illos done for me, huh, Harry?'

54

'Why shore.' I turned my back on him, set up my board, went to work. Time passed quickly; I didn't think of anything but the sketches; I didn't stop until I heard the sirens wail briefly for twelve o'clock. Then I stood up and went out into the hall. I looked in Stan Henrich's office and Louise was there, talking to a secretary named Helen Morrow from the fifth floor. I kept going and glanced in the stockroom and saw Vince working the stamping machine. I passed the doorway, then remembered the baseball pool. I went back. 'Who won the pool, Vince?'

He looked up, said, 'Francine Loes was high with Los Angeles. Stan Henrich was low with Kansas City. You in this week?'

'No. It doesn't interest me any more.' I went into the washroom and cleaned up. I returned to the bullpen and went around the glass partition, over to where Moe Crown sat facing the wall. 'How about lunch?' I said.

'I got to stick around till two-thirty,' Moe said without pausing in his paste-up work. He glued an advertisement into place on a dummy page of the science-fiction magazine. 'If you can wait that long, I'm your man.'

'Nope,' I said. 'I'm starved.'

Curt Sawyer called my name just then. I turned and went to his desk near the glass partition.

'You loused up those Italian starlet shots,' he said in a loud, nasty voice. 'You made one of them look flat-chested. I don't like it. Hear me, Harry? I don't like it at all!'

'Rough,' I said.

He jerked up his head and glared at me. His face looked tired, his eyes bloodshot. 'Rough? Who the hell do you think you're talking to? When I want a job done right – '

'You should stay home when you're hung-over,' I said.

'By God! I'm not going to sit here and take sass from a cheap – '

I stepped closer, leaned over his desk and murmured, 'You're a jerk. A stupid little jerk.' I smiled. I waited. I wasn't excited, I wasn't even angry. I didn't particularly want an argument; neither did I particularly want to avoid one. But I'd always disliked Sawyer, and now it just came out. 'What're you going to do about it?'

He opened his mouth, his face mottled red and purple. He worked his lips, and then half rose, fists clenched.

I turned my back on him. 'In the hall,' I said. 'I'll wait just one minute.' Everyone was looking at us. I walked by Francine and Ramona and grinned at them. They both dropped their eyes, faces frightened. They took it so damned seriously. As if a fist in the teeth was a big deal.

I walked into the hall and moved away from the door. I waited about five minutes; then went back into the bullpen. Curt Sawyer was sitting at Moe's desk, jawing away like mad. Moe turned his head, as if he'd been waiting for me to appear, and waved me over. I came around the partition and stopped at his desk.

'Curt says you're lacking in respect for the editors, Harry.'

I looked at Curt, who didn't meet my eyes. 'Fire me.'

Curt said, 'See? Now what can you do with – '

'Easy,' Moe said, and examined a paste-up critically. 'Harry, that photo you retouched, did you decide to fog the breasts on your own?'

'Who made the decision?'

'Stan Henrich.'

'And did he see the retouch job after you finished it?'

'Yes.'

'And did he have any complaints?'

'No.'

Moe looked up from his work at Sawyer. 'Curt, go fight with Stan Henrich. And remember, he's real close to the old man.'

Sawyer made a choking sound, got up and stamped back to his desk. I turned away from Moe, but he said, 'Do your baiting outside the office, Harry.'

I stood there a few seconds, and then said, 'Sorry, Moe. You're right, of course.'

He gave me a wide smile. It warmed me for a second, and then I left the bullpen. I walked by Stan Henrich's office again, and this time Louise was alone. I came inside the office and said, 'Lunch, honey?'

She was reading a magazine. She glanced up and shook her head. 'I'm eating in. Then I'm using my hour for a quick trip to Franklin Simon. They've got something I want.'

'And you've got something *I* want.'

She didn't smile. She just went back to her magazine and said, 'So long, Harry.'

It made me feel like an idiot. I tried to think of a reply, of a way to make her respond to me. I said, 'Don't forget our dinner date tomorrow night.'

She nodded and kept reading. I glanced over my shoulder, saw that the hall was empty, bent my lips to her neck. She jerked away, said, 'Maybe we shouldn't have dinner after all. Maybe you've got the wrong idea, Harry. I think we'd better – '

'I'm gone,' I said, and moved into the hall.

She shrugged and went back to her magazine, but her face was flushed and her tight blue sweater rose and fell rapidly. I walked away, annoyed, disturbed, excited. One of these days I'd have that little bitch begging for it! One of these days she'd do whatever I wanted . . .

But then the pangs of rejection disappeared, and I was left feeling empty. Why did I bother with her? Why didn't I just go along with my life as it was? What the hell was I looking for in Louise Gorden?

That night, I bought a complete Chinese dinner and took it to the apartment. I ate at the coffee table in the living room, watching television at the same time. Then I smoked Dad's pipe and felt myself getting tense, unhappy, tight as a wire. I got the bottle of Chablis and poured a water-glass full. I turned off the television and listened to some classical music on WNYC and drank the wine. I had a second glass and felt better. I went to bed.

I had a dream. About Dad. I was chasing him down the street, begging him not to go to work this once. I tried to explain that he would die if he got on the subway, but he wouldn't listen. And something stopped me so that I had to watch him walk away, his feet dragging, his head bobbing back and forth. When he got to the subway entrance he turned and waved at me. 'Good-by,' he said. 'Good-by, Harry. See you Friday. I'll bring a present for Debbie. We'll play canasta.'

I woke up then, and my eyes were wet. It was two-thirty. I told myself that tomorrow night I'd be with Louise Gorden; I'd be excited, competing, fully alive.

It helped drown out my heartbeats, and I fell asleep.

58

5

I worked well the next morning and finished Moe's three mystery-book illustrations by twelve-thirty. I brought them to his desk, and he examined them, smiled and said, 'Not the greatest, but they'll do. Thanks, Harry.'

I nodded. 'Okay. And don't tell me you expected the greatest from me.'

He got up. 'Lunch?'

'Yes.'

'Let's go.'

We went into the washroom and stood at the sinks together, and Moe said, 'About expecting the greatest from you – sure I do. Not that I ever get it. But I figure you're better than the work you turn out.'

I kept washing.

'Well?' he said.

I dried my hands on a paper towel. 'I never was any better than the work I hand in here. Never.'

'But your potential?'

'Who the hell knows, or cares? I don't paint at home. I do my work here, it buys the groceries and that's all.'

He used the paper towels and then lit a cigarette. He inhaled, coughed and said, 'Young fellow like you should have more ambition.'

We went out into the hall and over to the elevators. 'Written any good novels lately?' I asked, and grinned.

He coughed again, waved his hand, coughed on. 'Different,' he wheezed. 'I'm older. Different.'

'And when you were younger?'

He looked at me. 'I was running almost fifty magazines. *That* was my ambition, and I attained it.'

We got into the elevator, rode down to the lobby and walked out into the street. 'Automat okay with you?' Moe asked.

'Sure.'

We walked up Fifth Avenue to 42nd Street and the Automat. The hot-food counter was mobbed, so we bought sandwiches and pie from the glass cages, and iced coffee from the animal-headed spigots. We found a small table in back of the huge, below-street-level room and began to eat. Moe really wolfed his food; he was finished in about ten minutes. He lit a cigarette, looked around and absent-mindedly sucked his teeth.

'You're fast,' I said, starting on my pie.

He nodded and grinned. 'That's what the girls used to say. Ah, those were the good old days.'

I stopped chewing. 'The years went fast, didn't they, Moe?'

He inhaled smoke, shrugged, coughed heavily a few seconds. 'Yeah, I guess so. But I remember them all, and I know how they went. I have few regrets.'

I returned to eating my pie.

'But I didn't think that the years would pass quickly when I was your age, Harry. I thought of them as going on and on, forever. Correction – I got the grim outlook for a few days after my mother died, and then again, two years later, when my father died. But it went away.'

I nodded. 'And now?' I said around a mouthful.

'And now – hell, I might have twenty years more.'

'Or one year, or no years.' I didn't smile. I couldn't.

'True. But I don't think of it that way. I *can't*. If I could I'd probably throw myself under a truck.'

I was no longer hungry. 'Let's get out of here.'

60

'What's the hurry? We've got another half-hour, at least. And more if you feel like it. After all, I'm the boss.'

'Yeah, but I'd like some air.'

We walked upstairs to 42nd Street and around the corner to Fifth.

'Harry, you've really got to make an effort to stop thinking – '

I moved to a newsstand and read the headlines. When I stepped back to him I said, 'Any more illustrations coming up this week?'

'Listen, don't change the subject. You've got to talk it out in order to beat it.'

'You're dreaming,' I said, coldly. 'There's nothing to beat. I'm living, and I'll go on living. I work and watch television and enjoy all sorts of things. You're barking up the wrong man.'

For a minute his face showed doubt, but then he said, 'You're unwilling to share your thoughts.'

I opened my mouth to tell him he was wrong, but he held up his hand.

'I won't pry any more, Harry. Just remember that I'm a man who's seen a lot. Remember that I said it was dangerous to go on thinking the way you're thinking. It's dangerous because you might start doing things that you normally wouldn't do, things that at first glance seem only exciting and pleasurable. But they lead to other things, violent things, and you start treating your body cheaply, start taking chances with your life.'

'I've got to do some shopping, Moe. See you at the office.' I took advantage of the traffic lights and darted across Fifth Avenue. I walked west on 40th Street and wondered at his being able to read me so well. Except for that stuff about taking my life cheaply. I had no intention of subconsciously committing suicide!

And then the contradiction struck me – my intention wouldn't count if the suicidal tendencies were truly subconscious.

I stopped at a cigar store and bought fresh tobacco and a good panatella and smoked the long cigar on the way back to the office. When I entered the bullpen Moe was at his desk. He didn't turn, and I didn't go around to speak to him.

I was given some layouts on the crossword-puzzle magazines. The deadline wasn't until Thursday, so I went at it in leisurely fashion.

As five o'clock came closer I began finding it hard to concentrate on my work. Every other thought took a back seat to my going out with Louise Gorden. I tried to remember how she'd been dressed and realized that I hadn't seen her today.

At four-fifteen I got up from my desk, thinking I'd walk by Stan Henrich's office and look in on Louise. But I sat down again, telling myself I was acting the fool. I'd see her soon enough. I'd take her to dinner, dance with her a few times, and then drive her home. We'd have to take the subway to Brooklyn so I could pick up my car, but that was exactly what I wanted. Maybe she'd drop up to the apartment . . .

The excitement climbed higher, higher, and I day-dreamed of how she'd be in the apartment.

At a quarter to five my phone rang. It was Louise. 'I'll meet you near the 42nd Street Library about ten after,' she said.

'Sure. By the way, I didn't bring my car into the city. I figured we'd ride to Brooklyn – '

'Whatever you think best.'

I heard the click, felt chilled and wondered what sort of a girl she was. She'd showed interest in me at the Turtle Club, and was going out with me, but most of the time I felt as if she hated my guts.

I tried to shake the thought, but it lingered and I began to worry about the evening ahead. At the same time, my excitement increased. She was a puzzle, and a challenge, and a potential source of trouble. What more could I ask for? If anything could make me forget the steady process of dying, she could . . .

I was waiting in front of the library, scanning the rush-hour crowd, when Louise came walking up to me. I smiled and held out my hand, but she stopped short and said, 'Have you decided where we'll go?' She didn't smile. She didn't glance at my hand.

I nodded. 'Place on Lexington that has excellent Italian food and a small dance floor. Good band, too.'

'All right.' She stood there looking at something, or nothing, past my shoulder. She was wearing a form-fitting gray dress with thin white stripes. Her lips were bright red and her cheeks very white, very pale. She'd done something to her eyes – used mascara, perhaps – and they seemed deeper, larger, more expressive. Her shoes were backless, very high-heeled, extremely flattering to her legs. 'Well?' she said. 'Are we going or aren't we?'

I stepped forward, took her arm, said, 'Honey, what's wrong?'

She sighed and looked at me. 'Harry, you must have the wrong idea. I'm here to have dinner. *Dinner*, understand?' She moved her arm, and I let go.

I almost told her to run along home to mamma, but I controlled the impulse. 'Okay. Shall we walk single file or on opposite sides of the street?'

She smiled then – a brief smile. She put her hand on

my arm and we moved into the stream of people flowing along Fifth Avenue. Just as we reached the corner of 42nd I saw Curt Sawyer crossing Fifth, coming right at us. There was no way of avoiding him, and besides, he had already seen us. I turned my head and spoke to Louise about the Italian restaurant, and Curt Sawyer said, 'Good evening, Louise.'

She looked up and said, 'Oh, Mr – ' But he was past us. She shrugged. 'I hope he's not an office gossip.'

'Of course not. He's a friend of mine.' I turned. Sure enough, Sawyer had stopped a few steps behind us and was staring. When he met my eyes he smiled slowly, deliberately, and shook his head in ironic censure. I felt like going over and pushing his teeth down his throat. But hell, what could he do except say he'd seen us walking together?

We went to Lexington Avenue. The restaurant was almost filled, but we were shown to a booth against the north wall of the large, square room. The bandstand was empty, and when the waiter came to our table I asked about it.

'Music starts at six o'clock, sir. Will you have a cocktail?'

I looked at Louise. She nodded. 'Martini,' she said.

'Two,' I said.

The waiter went away.

Louise looked around the room. 'Nice place. Guess you were here with Ellie.'

It was like being doused with cold water. I began to wonder whether it wouldn't be wise to take her home as soon as we'd had dinner.

Then she stood up and said, 'Excuse me a moment, Harry.' She walked toward the entrance, and I watched her. Her body swayed provocatively, hips and buttocks

64

molded by the tight dress. I ran my eyes down her legs. Her heels, revealed by those backless shoes, got me. They were pink, the skin slightly wrinkled near the sole, and they lifted away from the shoe with every step. There was something intensely suggestive about their fleshy roundness, pinkness, up and down movement.

She spoke to the maître d', he pointed through the archway, and she walked from sight. I lit a cigarillo, and suddenly my feeling of inadequacy and defeat was gone. Louise had dressed up for our dinner date. She'd worn that form-fitting dress and those sexy shoes. She'd done something to her eyes. She wanted me to look at her, wanted me to be stimulated by her. No matter how she fought the feeling consciously, somewhere in her mind was the desire to excite me. And that meant I had a chance to reach her.

The waiter came with the drinks, put them on the table and asked if I wanted to order. 'Not right now,' I said.

I smoked and looked around the room and felt my heart hammering away. Only it didn't bother me now.

Louise came through the archway, and I watched her walk to the booth. I enjoyed every smooth step she took, every liquid roll of the hips. It was impossible to visualize a skeleton under that curved, solid flesh. It was impossible to think of anything but pulsing life while watching her.

She sat down opposite me and picked up her glass. I said, 'What shall we toast?'

She shrugged and looked into her glass. 'Happiness?'

'Yes. Happiness – tonight. Happiness for us, tonight.'

'Is that important?' she asked, eyes still on her glass.

'As important as anything in the world. Please believe that. *More* important than anything in the world, to me.' And I meant it, for the moment.

She raised her glass and sipped. I did, too. The Martini

was perfect. She kept sipping, and her eyes finally came up and touched mine. I looked into the golden-brown irises, and they were warm and inviting. At least that's how I felt. We sat there that way, glasses to lips, sipping the chilled, potent, gin-vermouth mixture, eyes blending, and we were suddenly very close. When I set my glass down it was empty. She was tilting back her head for the olive, throat stretched taut and white. I leaned forward, put out my hand and brushed my fingers along the side of her neck. Her throat quivered, but she didn't move away. She got the olive, lowered her head and put the glass on the table. 'What do you want of me, Harry?' she whispered.

For a moment, I wasn't sure I'd heard her correctly. 'What?'

She giggled, shook her head and said, 'Nothing.'

But I'd heard her, and I wondered what she'd meant. It bothered me a little. I asked if she wanted another drink, and she said yes. I beckoned to the waiter, and he came over and took our order. When he left, I covered Louise's hand with mine and said, 'Louise, I like you so very much. I have to say it. No matter what the circumstances, I like you so very much.' The alcohol moved through my blood. Louise's youth and strange beauty reached out and shook me. My yearnings multiplied, grew intense, and I squeezed her hand and looked into her eyes, and said, 'Please like me, Louise. Please.'

The waiter arrived with our Martinis and suggested we order dinner. I recommended the oysters marinara, minestrone and chicken cacciatore. Louise said it sounded fine, and that's what we ordered. After the waiter left we sipped our Martinis and looked around the room, and looked at each other. Louise's eyes were very bright. 'I like Martinis,' she said. 'I like you too, Harry, because you asked me to like you.' She giggled, drained her glass and giggled again. 'They work so fast – the Martinis, I mean.' She stopped giggling. 'I think I'm getting drunk.'

'Sure, and so am I.' Which wasn't exactly the truth and wasn't exactly a lie. Two Martinis always gave me a big lift. They must have really walloped her. I wanted to get up and go around the table and sit down beside her. I wanted to hold her in my arms and kiss her, and feel her body tight against mine –

I glanced at the bandstand, but it was still empty. Then the waiter began serving our dinner. Louise ate seriously, with obvious enjoyment, and she answered my few attempts at conversation with disinterested yesses and noes. Just as we started on the chicken cacciatore the band filed through a rear door and took their places on the stand. They tuned up quickly, and then went into a smooth, if uninspired, rendition of *Smoke Gets in Your Eyes*. Several couples moved onto the floor and danced to the foxtrot. I finished my chicken and pushed the plate away. Louise was still eating, and I curbed the impulse to ask her to put aside her food and dance. But I was shaking inside with anticipation, and it pleased me. Life was exciting at the moment, because of Louise.

Again I wondered at myself, wondered why I should want a girl so young, so difficult to approach, so far below the mental and educational level I admired. I looked across the table at her and reached for the answer, and for a second almost found it. But then she wiped her lips on a napkin, raised her eyes to mine and said, 'God, I'm full.' My thoughts dissolved, and I was smiling and thinking only of the dance-floor and of holding her in my arms. 'I'd like a cold drink, Harry. A Coke.'

'Sure,' I said. 'After we dance.'

She turned her head to the dance-floor and watched

the couples a few seconds, then said, 'I'm not so sure I want to dance.'

'Why?' I hoped she couldn't hear the sudden doubt and disappointment. 'It's a nice band – '

'Oh, it's not that, Harry. It's you and me. We're not on a date, you know.' She turned and looked at me. 'After all, you *are* married.'

I nodded. 'Yes. I am married. And you've known that quite some time now. And still we're here, and the music's good, and I want to dance.'

'Well, all right. If you want to.'

I stood up. 'I want to.' My knees shook as I came around the table.

She started to get up, then sat down again and grabbed a glass of water and raised it to her mouth. I was surprised to see that her hand was trembling. Ever since our luncheon date, when I'd shown her I was interested, she'd been sure of herself in my company. She'd seemed so cold, so damned contained by her little rules and regulations, that her being here with me had begun to mean nothing, had begun to seem the pure result of my forcing a dead issue. Maybe that's the way it actually was – but suddenly it didn't seem that way.

She got up and we moved past the tables to the dance-floor. I turned, and she stepped into my arms. My left hand held her right, my right arm closed around her waist and brought her close against me. She tried to pull back a little, but I danced backwards and dipped and tightened my hold on her. I felt her breath quicken against my neck, and my own breath quickened.

She was wonderful in my arms. She was curves and hollows of pure delight. She was sweet-smelling, soft to the touch, life and excitement and forgetfulness to me.

'Honey,' I said, whispering in her ear. 'Honey.' And

my lips pressed her hair, moved to her forehead. I kissed her briefly.

'Please,' she said, but the attempt at an outraged tone didn't come off at all. Her voice shook, and her movement to put some space between us was too weak to be more than token resistance. 'Please Harry, I don't – '

I didn't curb the fire rising in me. I danced, crushed her against me and put my lips to her fragrant hair. I danced and let everything go, and after a while she moaned under her breath and began to move against me. She wore no girdle. Our light summer clothing was the flimsiest of barriers. The music went on and on, and I felt the way I had when I was seventeen and eighteen. I wanted to look into her eyes, see the passion there, but she had her head down, her face pressed into my chest.

The music came to a sudden end. Louise jerked away and walked quickly toward the booth. I stood still for a few seconds, surprised at the way she'd left me. Then I followed. When I got to the table the band had started a rumba. Louise was already sitting, drinking from her glass of water.

'No more dancing,' she said, voice thick. 'I'd like to go now, Harry.'

I made as if to slide in alongside her, but she shook her head.

'No, Harry. I don't want – ' She left it hanging there.

I went back to my own side of the booth, sat down and pulled a cigarillo from my pocket. I lit it, puffed hard and said nothing. I didn't know what the hell to say. I wanted this girl more than anything else in the world. She was fire one second, and ice the next. But ice most of the time.

'Okay,' I finally said, and caught our waiter's eye. 'Okay.'

Anger must have showed in my voice because she looked at me and said, 'What's the matter?'

I stared at her. She meant it. She was genuinely puzzled at my anger. She felt she had the right to act any way she wanted to, because I was a married man.

I would never overcome her childishness, so why the hell bother?

But a few minutes later, as we walked onto Lexington Avenue, I once again realized that her childish attitude was the very reason I *did* bother. The challenge made me forget I was walking over generations of dead men.

We caught a West End Express. Louise said she'd been on the subway only ten or twelve times in all her life. She'd always lived out on Long Island.

We sat together, Louise near the window, and now she was talkative. I was content to listen to her chatter. She told me about her father and mother and older sisters. Her father owned a large electrical appliance store on lower Broadway. Her mother was afflicted with some sort of stomach ailment. Her older sister was married, had two children and lived in upper Westchester.

When she finished with her family, she told me about her high-school days, her two years of college, her desire to leave books and get into the world of business. And through it all came the picture of as uninspired, and uninspiring, a girl as I'd ever met. But it made no difference. She intrigued me.

It was seven-thirty, and still light, when we reached 55th Street. We walked down from the elevated platform to the street, and I was thinking that I hadn't planned this visit too well. If someone saw us entering the apartment –

But that was putting the cart before the horse.

'It's a two-block walk to my apartment,' I said. 'Like to drop up and see the place?'

She giggled. 'Got any etchings?'

'No, but I can whip up a few in a hurry.'

'No thanks, Harry.' She was looking around as we walked, examining the houses and people. 'This isn't what I thought Brooklyn was like. I thought it was – well, poorer.'

'Mean to say this is the first time you've ever been in Brooklyn?'

She nodded. 'I think so. Maybe I was here when I was a baby. My grandmother lived somewhere on Shore Road. But I don't remember visiting her. Of course, I've driven on the Belt Parkway, and that goes through Brooklyn. Anyway, I thought Brooklyn was sort of slummy.'

'It is, in spots.' I led her across 14th Avenue and away from the apartment house. I'd parked near the grammar school so none of the gossips would see us. If she'd been willing to come to the apartment I'd have taken my chances. 'Shore Road, though, is as nice as Riverside Drive.'

'I guess so,' she said. 'Grandma had plenty of money. But this is sort of nice too. Trees and all.'

'Did you expect me to live in a tenement?'

She giggled. 'I don't know what I expected.' She paused a moment. 'Maybe I didn't really think of you as living anywhere. Maybe I never gave you any thought outside of the office.'

'Gee, thanks.'

She shrugged. 'Well, why should I?'

'Don't start that again,' I said, and I was fed up.

'All right,' she said coolly. 'I won't. And don't you start asking me to have dinner again.'

'It's a deal,' I said, and stopped at the Dodge.

'Nice car.'

'Yeah, I borrowed it. Left my broken-down, slum-type, Model-T Ford back at the garbage dump.'

She giggled. 'Wouldn't surprise me.'

I opened the door and helped her in. I went around to the driver's side and got in beside her. I pulled away from the curb with a roar, and headed for the Bay 8th entrance to the Belt.

'You're angry,' she said, after about five minutes of silence.

'Not angry,' I said. 'Just tired.' And even that was a lie. Now that I'd had time to cool off I was sorry I'd snapped at her. The barriers were great, but my desire to play the game was greater. 'Do you blame me?'

She reached out and put on the radio, changing stations until she got a disk jockey and soft music. She leaned back. 'Yes, I blame you, Harry.'

I couldn't think of an answer.

We got onto the Belt. I stepped on the gas until we were doing seventy.

'You're driving too fast,' she said.

I slowed down. 'Sorry.'

She put her hand on my arm. 'We'll talk when we reach home, Harry.'

Her mood was changing again, and this time without the stimulus of alcohol. 'I don't think I should come into your house, Louise.'

'Neither do I. We'll talk in the car.'

My pulse began to quicken. 'Well, well, sitting in a parked car with a strange man. And it'll be dark.'

She hummed along with Perry Como. I put on my headlights and fought the impulse to speed again. The sky was darkening – the city on our left and the water on our right receding into shadows; the car turning into a snug haven of privacy. And, with the coming of night, Louise Gorden was changing.

There was an instant of clarity. An instant in which I felt all eternity pressing outside the car, howling for my life, Louise's life, everyone's life. An instant in which I looked at myself contemptuously.

Then another thought took its place – Louise Gorden was changing, but just how far would the change go?

That was at least as important as a malignant fate.

6

Louise lived in a new ranch-house development above Roslyn, having moved from Great Neck only a year before. I left the Belt at the Bronx Whitestone Bridge sign and used the Cross Island Parkway to the Roslyn exit. She gave me directions from there, and within ten minutes we reached her street. She pointed out her house and said, 'Drive a little further down to where they're building.'

I stopped in a pitch-black spot between houses. The night was complete; the sky overcast, the air hot and humid. I glanced back at Louise's home. It was large, and almost every window was lighted.

'Company, I guess,' she said.

'Looks very nice.' I had to clear my throat.

'Yes, I like it.' She seemed perfectly calm.

'I would too,' I said, and felt empty, afraid.

She hummed softly with the music.

I realized the engine was still running, and cut ignition and lights. I looked at her. She continued humming calmly and seemed to be a million miles away. The doubts rushed into my mind, and I didn't know what to do. 'Louise,' I said.

She turned to me – not just her head but her entire body – and her arms moved slightly. Suddenly, I knew she was waiting for me to reach out and take her. And I did.

'Harry,' she said, and her voice was thin and tight and nervous. 'Harry, you mustn't – '

It was so much easier than I'd expected. She was completely willing. Her lips opened under mine, her tongue flickered into my mouth time and again. And my reaction was stronger than I'd expected. I was wild with heat, wild with tenderness, wild with gratitude for the kisses she was giving me. We kissed for a long time, and I ran my hands up and down her smooth arms, afraid to explore further. Finally I moved one hand to her hip, the other to her breast. Her lips became softer, wetter, more responsive. We kissed again, and my hands caressed her, and the fire was white-hot. I began pushing her back, hearing my own breath rasping, hearing my voice repeating her name.

She resisted, and I put my lips against her ear and said, 'Louise, I love you. Louise, Louise – '

She went back slowly until she was lying on the seat, head propped against the door. Her thighs gleamed whitely, and her flesh was warm and damp as I touched her. She made no move to stop me, and I moved forward to press my weight on her. She murmured something that got lost under my mouth and allowed me to ease her legs apart. I felt the smooth, silky material of her panties. It was moist. I went on kissing her, barely able to contain my excitement as I gently slid my fingertips under the elastic of her panties. Her scent was sweet, and she shivered and seemed about to open her body to me.

Then she stiffened and shoved me back. 'That's enough, Harry.' Her voice was unbelievably cold.

'Louise – '

She twisted aside, sat up, straightened her dress. She turned to face the windshield and said, 'Please put on the light. I've got to fix my lipstick.'

I put my hands on her shoulders, unable to believe she

75

could suddenly, coldly, deliberately detach herself this way. She shrugged impatiently, slapping at my hands.

'It's late, Harry. If I don't get home my family will worry. Will you please put on the light?'

I put on the light and stared at her. She used lipstick and a compact mirror. She worked swiftly, closed the compact, picked up her bag from the seat and opened the door. 'Good night, Harry.'

I grabbed her arm. 'You're going?' I said stupidly.

She turned her head, looked at me and then smiled. 'Yes. It was a very nice evening. I shouldn't have let you kiss me, but thanks for the dinner.'

'Kiss you!'

She tried to step out, but I held onto her arm. 'Louise, wait a minute – '

'Now don't turn into a pest, Harry.'

I felt like a little boy who'd been slapped in the face. I was shocked and hurt by her chill tones, her sudden change. Change after change after change. And I wanted to crawl, to plead, to grovel and cry if it would bring her back to my arms. But I fought the feeling, ashamed of it, amazed at it. 'A minute ago you were letting me – And now – '

'And now you're acting like a pest.' She kept smiling. 'Ellie wouldn't like you to act like a pest, would she, Harry?'

Her smile, her words – she was deliberately baiting me, deliberately hurting me. I knew it, and that should have made me glad to be rid of her. But it didn't. I wanted to play along, wanted to feel the agony of rejection, wanted the shame and hurt and blocked longings. Because that was what she wanted me to feel, and it would lead to further meetings.

'Why do you treat me this way?' I said, thickness

76

choking my voice. 'Why, Louise? I could love you if you'd give me half a chance.'

'Good night, Harry.' Her eyes dropped to the hand holding her arm. 'Please.'

'All right. But let's have dinner again tomorrow night.'

'Tomorrow's Wednesday. I'm going out Wednesday night. I'm going to see a show with a boy from Great Neck.' She smiled again. 'He's almost twelve years younger than you, Harry. But he's still two years older than me – closer to three. You're fifteen years older than me, Harry. You could almost be my father.'

'You're sure of this information?' I asked, trying to keep my voice steady.

'Yes. I checked your personal file when I was down on the fifth floor. I've got a friend in the personnel department. So, like I said, you could almost be my father.'

'Sure,' I said, and I knew she was striking back at other men through me – men she wanted but who didn't want her. Single men, eligible men. 'Sure, I'm an old man.'

She giggled. 'Really. Thirty-five's pretty old. Another few years and you'll be forty.'

'Yeah, that's why I want to live it up now.' My attempt at humor flopped. I was helpless with this girl. Why did I bother with her? There were others – more mature, kinder. Why did I want Louise Gorden? 'Thursday?' I asked, and wondered at the depth of my pain, the extent of my lack of pride.

She moved her arm, but I held on. She sighed. 'I'll think about it. Now let go, Harry.'

'One good-night kiss.'

She shook her head, as if in amazement. 'And you're a father, Harry. Aren't you ashamed? Take my father now

77

– he'd never have run around like you're doing. How many other girls do you annoy, Harry?'

The extent of her viciousness surprised me. And the verbal counterattack that could easily have crushed her – simple crudities concerning her father, her mother, herself – just wouldn't come. I was going to hold onto this girl no matter how far she pushed me. I forced a laugh and said, 'I annoy dozens, honey. But you're lucky enough to be Number One. Thursday?'

'Like I said, Harry, I'll think about it.' She paused. 'But I don't think I'll say yes.'

I was very tired now, I let go of her arm. She got out of the car, shut the door and walked away.

I retraced my route to the Belt and drove home. In the apartment, I showered leisurely, put out the lights and sat near the living-room window. Lightning flickered weakly, briefly, in the east. The night was moist, heavy, but I was able to spot an occasional star. It wouldn't rain – yet. But when it did, the earth would grow muddy and fecund. The rich earth. The earth fertilized with rotting flesh –

I went to bed. I dreamt of Louise. We were back in the Dodge, but this time she didn't pull away, made no move to stop me. Instead, she helped me, reaching down to slip the panties over her thighs. She raised her legs to slip them off, and I saw the thick, dark thatch of her pubic hair.

'Now you can touch me,' she said. 'Touch me, Harry. I want you to touch me.'

I eased my hand between her thighs, and for a moment she closed them, squeezing. Then they parted and she moaned as my fingers found her moistness and began to stroke. She stared at me with those lovely golden-flecked eyes, her pink tongue flicking over the red lips. Then she pulled my head down and I felt her tongue probing deep into my mouth. I felt her hand slide down between us until it touched my crotch. My breath came faster as she began to fumble with the zip. Then my heart pounded forcibly as her hand closed on my erection and began to stroke.

She pulled her mouth away. 'I want you, Harry. I want you now.'

I took my hand from between her legs and rolled onto her. I felt the lips of her vagina moist against the tip of my penis. She gasped. 'Yes, Harry! Yes! Please.'

I pushed into her and she screamed.

I opened my eyes, and Louise's scream of ecstasy became the ringing of the alarm. I groaned, struggling with the sweat-dampened sheets. I had another day to face.

The next morning was hot and humid, and the subway ride to Manhattan was even more uncomfortable than usual. I came into the office at nine-ten, carrying my jacket over my arm. Mary Braken looked up from her proof and gave me the welcome-thrice-welcome routine. I laughed, sat down at my desk and looked through the glass partition. Francine Loes, Curt Sawyer and Ramona were at their desks. I nodded good morning to the girls, but not to Sawyer. He glanced away as soon as my eyes hit him. Moe Crown wasn't in yet.

I turned to my drawing board. There was a note pinned to the top frame. I unpinned it and read: 'Make up three double-spreads for western mag. First should have Apache Indians attacking ranch house in desert-type area. Second should have two cowboys – one blond, other dark – barricaded behind dead horses, firing down frontier-town street at villains in gambling-hall saloon. Third should show woman with rifle, standing courageously in front of a little boy, defending him against unseen menace off in distance. (Make this gal dark, attractive, somewhat sexy. Tear her dress, muss up her hair, etc. She's been in action.) Got to have this by four tomorrow, Harry.' It was signed Stan Henrich.

I crumpled the note, tossed it into the waste basket and pulled out my pipes and equipment. I was burning. Three double-spreads in two days! That was really pouring it on! Henrich could have farmed the illos out to free-lancers, or he could have given me the usual week. I wasn't in shape for tight deadlines. Hell, it wasn't fair.

I got up and walked out past Mary Braken, slamming the door behind me. I stalked down the hall and went into Stan Henrich's office. I was ready to tell him off, but he wasn't there. Louise looked up from a danish and container of milk. 'What's the matter?' she asked.

I took a deep breath. 'Nothing,' I said, and I was glad Henrich hadn't been there to catch my fit. He might have gotten me canned. 'Just wanted to see Stan.'

'About those double-spreads?' She smiled. 'I knew you'd love it. He messed up on his schedules. He was in before me this morning, trying to work something out to beat his deadline.'

'He worked something out, all right.'

She laughed. 'Yes. And you'd better produce, Harry.'

I sat down on the corner of her desk, my anger gone, my interest turned from work to her. 'Really? And if I don't?'

'If you don't, he'll get you blamed for the magazine being held up. I know Stan. He'll do anything to protect his two-fifty a week.'

'He makes that much, huh?' I said, but I'd known it before. I just wanted to keep her talking. It was the first time she'd relaxed with me in the office. 'Guess I'd do the same for that kind of money.'

She took a bite of danish, chewed, swallowed, raised her eyes to mine. Her face was composed as she said, 'You'll never make that much, Harry. You spend your time chasing women instead of trying to earn a decent living for your wife and child.'

I felt as if I'd been kicked in the guts, but I forced a smile. 'Think so? Interesting observation. Tell me more.'

'What more is there?' She took another bite of danish.

I should have walked out, but I heard myself say, 'There's lots more. Like telling me when we'll be going out again.'

She put down her pastry and giggled. 'You don't have any pride at all, Harry. God, if anyone spoke to me that way – '

'How about it?' I said, raging. And yet I was also dying to hear her say she'd see me. The more she stepped on me, the more I wanted to get her. 'Tomorrow night?'

She shook her head and giggled again and sipped her milk. I waited.

'Tomorrow is Thursday – ' she began.

'And on Thursday,' I interrupted, 'you have a date with a young man from North Islip who will take you to the Junior League dance at the country club and buy you champagne and caviar.' I grinned to cover the irritation, the frustration.

'No,' she said calmly. 'On Thursday I usually see someone, but he hasn't called this week. Mainly because I was mean to him last Thursday. But he still might call today. If he doesn't – ' She finished her milk. 'Well, maybe.'

I was suddenly very happy. No matter how vicious she acted, she *wanted* to go out with me! 'Where would you like to go?' I ran my eyes over her nylon blouse, which showed the white brassiere underneath, the full cups straining tight. 'Dancing, a show, a drive-in – '

'I only said *maybe*, Harry. Now you'd better go.'

The chill was on again. I shrugged and got off the desk. 'Where *is* Stan?'

'In the boss's office. Something about the last cover for the men's book.'

Footsteps sounded, and then Stan Henrich was in the doorway. He looked unhappy, his long, thin face set in sour lines. Louise immediately picked up papers and began sorting them. 'Yeah?' Henrich said to me. 'What is it?'

His big-boss attitude irritated me, brought back my anger at the short notice he'd given me on the double-spreads. 'I might be late with those western illos, Stan.'

He moved past me to his desk and sat down. 'No, you won't,' he said. 'You can't. They *must* go out. It's a deadline. Got that, Harry? A deadline.'

'I got it. But my hours are nine to five. If I can manage – '

'Now listen,' he said, leaning forward, face paling with anger. 'I told you what to do. Just get out and start doing it!'

I felt as if my head were exploding. And yet, at the same time, I knew I *wanted* it this way. I wanted things to fall apart, blow up, crash around me. I didn't understand why, but I felt as if it was the way things should be. I stepped forward, then realized he'd stopped talking and was holding up his hand.

'Hey,' he said, and leaned back and away from me. 'Hey, take it easy!'

I stopped and cleared my throat and said, 'I'll do as much as I can. As much as I can and no more. And remember, I got the notice this morning. This morning, Stan.' I turned and went out. I went back to my desk and sat down.

'Anything wrong?' Mary Braken said.

'Yeah. I got a deadline. No talking, huh?'

She didn't answer right away, and I felt I'd hurt her with my brusque manner. Then she said, 'Sure. Only ease up, Picasso. You're not your old laughing self today.'

I got my board set up and went to work.

Some time later, Moe Crown came in and stopped at my desk. 'I was walking by Stan Henrich's office, Harry. He called me in and chewed my ear off.'

I sighed, put down my inking pen and looked at him. 'So?'

'So nothing, Harry. You're losing your grip on reality. You've got to stop cutting your throat.'

'No lectures now, Moe. If you spoke to Stan, you know what I have to do.'

'Yeah. And do it. He'll calm down then.'

'Okay.' I went back to work, but Moe's shadow still fell across my board. 'Well?' I said.

'How about dinner tonight? And a few drinks at my place?'

'Fine,' I said, suddenly glad of something to do while Louise was out with her boy friend from Great Neck.

He slapped my back and went around the partition to his desk. I worked until Mary Braken came over. 'It's twelve-thirty, Picasso. Want me to bring you a sandwich?'

'That's a good idea, Mary.' I gave her a buck and asked her to get me a chicken salad on rye and a large coke. Later, when she brought me the food, I ate and worked at the same time. By five o'clock I'd finished two double-spreads, leaving the tough one – the Apache attack – for last. I'd surprised myself by working faster than I'd ever worked before.

I would make my deadline easy. I would keep my job. It didn't mean a thing.

As I was getting up from my desk, looking through the partition to catch Moe's eye, Louise Gorden came through the door and stopped beside me. 'I didn't hear from my friend,' she said, and though her voice was cool and her face composed, she was twisting her hands together.

I made it easy for her, afraid she wouldn't make the date on her own. 'Then I'll be seeing you tomorrow after work. We'll meet at the library again, right?'

She shrugged. 'I guess so.' She looked at my board. 'How's the work coming?'

'Finished two double-spreads.'

She turned away, then said, 'Stan Henrich was plenty mad, but he won't do anything. He's said many times that you're the fastest artist he's ever known – perfect for house-work on deadlines. So you don't have to worry.'

'I'm not worried about anything but you.'

'And I'm no concern of yours, so you're free of *all* worries.' She went through the door, not giving me a glance. She was showing me the date meant nothing. But the way her body moved, hips swaying, proved she was aware it meant plenty.

Moe and I went across the street to a medium-priced restaurant that served reasonably good food. We took a booth in back and ordered the same meal – spaghetti and meatballs, cold beer, pie and coffee. We ate quickly and didn't do much talking. Then I went to the cashier, bought a good cigar and returned to the booth. Moe was sucking on a cigarette. He coughed, sucked smoke again and coughed again. He pressed his hand to his chest and

84

said, 'Damned gas.' He looked around the room, his loose-skinned, narrow face changing expression as he frowned and relaxed, sucked his teeth and did other things. He was never still a minute – his face or eyes or hands or body always moving, moving. He'd made me nervous when I'd first come to work for Lobert Publications. Now I was used to him.

'You living it up lately, Harry?' he asked, fiddling with his empty coffee cup.

'So now I'm supposed to tell risqué stories. You got the wrong man. Curt Sawyer's your boy.'

He laughed low in his throat. I puffed on my cigar. Then his laughter went away, and his pale blue eyes came up to mine and dug deep.

'I mean you running around,' he said quietly. 'Looking for trouble, busting up your life at home like you're trying to bust up your life in the office.'

I wanted to laugh it off, change the subject, but he didn't give me the chance.

'That business with Sawyer the other day. And today making fists at Stan Henrich. And I figure you're using girls, the same way you use your fists, when it comes to your wife. I mean, you're trying – '

'I know what you mean,' I said, and suddenly wanted to admit it, tell him he was right and what of it. Ask him what the hell difference it made. But I held back. 'I've been a little edgy lately – my father, as you guessed. And I've always been a horny skirt-chaser. So where do you see me walking the plank?'

'Always a horny skirt-chaser? Okay, so was I. But I was always scared I'd be caught and my wife would run out on me. And so were you. *Were*, Harry. Because now you're losing your fears, losing your survival instincts.

You're getting obvious, Harry. The office is going to start talking soon. And you don't care.'

The chill feeling lasted only a second. He was right. I didn't care. Not enough. 'If I'm that obvious, who's the girl?'

He snorted. 'I gotta spell out Louise Gorden? And those near-fights weren't normal results of edginess.'

My cigar didn't taste so good any more. I looked at it. 'Moe, stop trying to psychoanalyze me. You're out of your field. You're wrong about Louise Gorden – '

He leaned forward, grabbing my left wrist with both his hands. 'You think I'm jabbing you so I can have juicy gossip? You think I make a habit of interfering in other people's lives? You think I like begging for confidences, begging to hear your troubles, when I got enough of my own? I – ' He wet his lips, let go of my wrist and looked at the table. 'I like you, man. I think you're good somehow. Maybe the very fact that you can get so sick of life shows you're intelligent and perceptive and sensitive. Maybe I think you're like I was twenty, twenty-five years ago. Maybe I think you're the son I should've had. Maybe I'm just an old jerk. But whatever it is, I see you clearly, Harry. I see you going down, and I see you going down in a way that means trouble.'

I was sweating. I didn't want to hear the end of his spiel. 'Moe, let's get out of here. You can't drink beer.'

His head jerked up. He whipped the cigarette to his lips, inhaled smoke and barked once in arid laughter. 'Drink? Christ, I can drink all night – gin, rum, brandy, rye, bourbon, Scotch, anything! Drink? Man, I was raised on it. The Village was my kindergarten; the intellectual rumdums my nursemaids. Drink? I could tell you stories – ' And then he sighed and beckoned the waiter. After our check was on the table Moe said quickly, 'Harry,

86

you're going to die. That's why I'm scared for you. You're going to die.'

I nodded. 'Sure. That's the whole point, Moe. I'm going to die. So I'll live it up – right?' I laughed.

'That's not the point,' he said, putting change on the table. 'I don't mean you're going to die when your time comes. I mean *soon*. As soon as you can manage it in your roundabout, subconscious way.'

So now I had it. I looked at him, grinning, knew he was right and felt nothing. And feeling nothing was proof positive he was right. But then I stopped believing he was right, and I kept grinning until he was forced to answer with a smile of his own.

'Okay,' he said, the smile playing around his full lips. 'So maybe I'm nuts. But I don't think so.'

He walked to the cashier, split the check, walked into the street. We strolled leisurely to Seventh Avenue and the Broadway IRT, uptown. Even at six-ten it was too crowded to find a seat. We changed for the local at 72nd Street, got off at 86th, walked to West End Avenue and then three more blocks to a huge old apartment house.

I was surprised at the fine neighborhood, the good condition of the old apartment house. West End Avenue in the eighties was still an expensive proposition. Moe earned a good salary, all right, but he always seemed to be broke, and I hadn't expected him to be in the two-hundred-a-month rental bracket.

We went into a small, marble lobby and then into a narrow elevator operated by a young kid in black trousers and white shirt. We didn't talk, but something warm had come alive inside me, something for Moe, something like the feeling I'd had for my father. It worried me. I pushed the worry away, but it came back as we got off at the eleventh floor and walked down a spacious hallway. I glanced at him and he glanced at me, and we both smiled. The warm feeling grew with a rush, and so did the worry.

Why should liking Moe worry me?

7

Moe didn't reach for a key when we stopped in front of a door at the end of the hallway. He pressed the bell-button, then dropped his cigarette and stepped on it. 'What's the time?' he asked and cleared his throat loudly.

'Just about seven,' I said, sensing his nervousness and wondering at it. I tried to remember what he'd told me about his family, what I'd learned about his private life during the past four years. It wasn't much, not when compared with the details that some people handed out day by day. I knew more of Francine Loes, her mother, father and fiancé, than I did of Moe. I knew more of Mary Braken and her husband. I knew more of Louise Gorden. And I was sure Moe knew more of me and Ellie and the baby.

It had been a long time since he'd spoken of his family, most of it during my first year in the office. I knew his wife had died of a cerebral hemorrhage about five years ago; that he had a sister and brother; that he had two children; that he had a girl friend who continually pressed him to get married. Of the children, one was a twenty-five-year-old son who lived with him, and the other was a seventeen- or eighteen-year-old daughter boarding out in a junior college.

Thinking back, I realized he'd talked most about his tragi-comic relationship with Wanda, his violent-tempered girl friend. And once, in trying to explain why he was always broke, he'd spoken of his daughter Grace and of how expensive it was to send her to the private school in upper New York State.

As footsteps approached us from inside the apartment I searched my mind for information on the one person he should have talked most about – the son living with him right here. And I couldn't find a single fact. I didn't even know the son's name.

When the door opened I understood why.

'I'm busy now,' the short, heavy man said. He was young, but his face sagged in loose folds and his eyes didn't focus on either of us. His clothes weren't worn right; his hair wasn't combed right; he just didn't look right. 'I got to finish my airplane. It's a rotten airplane. It falls apart when I put the glue on the pieces. I think maybe I'd better get another one. Give me some money and I'll get another one. I'm going to throw this one away.'

'Okay,' Moe said, voice low and quiet. He moved inside without looking at me. The man, or boy, stepped aside and I followed. The door slammed behind us. Moe stopped in a narrow foyer and said, 'David, this is Harry Admer from my office. Shake hands.' He still didn't look at me.

David put out his hand, and I shook it and then let it go. He turned suddenly and ran inside the apartment. He yelled back, 'I'm going to break it! I'm going to tear it up and rip it and – and – I'll *kill* it!'

'All right,' Moe called. 'Just don't make a mess.' He finally looked at me. 'Since he was ten. Up to then he was a brilliant kid. His teachers thought he was a genius. His IQ and grades were so high they put him in special classes. But then something went wrong and his mind stopped developing. He's still brilliant, for a ten-year-old. It's not his fault his body is twenty-five.'

'Have you tried – '

'Everything,' Moe interrupted quickly. 'Everything, everywhere. I spent a small fortune, but it's hopeless. I'm just thankful that he's easy to handle. He goes to my sister's every day while I'm at work and helps her around the house, and he's no trouble. And best of all, unlike most of these cases, he's not interested in women. Thank God for that! Once sex crops up it means an institution, and I think he'd be lost there.' He suddenly grinned. 'Skeleton's out of the closet, so now we can open a bottle of Scotch. C'mon.'

I followed him into a huge living room, and the warm feeling inside me grew stronger – the warm feeling for Moe. And the fear of that feeling grew, too. I was pulled both ways at once, and I couldn't understand it. Why be afraid of liking a nice guy?

And then it came to me. I didn't want any more fathers. I'd lost one, and the pain of that loss had been enough. I didn't want any more pain. If I grew to care for Moe I'd eventually suffer. He'd die, and then I'd be involved and I'd suffer.

But I drank the stiff Scotch Moe gave me and shook the thought away. Moe was just too old to be my friend. Why complicate matters? I had more than enough people cluttering up my life as it was.

Moe poured us each a fresh drink and said, 'C'mon, we'll take a look at my sanctum sanctorum – my study. Wanda was up the other night and used it as an example of the evils of not being married. She said she'd clean it up and turn it into a neat and attractive room.' He slapped my back. 'She'd kill it. Hell, it's perfect now. Wait'll you see – '

He went on talking, and then we were in the small room. He showed me his books, played some classical records and told me stories of the writers he'd known, an imposing list of old-time avant-gardists of the Maxwell Bodenheim school. He owned a good library, but most of the new books were on psychology, showing the effect David had on his life. He drank and talked and everything was interesting, intelligent, highly amusing.

But then his talk took a turn I'd been expecting – and dreading.

'Lots of those writers I knew in the nineteen-twenties and thirties were talented, all right, but they lacked discipline. Of course, they also lacked belief in God, but that wouldn't have been enough to destroy them if they'd had some sort of knowledge of self – some sort of schedule of life. A man has to know just how far he can go in drinking, running around, playing with women, staying up late. A man has to understand that the body is as important as the mind; that it must be protected, nurtured – '

I saw what was coming and tried to turn it aside. 'Did *you* ever do any writing, Moe?'

He nodded, got up from the couch and went to the bookcase. He ran his fingers over the top shelf and pulled out a volume. He searched again and pulled out two more. He brought them to the couch and dropped them in my lap. 'I wrote maybe ten stories in my life, Harry – all before I was thirty. I published eight of them in avant-garde little magazines, and these three were picked up by collections. Not a bad batting average, eh?'

I opened one of the books to the contents page and found his name. I did the same with the other two, then looked up.

'If you were able to get placed in important collections like these why didn't you go on? Why didn't you write more?'

He took the books from me, put them back in the bookcase. 'Didn't care to. Not enough drive. Wanted a good job and money and fun. Wanted my evenings for pleasure. Fame and fortune, if they were attainable, were too hard to get, required too much work. Hell, boy, I wanted to *live!*' He turned to me, standing in front of the wall of books, and grinned. 'And I *did* live. I regret nothing. I had fun, I had a reasonably good marriage, I had children. Yes, even David brought me pleasure. Looking back, I feel the pleasure far outweighed the pain. It does even today.' He looked at me, hard. 'You've got to remember the good times, Harry. If it seems that everything in life is grim, everything part of the long process of dying, you've got to think of the good times and understand that they'll come back. They always come back; especially at your age. So get off the self-destruction kick. Get back – '

I got up from the chair. I'd had enough. 'Good night, Moe.'

His eyes blinked unhappily. 'Sorry if I pushed you, Harry. One for the road?'

'No, thanks.'

He held out his hand. I shook it, then left quickly. I rode down in the elevator, and by the time I reached the street I was angry. Old meddler! He must be in his second childhood. What the hell did he know about me, about what I was doing with my life? I had a lech for Louise Gorden, so he saw me putting a rope around my neck. I got hot at that jerk Curt Sawyer and stood up to Stan Henrich's big-boss histrionics, so I was sawing my wrists with a razor.

Christ, the old idiot wanted to play father, with me as baby boy! Well, we'd see about that. From now on he could talk to me about work, and nothing else.

* * *

The next morning I got to the office before nine. I was working when Mary Braken came in. 'Now I've seen everything,' she said. 'Harry Admer, boy somnambulist. And you made it right to your desk. This should be reported to the AMA.'

I laughed and continued working on the last of Stan Henrich's double-spreads. Francine Loes, Ramona, and Curt Sawyer came in during the next ten minutes. I nodded at each of them, forgetting myself with Curt. The others gave me their good-mornings, but Curt jerked his eyes away from mine as if the sight of me hurt.

Moe came in at nine-forty. He stopped at my desk. 'Make it home all right?' he said.

I was immediately angered. 'No. I dropped dead on the subway.' I kept working.

He laughed. 'How about dinner?'

'Sorry,' I said, the irrational anger climbing higher. 'Got other plans.'

'You think about what I said?'

I put down my pen. 'Now listen, I've got to finish this double-spread.'

'And you will. Everyone here knows you're the fastest artist in New York. Maybe not the best, but the fastest. Why, it takes most artists a week to do *one* double spread. 'Course, you're a little sloppy, but you could double your salary in a few years if you applied yourself – '

'I will apply myself, soon as you let me.'

He was silent a moment, digesting my words and tone of voice. 'You telling me something, Harry?'

'I am,' I said, and just sat there, looking at my desk.

He made a sudden, angry sound and stalked around the partition to his desk. I got back to work. I felt bad, but not too bad.

About half an hour later Moe came back to my desk. He said, 'If you're free sometime this week, Harry, there's a good foreign film at the Trans-Lux. Italian, with English titles.'

'I don't go for foreign films, Moe. Not for Italian ones with English titles, or Russian ones with Italian titles, or English ones with French titles. Fact is, I don't even like American films with American titles.'

'What the hell did *I* do?' he said, voice loud.

I got up from my desk and walked away from him, out into the hall past a startled Mary Braken. I went to the john and then to the elevators. I went down to the fifth floor and walked to the right, past the accounting department and the movie mags and the pocket books. I went clear around the entire floor to the stockroom, not saying anything to anyone, not really seeing anyone. Sol Kaplan, senior stockroom man, was sitting on a high stool, his tall, corpulent body slouched over a cheese-cake magazine. 'You raiding us again, Harry?' he said, barely glancing at me.

I nodded, went into the back and picked a few new soft-cover titles off the shelves. I went back upstairs.

Moe Crown was at his desk and swiveled around as I came into the bullpen. He looked at me through the glass partition, then turned back to his work. But not before I saw something in his face, saw that he understood exactly what I was doing.

I got busy on the double-spread, glad that the worst part of the brushoff was over.

I worked steadily and Louise Gorden came into the bullpen. I said, 'Good morning, Louise,' and she smiled as she swung by. The smile warmed me, and so did her outfit. She wore a checkered blue-and-gray dress, snug from neck to waist, accenting her high breasts, flaring from the hips and held out by crinolines. She sure as hell wanted to look good on our date tonight!

I watched as she brought something to Moe's desk and headed back to my side of the partition. I crooked my finger at her, intending to find out if she was doing anything for lunch, but she merely lifted her eyebrows and kept going. This time there was no smile; this time her expression was cold and contemptuous.

So the smile warmed me and the rebuff chilled me, and that's the way it always was with Louise. Hot and cold.

I wondered what she really thought of me.

Maybe I'd find out tonight. Maybe she'd come up to the apartment –

The Indian attack illustration required plenty of detail, and I wanted to finish it and get back to my layout work on the crossword mag. I thought of what Moe had said about my being the fastest artist in New York, and of Louise saying Stan Henrich held a similar opinion. For a minute I felt myself vastly underpaid and realized I could make much more money by concentrating on quality and getting myself into a better bargaining position. But the thought slipped away, seemed trivial.

Why the hell bother over a few lousy bucks? I belonged to a burial society – my father had placed me as a member, and I paid a small annual fee. So I was all set for the future. What more did I need? What more, in the final analysis, did anyone need?

My phone rang. It was Audrey, the switchboard operator and receptionist. 'There's a Miss Terry Drego to see you, Mr Admer.'

'Who?' I said, and then remembered Mort Brenner's call about an ex-model who wanted to be a writer. 'Oh, yes. Tell her I'll be out in a minute.'

'Hurry, feller,' Audrey murmured. 'This one you wouldn't want to miss.'

I got up, slipped into my jacket, straightened my tie.

There was only one person in the waiting room, a girl of about twenty-five who sat on the couch, long legs crossed, head tilted back theatrically, cigarette held unlighted in gloved right hand. She looked up at me and showed a perfect set of white teeth in an attractive smile.

'Mr Admer? Harry Admer?'

'Yes,' I said, and sat down beside her. She was something, all right. About five-six or seven, with the type of figure that makes men hungry – lean every place except breasts and hips and buttocks. Her hair was worn long, almost to her shoulders, and was much too blonde to be natural in a girl of otherwise brunette coloring. But knowing she dyed her hair didn't detract from her looks. In fact, it was exactly what a man would want in her – an extra sign, another tip-off that Terry was specifically for the boys. She had a longish face, large brown eyes, good features. She was pretty, but it was her body that took all the prizes. I knew she'd look wonderful in nothing but high heels. I knew it because she wanted me to know it, wanted every man to know it. That's why she wore the tight, figure-molding, blue knitted dress.

'Mort Brenner called about me?' she said, her voice soft, low, carefully trained to sound exactly as she looked.

'Yes,' I said, enjoying myself. The Predatory Female was here in the waiting room with me.

And then the image grew weak as I noticed her cigarette trembling, looked at her lips and saw that she was biting the lower one, and heard her say, 'I really shouldn't bother you, but Mort said – '

She stopped there, floundering, smiling weakly, begging me to help her along. And I did.

'Yes,' I said. 'Mort called and told me all about you.'

That gave her the opening she needed. 'Really? I hope he held a *few* things back.' She gave me a sly, sexy smile.

'Not much,' I said, and returned her smile.

She reached for a brown manilla folder lying on the arm of the couch. 'I write,' she said, still smiling. 'Not very well, I'm afraid. But if you could look these over – '

'I'm an artist, not an editor, Miss Drego.'

'Terry,' she said, and that sexy smile was on her lips to stay. 'And I know your position, Harry. I'd still like you to look these over. Use your own judgement. If you feel they stand a chance, hand them on to the science-fiction editor. If not, return them to me. Either way, I'll want your opinion.'

'You're very flattering.'

She held out the folder, and I took it and placed it on my lap. She put both her hands over my left hand, which was resting on the couch. She said, 'I'd do almost anything to get published in science fiction, Harry. It's been a dream of mine so long – '

She went on, telling me that she'd always wanted to write, and I believed her. I also believed that she'd do almost anything to get into print. She was trying to prove it by changing position as she talked, posing, thrusting her obvious assets in an obvious way. And her eyes moved over me, alive, excited, genuinely interested. She was a hungry gal – hungry for all men. But she was quite nervous, quite sincere, quite frightened.

I felt sorry for her. I knew I shouldn't because men would always be doing things for Terry Drego.

They'd also be doing things *to* her. And somewhere between those two lines of action, Miss Drego would get her lumps. She was gorgeous and knew it. I felt that she wanted more from life than most girls, and was getting much less. She seemed happy, and unhappy . . .

But why the hell was I sitting here, analyzing her? Moe had done the same with me, and he was way off. I was probably as far off with Miss Drego. Just because I happened to be untouched by her sex-machine tactics I began to go cerebral and analytical. She probably promised all, gave nothing and had a neat young banker-type guy stashed away for marriage.

' – have dinner as soon as you're ready to tell me what you think, Harry.'

'Dinner?' I said, and then decided to test my theories. 'Of course. At my place. I'm a good cook. We'll have the convivial artist's special – Martinis, sandwiches, Martinis, canned peaches, Martinis. And after a final round of Martinis – ' I grinned. 'After so many Martinis, there's only one thing a red-blooded American couple *can* do.'

She laughed, low and deep and carefully controlled. But her eyes held mine with considerable warmth. 'It's all right with me, Harry.'

There was no mistaking the promise in her voice. Terry Drego was ready to go all the way, and then some to sell her stories. I had no doubt that if I suggested a date there and then, she'd have agreed. All I had to do was open my mouth and say a few simple words, and I could have this gorgeous girl.

I got one of those flashes of imagination that cover a whole panorama of activity, but last only an instant. I saw us in the apartment, drinking Martinis. I saw Terry peel out of her figure-hugging dress to stand as I had first imagined her, wearing only those high-heeled shoes. I saw myself, naked, holding her, kissing her. I saw us tumble onto the bed, Terry positioning herself so that those magnificent breasts hung temptingly above my face.

I felt, rather than saw, Terry ease herself down onto me. My hands were on her hips as she began to move slowly, rhythmically, her blonde hair falling in a curtain about my face. I looked up at her. Her eyes were closed, but her lips were parted in a sensual smile.

Only her eyes were open, and the smile was expectant, waiting for my answer.

I nodded, but I knew I wouldn't do anything about it. I didn't want her. Just didn't. And it worried me. I said something about working on a deadline, and she took off her right glove and gave me her hand, and her fingers pressed mine. We went out to the elevators and she walked like a model, head high and hips swaying. Her elbow and hip and thigh brushed my body continuously, and she gave me her hand again and said she was looking forward to the convivial artist's special.

Then I remembered to ask her if she'd ever published anything before. She surprised me.

'Yes, Harry. Oh, nothing much. I sold a few shorts to pulp detective magazines about two years ago. But then I lost taste for them and went back to trying my first love – science fiction.' She gave me a smile, and it wasn't sexy this time. 'I guess it's my way of dreaming – rocket ships, inhabited planets and such.' An elevator opened its doors and she stepped toward it, saying, 'See you soon.' She was gone.

I went back to my desk and put the manilla folder in the top drawer and got to work on the double-spread. But I kept thinking of Terry Drego – or rather of why she didn't reach me, didn't excite me. She certainly had it over Louise in looks and intelligence and ability to interest a man. And she could be had without too much trouble.

The twelve o'clock sirens sounded, and I asked Mary

Braken if she'd bring me a sandwich and coke when she came back from lunch. She said okay and walked out.

I filled a pipe and lit it, and thought of myself and Terry Drego and Louise Gorden. I took the manilla folder from my desk drawer, opened it and read the covering letter. It gave a list of her mystery sales – six – to pulps, none of them ours. I leafed through the stories, and of the five one was a seven page short-short. I leaned back and read it in ten minutes.

It was good – about a Martian who lands on Earth a few hours before dawn, prepared to contact the Prime Minister of England. The Martian has learned English, knows the history and traditions and modern-day customs of England. And so he figures to overcome the effect his octopuslike shape will have on the people he meets. The kicker is that he's made a tiny miscalculation in navigation and lands on the wrong side of the channel – in a small town in France. And so dawn comes and he is destroyed as a monster, all the time murmuring soothingly, 'I say, but this is awkward, old fellow. I represent the first – ' and so on.

I wasn't sure, but I figured Moe would buy it. I'd certainly pass it on to him, along with the others.

And so I had a higher opinion of Terry Drego now than I'd had before. And I still didn't have the slightest interest in seeing her again.

Why?

I worked, and thought, and it came to me. Not all at once, but it was there, and I pulled it from the back of my mind and put it into words.

The Terry Dregos were certainly physically satisfying. But physical satisfaction was about the easiest thing in the world to find, at least for me. Ellie was satisfying physically, if it came to that, and I didn't have to step out

101

of my own home. So there was no reason for me to take the Terry Dregos, easy as they were to get. No reason at all. Louise was different from Terry. Louise had different values, *moral* values she'd call them. They seemed child-ish, stupid, out-moded to me, and yet if *she* valued them they gained importance in our relationship. If she valued them I would have to assume even greater value in her life to overcome them. And that constituted the great game, the great challenge.

There was rarely any real excitement, true eroticism in making love to a woman who thought like a man – who used men as men used women, as a source of sexual gratification. No matter how these women embellished the act – with intellectual acumen and creativity, with mature approach and open explanations – it lost its magic. At least to me, at this stage of life. The only true pleasure, true excitement, would come from a Louise Gorden, with all her fears and prejudices and moral shibboleths. To become more important, more powerful, than these learned-by-rote taboos would provide the thrill I wanted, the thrill I needed. Otherwise, why bother with women at all?

That was it. I repeated it to myself, rephrased it, accepted it.

And then I laughed at myself and dismissed it. Hell, Terry Drego just didn't hit me, that's all.

Mary brought my lunch, and I ate and worked at the same time. I was finished with the double-spread by three-thirty. I worked on the crossword layouts until ten to five, then washed up and put my desk in order. I got out of the office a few minutes before the mob, mainly to avoid contact with Moe Crown.

I just didn't feel like facing him at close quarters.

8

I stood on the steps of the 42nd Street Library, looking at the people flooding Fifth Avenue. The sun beat down. It was hot, and the air was full of automobile exhaust-fumes. The city boiled and roiled and stank. But it was exciting. Louise would be here in a few minutes, and that made it exciting and worth-while.

I remembered my inner searching about Terry Drego, my worries about Moe Crown – and I laughed at myself.

Psychology, hell!

A man got hot; a man got the yen to bust someone in the teeth. It was normal.

Then I saw Louise, and I stepped down to the street to meet her. 'Hi,' I said, and took her arm. 'Want to try a French restaurant this time?'

She kept walking, so I fell in beside her and we headed uptown on Fifth. She shook her head.

'Chinese?' I said.

'No, Harry. Just a sandwich.'

'Don't be silly,' I said, trying to slow her down. 'We'll go back to the Italian restaurant on Madison. That band was pretty good – '

We were at the corner of 42nd. 'Just a sandwich, Harry.' Her voice was tight, ugly. 'I want to eat quickly and get home. I don't feel like going out tonight. Anyway, I'm not on a date.'

'Christ!' I said, and we stopped and looked at each other. 'If I have to hear that spiel once more – '

'Then let's just call the whole thing off,' she said, eyes

103

cold. 'Good night.' She turned and began crossing the street, heading for Penn Station.

I ran after her, caught up with her, took her arm. 'Wait a minute, honey.' I didn't want it to fizz out like this. I couldn't face the prospect of going home, sitting around, watching television and thinking, thinking, listening to my heart beat and thinking. 'We'll have a sandwich. There's a coffee shop just down the street.'

'All right,' she said, walking on, staring straight ahead. 'A sandwich and I'll catch a train – '

'At least let me drive you home.' I was begging. 'I looked forward to our date all day yesterday and today. Don't be that way, Louise.'

She sighed and kept walking and finally nodded. 'All right. You have your car in the city?'

'No. It's in Brooklyn, like last time.'

'Don't expect me to come up to your apartment. I don't feel like looking at pictures of Ellie and the baby.'

I wanted to slam her in the face. I wanted to tell her what a confused, ignorant, vicious little bitch she was.

But I didn't.

I was so muddled that I took her past the small luncheonette. 'Wait a minute,' I said when I realized we'd walked too far. 'Back there.' We turned, and we both spotted Curt Sawyer. He wasn't more than fifteen feet away.

As soon as I saw the startled, frightened look on his face I knew he'd been tailing us. And to make it even more obvious, he swung suddenly to his left and crossed 42nd against the traffic, almost getting clipped by a northbound taxi.

'Following us!' Louise said, and there was satisfaction as well as fright in her voice. 'Mr Sawyer was following us! Now you've got something to worry about, Harry.

Now maybe your wife will hear about your running around.' She giggled nervously. 'Happy now, Harry?'

I shrugged to show her it meant nothing to me. And, strangely enough, it didn't. It annoyed me, but not because I was worried about what anyone – including Ellie – might think of my spending time with Louise. I just didn't like Curt Sawyer's spying.

Of course, I didn't really have proof –

But his face, and the way he'd run from facing us, was proof enough. Still, that didn't mean he was going to do anything with whatever he'd learned or hoped to learn. Hell, he wasn't jerk enough to go telling my wife. And after all, exactly what could he tell her? That I'd been walking along New York's busiest streets during the rush hour with a girl from the office? Hell, a million men walked a million girls to subways and trains and buses every day.

I laughed and said to Louise, 'Honey, if it doesn't bother you it doesn't bother me.'

We were at the luncheonette, and she turned to stare at me. 'You really mean that,' she said, surprised.

'Sure. Just be nice to me and I won't care if the whole city sees us together.'

She kept staring. 'I'm single,' she said. 'It can't hurt me – not too much. But you – you can lose a lot, Harry.'

People were rushing past us, and the roar of traffic was in our ears. It was the worst possible place to say what I wanted to say, but it was the right time for it. Louise was waiting to be convinced, and the game demanded that I convince her.

I dropped my hand to hers, squeezed her fingers, said, 'I want you, Louise. I don't give a damn if I lose wife and kid and job and anything else. You're more important to me than the works.'

105

Her face went pink. 'You're crazy. You're crazy, Harry.' But her hand stayed in mine and she swallowed, and I knew she'd been reached, flattered, impressed.

'Change your mind about dinner and dancing?' I asked softly.

She shook her head. 'No, Harry. I – ' She let it hang there.

I decided not to press the point. She couldn't very well reverse herself completely within five minutes. 'Okay,' I said. 'Food's pretty good here.' I led her into the long, narrow room and to a booth in back.

The place was busy, but not packed. We ate, and I kept looking at her, drinking in the strange beauty of her face, feeling desire build higher and higher.

She met my gaze once or twice, but most of the time she looked at her food, or around the long room. Again I felt her slipping away.

I finished, lit a cigarillo, tried to take her hand. She jerked it away. 'Listen, Harry, none of that.'

'Why the hell do you even bother talking to me!' I said, almost shouting, and was immediately sorry.

She put down her fork. 'Yes, why do I? Want me to stop – as of now?' She looked me right in the eye, and it was as if we were enemies.

I forced a laugh, puffed on my cigar and said, 'You're quite a gal.'

She shrugged, picked up her fork and continued eating.

'Quite a gal,' I repeated, grinning like an idiot.

I meant she was nutty as a fruit cake; I meant she'd lost most of her marbles somewhere along the road.

But I'd stick with her. She was my little insurance policy – insurance against thought, against the knowledge of fecund earth waiting, waiting . . .

As soon as we left the luncheonette, I told her a mildly

sexy story. She laughed at the punch line, and I was 'reminded' of another story, much stronger, with a great deal more pornographic detail. We were on the BMT platform by the time I murmured the punch line into her ear. It really broke her up. She put her hand over her mouth and colored clear to her cleavage and laughed until her eyes were damp. She was still laughing as we settled ourselves in a West End Express. Our end of the car was nearly empty, and I took her hand, laughed with her and pressed closer to her.

When she stopped laughing she tried to free her hand, but I held on and launched into a new story, over her protests. It wasn't nearly as funny a story as the first two, but I built up the seduction scene carefully, aiming to excite her. She laughed at the punch line, laughed more than it deserved. She crossed her legs, uncrossed them, shifted weight, said, 'Harry, I don't like to hear dirty stories.'

'Okay,' I said. 'No more.'

We came up onto the elevated in Brooklyn at seventen, and it was still bright and sunny. Louise looked out the window, and I looked at Louise. I held her hand and felt the moist warmth. My shoulder, hip, thigh and leg pressed hers, and there was no withdrawal from the pressure. She was breathing rapidly.

When we reached 55th Street I rushed her to the doors, saying, 'Hey, we'll get locked in!' I put my arm around her waist and squeezed, and then let go as we made the platform.

We walked down the steps into the street, and I was talking steadily, making her laugh. But I wasn't paying any attention to what I was saying; I was trying to think of a way to get her to my apartment. Even if she walked

107

in and walked right out again, it would be breaking a barrier, establishing a precedent.

We'd reached 14th Avenue and my Dodge when the idea came.

I searched my pockets, said, 'Hell! Forgot my car keys!'

She gasped. 'You mean you left them in the office?'

'No. At the apartment this morning. We'll have to walk a few extra blocks.' I took her arm, hoping she'd come along without protest. 'It'll only take a minute. It's just two blocks from here, and we'll be in and out like a flash.'

I began walking, and she came along. Excitement rose in a near-sickening wave, and I let go of her arm so she wouldn't feel how I was trembling. At the same time I thought of the women who sat around in front of the house on warm summer days, ready, willing and able to gossip about husbands whose wives were out of town.

The back entrance. If we came in the back, and no one was waiting for the elevator . . .

We reached 15th Avenue and crossed it, and I saw three women sitting near the lobby entrance. I kept walking, leading Louise toward the back entrance.

'We'll use the alley,' I said. 'I want to see if the super is around back. He promised to fix a screen in the bedroom.' I walked her quickly down the side street.

She giggled. 'How naïve do you think I am?'

'No, really,' I said, feeling ashamed, and laughed. 'Want to go in the front?'

'Yes.'

That took me by surprise. I stopped near the wrought-iron alley gate and said, 'Okay.'

'Well, we'll forget it this time.' She was smiling cynically.

'No, honey. We'll use the front.' I pulled her a few

steps back the way we'd come. 'I shouldn't have tried sneaking in this way, and I'm going to show you – '

She stopped smiling. 'You're bluffing, Harry.'

She was right. At least I *had* been bluffing. But now I saw a way to make some real progress with her. Now I'd be able to prove that my feelings for her were of the strongest kind.

Somehow, the thought that I'd be risking trouble with Ellie didn't mean much.

'Am I?' I said. 'Test me.'

She took my arm, snuggled up close, nodded. 'All right, lover, I will. Let's go – like this.' Her breasts pressed my arm and her face turned intimately to mine. 'Just like this.'

I bent suddenly and kissed her on the lips. She jerked back, but only for a second. 'Just like this, lover,' she said.

And that's how we walked to the corner. Excitement was once again pounding through me, but now it was much stronger than before, much more complex. I was afraid of being seen by people who knew me. And in some crazy way I was also anxious to be seen by them, anxious to get the inevitable over and done with . . .

Wasn't that what Moe had warned me about?

I was angry at myself. Thinking, always thinking, always examining myself.

I must have muttered something because Louise said, 'What?'

'Nothing,' I said.

She let go of my arm and stopped short of the corner. 'I was only kidding, Harry. I don't want your neighbors gossiping about you.'

I was relieved, disappointed and unsure of what to do. 'I don't want you thinking I'm ashamed – '

'What difference does it make what I think?' she said. 'It's not going to affect anything. I mean – one way or the other, nothing can come of our being together.'

'Honey – '

'Let's go in the back way, Harry. I don't want to stand out here all night.'

Her tone of brisk finality showed me she'd slipped away again. I led her through the alley.

We reached the third floor without meeting any tenants and entered the apartment. 'Well,' I said. 'Here we are.'

'And no one saw us. Aren't we lucky, Harry?' She laughed coldly.

'Yeah.' I snapped on the foyer light. The place had a slightly musty smell because of the closed windows. 'I'd better let some air in. Look around. There's no chance of your getting lost.'

I walked ahead of her, past the kitchen on my right, into the living room. I opened both windows and heard a light-switch snap behind me.

'Not bad at all,' she called. 'Small, but nice.'

I walked through the tiny foyer leading to the bathroom on the left and the bedroom straight ahead. 'Thanks,' I said. I opened the windows in the bedroom, started back toward the living room, then decided to lower the Venetians. Louise came in while I was doing it. She said, 'It's hot in here, Harry. Why lower – ' And then she looked at me, flushed and said, 'You're going to take me home in a minute.' She went into the bathroom and closed the door.

I yanked the blinds up savagely, went to the kitchen, took out ice cubes and put them in tall glasses. After pouring Chablis over the ice I carried both glasses to the living room, put one on the coffee table and took a long drink from the other. Thunder rumbled far off, then rumbled again much nearer. I walked to the windows and saw the sky growing dark with night, and also black with storm clouds in the east. Lightning flickered briefly; the air was hot and heavy. The black clouds drew closer, and the smell of rain grew stronger.

Water began running in the bathroom. I went to the couch and sat down. Louise came into the living room and said, 'Was that thunder I heard?'

I nodded.

She walked to the windows and looked out. 'It's going to storm. We'd better leave right away, Harry.'

'Why?' I said, and finished my wine. 'What difference does it make as long as we have the car?'

'We could get soaked walking to the car.'

'You can wait in the lobby, if necessary. I'll pick you up right at the door.' I motioned at the wine. 'C'mon.'

She sighed, looked around and said, 'It's getting dark, Harry. Put on a light.'

I didn't move. 'In a minute. Sit down.' I felt the wine warming my stomach, warming my blood. I slipped off my jacket and threw it over the arm of the couch. 'Don't you want a drink?'

She came to the couch and sat down, leaving plenty of space between us. She picked up her glass, sipped it and said, 'Good.' She took a long swallow, put the glass down on the table, leaned back. 'This is a nice little place, Harry. It's – it's snug.'

Thunder pealed suddenly, making her jump. It began to rain. In a minute it was pouring.

The room was quite dark now, but I could see her clearly enough. I saw her face turning to me, saw her tight bodice rising and falling, heard a little sound she made – a wet swallowing sound. I slid over quickly and put both arms around her.

111

'No,' she said.

I kissed her.

For a second she was stiff, unyielding. Then her body relaxed, her lips opened and she began returning my kisses. The rain pounded down, and the room was cool with the smell of it. I pressed her back, letting my hands wander over her body. I touched her breasts through the thin material of her dress and felt her tense for an instant. Then she seemed to relax, kissing me hard as I fondled her. I transferred my hand to her thigh, squeezing gently, then working down until I felt the hem of her dress and lifted it. She wore no stockings and her skin was smooth and soft to my touch. I felt my own excitement mounting to an almost unbearable level as the very scene I had dreamt began to materialize.

Now, I said to myself. Now it happens!

I moved my hand to her inner thigh. She moaned a little, but made no attempt to stop me. I moved my hand higher, until I felt the material of her panties. Was I imagining it, or were they really wet with excitement? I began to touch her through the material, and she made a kind of purring noise deep in her throat. Her body tautened against me. I kissed her harder, my touching becoming more urgent.

Then she began blocking my hands, began moving away. And yet it wasn't at all like her withdrawal in the car. She didn't detach herself and end it right there. She sat up and straightened her clothing – and at the same time continued to take my kisses and give me hers. Her hands began to move, and I gasped as I felt her unfastening my fly.

'Louise,' I said, my voice a thick whisper, and reached for her again. But she blocked me, drew herself together – legs tucked under her, leaning back. There was distance

112

between us, and she would not let me kiss her. Only her hands were intimate, terribly intimate. And expert. They opened my pants and released my erection. By now it was too dark to see her clearly, the expression on her face unreadable. I groaned as she began to move her hand over the length of my penis. I was torn between overpowering desire and a kind of self-disgust. This wasn't what I wanted, but it was better than nothing. I tried to reach for her again, but again she held me off. Her hands continued their work, one cupping my testicles, the other stroking me. I felt helpless, held to the couch by the sheer weight of longing rising inside me. I let her touch me. It felt so good. I murmured her name.

She made no response, except to quicken the stroking of her hand. I felt my heart beating, my need mounting. It was almost unbearable now, the pleasure exquisite. And yet there was still that feeling of powerlessness, of disgust at the ease with which she could manipulate me.

I heard her giggle softly, and wanted to stop her, wanted to stop myself, because she was aloof, unexcited. She was performing a job, ridding herself of a problem.

But that couldn't be. I twisted my head, peered through the darkness and couldn't see her face. I said, 'Stop.' But she didn't, and it was too late for me to do anything. My legs and stomach were growing heavy, heavy, swelling with warmth. My head sank back, and I told myself she was making love to me, and then the lightning flashed and I saw her face emerge for a second.

She was laughing. She was laughing at me. And I could do nothing.

Then her hands jerked away, and I was completely alone, and I said, 'You, bitch!'

She giggled and got up and went into the kitchen. The light came on and she said, 'Harry, I want to go home.'

I got up and took one step toward the kitchen, wanting to use my fists. But I was ashamed to look at her, and I had to change my clothes. I went to the bedroom, put on gray denims and a polo shirt and walked to the kitchen. She was standing near the sink, drinking a glass of water. She kept her eyes down and said, 'Ready?'

'Yes.'

'Got your keys this time?'

'Yes.'

'Fine. We can go.'

'Yes.'

She raised her eyes and looked at me, smiling. 'Do you know, most men would be very grateful, very happy.'

'No, they wouldn't,' I said, and I was no longer angry. I was just sick. 'They would slap your ears off.'

'Oh? Not the men I know.' But she continued to smile. 'How much farther can you go in petting?'

'Holding hands is farther than that,' I said. 'Looking at each other is farther than that.'

She just smiled.

'And you know it,' I said.

'Do I?'

I was going to ask her if she hated me, but then changed my mind. I couldn't risk the answer.

I merely nodded.

And suddenly she was angry. 'What right do you have to expect anything from me?' she said, voice shrill. 'You're married, you've got a child, you've bothered me and made me do things I didn't want to do! What right have you got to even talk to me? Tricking me up here and doing things and then saying crazy things when I – ' She stopped and glared at me.

'All right,' I said, sick of her. 'Let's get out of here . . .'

We didn't say one word to each other all the way to

her home. It continued to rain, though it eased up about the time I parked in front of the ranch-house.

I felt better by then. 'Well,' I said, 'see you at the office.'

'Not if I see you first,' she said, and opened the door.

'That's original,' I said, and let her go. She ran up a paved path and disappeared into the house. I U-turned and drove back to Brooklyn.

I showered and went to bed. I thought of Louise, but didn't worry about her. Somehow, I felt she'd be back playing her game with me tomorrow.

What had happened tonight was only one battle in a long war.

9

It was Friday and I was heading for the lake after work, so I drove my car into the city and left it at the 39th Street parking lot. I was in the office at nine-twenty. As I was setting up my board for the crossword-puzzle layouts, the phone rang. It was Stan Henrich. I hadn't seen or spoken to him since our argument, and he sounded embarrassed.

'Harry, just wanted to say that you did a good job on those double-spreads. Good job, man.'

'Thanks,' I said, and hoped he'd drop the subject.

'Fastest work in the field. Fastest work I ever heard of.'

It took a certain amount of courage to say nice things to a guy you'd fought with a day before, a certain amount of honest humility. I began to like him again, and I didn't want to.

'Yeah? Then you'll plug for that ten-dollar raise I've been wanting.'

He cleared his throat. 'Well, we'll see. Things are tight but – ' He laughed briefly, uncomfortably. 'Anyway, you must've set a record.'

'Hope I get a little more warning next time.'

He spoke quickly. 'You certainly will, Harry. I don't mind admitting it was my fault. I screwed up on the deadlines.' He laughed again. 'There. Got it off my chest and I'm glad. Now I'll let you get back to work.' He hung up.

A few minutes later, Ramona brought our pay checks

from the fifth floor. I stuck mine in my wallet and dutifully laughed at Mary Braken's crack about being able to get by on her check – if it would come every week instead of every second week.

I worked on the crossword layouts until eleven, then put them aside and took out Terry Drego's folder. Besides the short-short which I'd read yesterday, there were four shorts. I read them all, finishing at a quarter to one. They were good.

I wrote a brief note, stating that they merited serious consideration. I stuck it in with the stories and looked through the glass partition at Moe's desk. He was out to lunch, as were Francine, Curt and Ramona. I went around the partition and put the folder on his desk.

I was out of it now. I wouldn't get in touch with Terry Drego. I didn't want to.

I went out to lunch, cashed my check at the bank on Madison and returned to the office. I entered the bullpen just as Louise Gorden was leaving it. She wore a tight blue skirt, tighter gray sweater, open-toed high-heeled shoes. She looked good to me, so good that I wanted to reach out for her right there.

'Hi,' I said, blocking her path by stopping in the doorway. 'C'mon over to my desk and we'll talk a bit.'

She glanced at Mary Braken's desk. Mary was busy on proof and didn't even raise her eyes.

'No thanks,' Louise murmured. 'I've got letters to type.' She stepped forward. 'I can't climb over you, Harry.'

Her eyes were cold, so I shrugged and moved aside. I lowered my voice and said, 'Why don't we have dinner Monday?'

She walked past me, hips swinging beautifully, and

looked back over her shoulder. 'Monday's the Fourth of July. Or don't you believe in holidays?'

I was shocked. Time was when I'd be looking forward to a holiday a month before it came along. And here I hadn't even remembered the Fourth.

'Tuesday then.'

She stopped, half turned, laughed. 'You're a glutton for punishment. But no thanks, Harry.'

'We'll talk about it again,' I said.

'Will we?' She walked into the corridor.

And suddenly I was angry. I walked quickly after her. 'Just a minute!'

She walked faster, turned her head and said, 'You must be crazy!'

I almost ran up to her, almost slugged her.

She was right – I must've been crazy. Everything piled up; everything became too much; everything asked to be slugged and ripped and destroyed.

But then the feeling passed, and I took a deep breath. Louise was gone. Luckily, no one else had been around to see and hear me. I'd talk to her again. Maybe I'd put it off until Tuesday. But I'd talk to her again.

I went to my desk and worked on the crossword layouts. I made a minor mistake, lost my temper and slammed my fist on the board. The anger I'd felt a few minutes ago returned, stronger, only now it wasn't directed at Louise. It was directed at the board, my work, myself. I wanted to walk out and get plastered.

I went to the men's room and washed my face with cold water. I was shaking all over, sweating with rage. And it frightened me. Nothing had happened to make me *that* angry . . .

At four o'clock my phone rang. It was Mort Brenner.

'Hey,' he said, 'was Terry Drego up to see you?'

'She was. Gave me five stories. I read them, and they're pretty good. I passed them on to our science-fiction editor.'

'Yeah, yeah,' he said impatiently. 'But what about *her?* Some hunk, eh?'

'Yeah. Sorry to rush you, Mort, but this is Friday and I've got – '

'Friday, or Monday, or Tuesday – lately you're too damned busy to spare me five minutes! What the hell's got into you?'

He was right. I'd brushed him off the last two times we'd spoken, and he was my best friend, my *only* friend. But I just didn't feel like batting the breeze.

'Sorry,' I said. 'I'll call you soon as I get back from the lake.'

'Yeah,' he said flatly. Then, 'What about Terry? You going to cash in on your opportunity?'

'No. She's not my type.'

He didn't answer for a good ten seconds. 'You must be sick, Harry. Hell, boy, a year ago you were begging me to throw some friendly models your way, and now – ' He made a sad, whistling sound.

'Okay,' I said. 'So I'm sick. So you grab her. I'll lend you my apartment. Now I've got to finish my work.'

'Keep your apartment,' he snapped. 'I wouldn't take the chance of catching whatever it is you have.'

'Ever figure I might have a small case of loyalty to my wife?' It was an inexcusable dig at someone with whom I'd been exchanging confidences for more than two years, and I wanted to take it back. But I didn't.

'Thanks,' he said quietly. 'Give my regards to Ellie and the baby.'

'Same to Laura – ' I began, but he'd hung up.

I felt like hell, then I felt angry, and then I got up and

119

put on my jacket. I couldn't work another second. I had to get out of here. I'd start for the lake an hour earlier. If they wanted to can me for that they could!

I cleared my desk, and Mary Braken said, 'Slipping out early, Picasso?'

'Not slipping, leaving.'

She swiveled around in her seat and looked at me. 'Aren't we temperamental today? Maybe I'd better run to the ladies' room and hide before you hurt me.'

I went around the glass to Moe's desk. He was reading Terry Drego's stories. He looked up and began to smile; then he cut it short and said, 'Well?'

'I'm leaving early. Want to beat the traffic up to the lake. Okay?'

He shrugged. 'Would it make any difference if I said no?'

I shook my head. 'Like the stories?'

'Yes. One of them – the short-short – I'll buy. Maybe another, if the ending can be tightened.'

I turned away.

'Harry.'

I turned back, afraid that he was going to ask me questions, afraid that he was going to show his hurt and try to get back on a personal footing with me. I didn't want that. I was afraid of that.

And he must have read my feelings because all he said was, 'Have some fun. You need it.'

I nodded and left the office . . .

I reached the West Side Highway at four-twenty, and it wasn't too crowded for a Friday afternoon. There was a slight delay before the George Washington Bridge and each of the two Westchester tolls, and then traffic thinned out and I was able to open the Dodge wide. I hit seventy on the Taconic and maintained it until I passed a motorcycle cop giving some poor bastard a ticket. That made me slow down, and it was lucky I did because my left rear tire went flat just as I passed exit P-2. I pulled up on the grassy shoulder and got out and looked at the pancaked tire. Of all the lousy luck!

It was over ninety degrees, according to the radio. It felt closer to a hundred standing there in the blazing sun with cars whizzing by only a foot away. I already had my jacket and tie lying on the seat, and I took off my shirt. I got bumper jack, lug wrench, and screwdriver from the trunk and took out the spare. I squatted in the grass, back to the highway, and loosened the bolts on the tire. Then I secured the jack and raised the car high enough to remove the flat. By that time I was sweating like a pig and had to wipe my face and neck with a handkerchief. My heart was banging away like mad, and the pulse in my temple was incredibly loud.

Heart pounding, pounding, and some day it stops. What if it stopped now? What if I suddenly felt a terrific pain in my chest, and the world went black and I fell and I died –

I went to the front seat and sat down and cursed myself. But the fear remained, and I couldn't sit there all day. I got up and went back to work and removed the flat. I had trouble mounting the spare; the damned bolt-openings wouldn't line up correctly. Finally, after ten agonizing minutes, I got it right and put in the bolts and turned them by hand until they were secure. I lowered the jack and used the wrench on the bolts and reached for the hub-cap. Before I could slap it on, a voice yelled right behind me, 'Hey, that's a pretty good job, buddy!'

I turned, saw a Chevvy convertible crawling past, saw a young guy grinning at me. The girl sitting beside him was laughing at his stupid crack.

Without having to think, I found the wrench with my right hand and leaped to my feet and whirled to face them. The kid's face twisted in sudden fear and the girl's mouth opened, and then I was swinging the wrench and screaming things. The convertible shot forward and I swung down with the wrench and my arm went numb as I slammed the rear fender. But I didn't drop the wrench. I raised my arm again and threw as hard as I could. The wrench hit the Chevvy's trunk and bounced into the highway. The convertible kept going, even though I'd put two good dents in the pale-blue body. I stood there, screaming obscenities at them, and they were almost out of sight and going faster every second.

I sucked lungfuls of air and wanted to kill that wise-guy bastard, and then told myself to take it easy, I told myself I was losing my grip. Violence like this could only end in my being hurt . . .

Wasn't that what Moe had said? Wasn't that his theory – that I was moving toward self-destruction?

I looked up the highway, saw my chance and ran into the road. I got my wrench, made it back to the grass and put everything in the trunk. After slapping on the hub-cap I pulled off the grass and drove at a steady forty-five until I reached a gas station. I told the attendant to fix my flat and walked to the restaurant-bar attached to the station.

It was dim and cool in the long room. There were only two other people there, a middle-aged couple eating at a rear table. I took one of the four stools at the small bar and looked around for service. A tall, thin man wearing a white apron and yellow polo-shirt came through the swinging doors facing me. He smiled and said, 'What'll it be?'

'Beer.'

'Bottle or glass?'

'Bottle of Bud. Quart, if you've got it.'

He shook his head. 'Regular size only.'

'Okay then. Open a few.'

He gave me a sidelong glance as he bent to a waist-high refrigerator. It made me uncomfortable. I wondered if I looked wrong in any way. I dropped my eyes, saw my hands and realized they were filthy. I hadn't washed up after changing the flat.

The bartender placed two open bottles before me, poured from one into a tall pilsner glass, lit a cigarette. I drained the glass in three long swallows and said, 'You got a washroom here?'

He jerked his thumb at a door to my right, down where the middle-aged couple was sitting. I walked to the door and went inside and washed up. I reached for paper towels, but the dispenser was empty. I used toilet paper instead.

I went back to the bar. The tall, thin guy was still there, still smoking his cigarette. He dropped his eyes as I sat down, and again he managed to annoy me.

'You're all out of paper towels,' I said, and refilled my glass, killing the first bottle.

He nodded. 'Yeah. I know.'

I'd emptied the glass and was pouring from the second bottle, but his cool tone of voice stopped me. I looked at him. 'You don't sound very concerned,' I said, and wanted to stop right there. But I didn't. 'You don't sound like a man who has any interest in keeping his customers happy.'

He dropped his cigarette, stepped on it and sighed. He kept his eyes down. 'Listen, I only work here. The boss is somewhere around the station. If you want to fight with someone fight with him.'

He was right, but it made no difference. I still couldn't stop. 'What kind of answer is that? You could get in trouble with answers like that.'

His head jerked up and his face was red. 'And you could get – '

I leaned over the bar, grabbed a handful of his yellow polo-shirt and yanked him forward as hard as I could. The glass and bottles toppled and beer splashed over my pants as I drew back my right fist.

'No,' he said, and his voice was shaking. 'No, mister, I didn't mean anything.'

I heard a woman cry out and knew the couple in back was watching us, and I didn't give a damn. But the bartender wouldn't play. Curt Sawyer wouldn't play and Stan Henrich wouldn't play and this bartender wouldn't play. But sooner or later someone *would* play, and then the fun would start. Then I'd find out where I was going.

I let him go and got up and brushed at my pants. It didn't do any good; I smelled like a brewery. 'How much?' I said, and glanced to the rear of the long room. The man and woman were standing near their table, poised as if to run.

'Sixty cents,' the bartender said, and his voice was low, weak.

I put a dollar on the wet mahogany and he picked it up. He fumbled at a cash register with trembling hands and couldn't seem to punch out the right figures.

I suddenly wanted to say something – beg him to forgive me and tell him I wasn't the kind of guy he thought I was.

He finally opened the register and gave me my change. I went out into the blazing heat, walked to the station and watched a colored guy fix my flat. It took about fifteen minutes, and then I was on my way. I was calmer now. In fact, I was almost dead inside. I didn't know if I was happy or unhappy to be going up to the lake. I didn't know what I would get out of my three-day week end. But something had to happen. I had to *make* something happen. I couldn't sit around like the last week end, doing nothing but think.

There'd be dancing at the recreation hall this Friday and Saturday night. Sunday night too, since Monday was the Fourth. Ellie and I would have fun. Sure, just like the old days.

It was broiling, and I drove faster, thinking of the icy lake water. Soon as I got up to the cabin I'd change into shorts and take a long swim.

I reached the lake at seven-thirty and walked up the hill. There were a lot of people around now; almost every cabin showed signs of occupancy. There was also a great deal of noise.

As I reached our cabin, I saw Debbie playing with her doll carriage. 'Hey, sweetie,' I yelled.

She turned and screamed, and came running to meet me. I picked her up and hugged her, overwhelmed with sudden affection. And I wondered how a guy who wanted to cheat on his wife and kick out his friends could love a little hunk of innocence like this.

I kissed her, and she squealed and said, 'Daddy, I smell you! I smell you!'

The beer. I put her down, and Ellie was coming through the screen door. She kissed me and said, 'I smell you too, Daddy.' She laughed. 'But after a whole week without you, it's okay. I've missed you, Harry. I never knew I could miss anyone so much.' She kissed me again, hard, and I was ashamed. I hadn't missed her at all. I hadn't given her or the baby a thought.

125

'What *is* that smell?' she said, when we were inside the cabin and I was changing into bathing trunks. 'Liquor?'

'Beer,' I said. 'Spilled some on myself when I stopped at a restaurant on the way up here.'

'Lucky you have an extra suit in the closet. Didn't I tell you we'd need one for emergencies?'

I nodded, got into my trunks, picked up the towel she'd draped across the chair. 'I'll be back in about twenty minutes.'

'No later, Harry. I've got a roast in the oven.'

Debbie was outside, rocking her carriage. She said, 'My baby's sleeping, Daddy. Don't make noise.'

I nodded solemnly. 'Okay.' I walked away.

She made a crying sound, and I turned. She'd left her carriage and was running toward me. 'Take me, Daddy! Take me!'

I bent and caught her. 'Daddy's going for a swim. You wait here.'

'No!' she screamed. 'Take me! Take me!'

'But I'll be swimming and you'll be alone.'

'Debbie swim too! Debbie swim too!'

I began to get irritated. I couldn't leave her alone near the lake, and I wanted that swim badly. I pushed her back and stood up. 'I'm sorry, honey. Daddy'll take you swimming tomorrow.'

'Now! Now!' She came after me, screaming at the top of her lungs. 'Now! Now!' And the tears began to flow.

I stopped and said sharply, 'No more nonsense, Debbie! Get back to the cabin!'

She shook her head violently, making her blond hair fly. This type of behavior wasn't unusual with her, with any child, and I knew it. But somehow, I couldn't take it right now.

I reached out, jerked her forward, saw her eyes widen

126

with fear. I swung her around and slapped her across the bottom, hard. I didn't stop with one blow. And all the time I kept telling myself to stop, and all the time I couldn't stop, and I was hitting her harder and faster and she was screaming in fear and pain.

Then Ellie was with us, pulling Debbie away, picking her up and holding her tight and saying, 'Harry, for God's sake!'

I was panting. 'She needed it. Little brat needed it.'

'But so much, so hard!' Ellie said, trying to soothe the screaming child. 'It's wrong, Harry.'

'You trying to nullify the whole lesson?' I said, and I wanted to shout. 'You trying to confuse the kid?'

'No, of course not.' She looked at the baby, her own eyes full of tears, and she said, 'Debbie was a bad girl – that's why Daddy spanked.'

Debbie was sobbing convulsively, and she nodded.

I felt ashamed, sick of myself, but I was still angry. I turned and went down the hill to the lake. There were about twenty people bathing – spaced out in five or six groups. I took off my tennis shoes and dropped my towel and walked into the water. It wasn't nearly as cold as it had been last week, but it was cold enough. I dived in, gasping with shock and pleasure, and came up spouting water. I put my head down and stroked furiously until my breath gave out, then went into a normal Australian crawl. There was a float about fifty feet out. I swam there and rested a few minutes, then dove back, heading for shore. I enjoyed the swim, stopping twice to roll over on my back and float in the rapidly failing sunshine. About ten feet from shore I spotted the teen-age kid who had spoken to me last week end. He was splashing around with the girl who'd grown two inches over the winter –

Arlene, I think he'd called her. They were really having a ball, wrestling and ducking and mauling each other.

I swam by slowly and saw that the boy was putting his hands all over that ripe little girl. Then they noticed me and jerked away from each other, and the girl swam a little farther out and the boy said, 'Hi,' and quickly followed her.

They began their play again and I went in to shore. I dried myself with the towel, put on my sneakers and watched them.

God, to be able to change places with him!

When I went up the hill and entered the cabin Ellie was setting the table and Debbie was lying on the kitchen cot and sucking her thumb. The baby sat up and said, 'Debbie's sorry, Daddy.'

I went to her and kissed her and felt like a monster.

'Might as well change into your suit,' Ellie said. 'That is, if you want to go to the dance in the recreation hall tonight?'

'Sure,' I said. I showered, dressed and sat down at the table. We ate and talked, and Debbie lay on the cot and murmured to herself. Ellie was letting her stay up late because of my arrival, and also because of the spanking.

We finished at eight-thirty, and Debbie was ready for her crib. I went outside and sat in the contour chair. I smoked a cigarillo and looked up at the sky. It was still too early for a moon and full display of stars, but the North Star – or what I took for the North Star – was already present. I enjoyed my cigar, and began to look forward to the evening ahead.

10

Ellie came out of the cabin at nine-fifteen. She was wearing a tight-waisted, flare-skirted dress of blue-checked cotton. Her hair was swept up and back, showing her small neck and perfect ears to best advantage. She looked cute and young and utterly appealing.

'I'm ready,' she said, patting her hair. 'Now all we have to do is wait for the sitter.'

We sat talking for another five minutes, and then a dark-haired girl in levis and white shirt came across the grass and into the light streaming through our screen door.

Ellie and I got up, and Ellie said, 'Stephanie, this is my husband.'

I said hello, and Stephanie smiled, and I was surprised to see she was a real dish, a truly attractive girl with a full, curvy figure. 'How come you're passing up the dance tonight?' I asked. 'Money can't be that important to you.'

Ellie said, 'Now, Harry, don't embarrass – '

But Stephanie interrupted. 'Oh, it's all right, Mrs Admer. I don't mind telling why. I can use the money – three dollars a week allowance doesn't go very far on vacation.' She giggled, looking at me. 'Anyway, a friend from the boys' camp across the lake is going to drop over a little later. We'll sit out here, and I'll still be able to hear if the baby wakes up.'

'Aha,' I said.

'And there are three dances this week end, Mr Admer. Tonight, tomorrow and Sunday. I'll go to one of them.

And I'll go to one of the two dances given each week end all summer long.'

'Yep,' I said. 'You've got a racket, all right.'

She laughed and her eyes flickered over me, and she sure didn't look like a kid. I envied her friend from the boys' camp.

'We'll check with you later on,' Ellie said, and we walked away.

We went down the hill, moving carefully in the darkness. The recreation hall was near the lake and over toward the road on our right. It took a good ten minutes to reach it, and then Ellie paused outside the doors to pat her hair and smooth down her dress.

'Let's dance,' I said, and led her inside. The place was as large as a barn, with a bandstand at the opposite end, a bar to the left of the stand, and gay streamers and balloons hanging from the rafters. A hot five-piece combo was pounding out a mambo and doing pretty well. The floor was huge but already crowded with dancing couples.

Ellie's frown disappeared as she took everything in. 'This is much nicer than I expected!' she said. And then, 'There's Leo Brun and his wife, Mirinda. You remember Leo, don't you?'

I nodded. 'Sure. The boy who liked you so much.'

She smiled weakly. 'Harry, please don't say that. It – it makes me uncomfortable.'

I searched the crowd and spotted the short, stocky man and his wife. Mirinda Brun was about Leo's height, quite heavy, but with a clearly defined waistline and good legs. Her figure wasn't bad for a heavy woman, and her face was pretty in a round, strong-featured way. Leo saw us and waved.

'How are you, Harry?' he bellowed, pulling his wife along. From his greeting you'd have thought we were the closest of friends. He shook my hand. 'Wantcha to meet my wife, Mirinda. Mirinda, this is Harry Admer.' She smiled at me.

'Hey, you oughta try the bar, Harry,' Leo Brun said. 'That man mixing the drinks knows his stuff. Best Manhattans I ever tasted.'

Mirinda Brun freed her hand from Leo's. 'And he's tasted plenty. Must've had three already.'

'Well then,' I said, 'Ellie and I will have to catch up with him.' I give Mirinda a brief once-over, and she patted her hair quickly, instinctively. When she raised her hand that way it brought her large breasts tight against the thin fabric of her white blouse. She wore a snug gray skirt and spike-heeled, ankle-strap shoes. I glanced at Leo, and he was saying something to Ellie. His eyes were busy admiring every inch of her, and I said, 'Isn't that right, Leo?'

'What?' He looked at me, dropped his eyes and acted as if I'd caught him making a pass. 'I didn't get what you said, Harry.'

'I said that Ellie and I will have to catch up with you.'

'Yeah. Sure. C'mon, we'll all go over and have a drink!'

'Leo,' Mirinda said softly. 'Maybe you've had enough?'

'Hell,' Leo said, and then glanced around apologetically. 'Sorry. Anyway, I can handle my half-dozen. Trouble with you, Mirinda, you don't drink enough. Gotta liven up a party. After all, it's summer and we're on vacation, and you only live once. Right, Harry?'

I gave him the support he wanted by nodding emphatically. But his eyes were a little too bright, almost glassy, and he was slurring some of his words. His wife had probably helped him to bed many a night, and coped with his hang-overs the following mornings. Leo didn't look like much of a drinker.

We walked around the dance-floor to the bar. Ellie ordered a rum and coke, Leo and I had Manhattans, Mirinda surprised me by asking for Scotch and water. As we stood with our glasses, I moved to Mirinda's side and said, 'That's an educated drink.'

'I waited on tables for three years – in a tavern. I found out what was good for me, and what wasn't. Scotch is good for me.' She smiled. 'At least I can handle it.'

'And how does Leo handle it?'

Her smile widened. 'He doesn't. He's just a big baby. But I like him that way. I had enough of hard-drinking wise guys.'

I finished my Manhattan and stepped to the bar for another. When I turned back to Mirinda, she pointed at the dance-floor. 'Leo is feeling his oats.'

I looked. Leo was dancing Ellie across the floor, holding her very close, jawing away into her ear. Ellie had a fixed smile on her face. I hoped she wasn't too unhappy.

I laughed and gulped my Manhattan.

'Hey,' Mirinda said. 'You trying to follow in Leo's footsteps?'

I took the glass from her hand, put both glasses on the bar and nodded. 'Yes. He's dancing with my wife, so I'll dance with his.'

I took her in my arms as the combo beat out a lively fox trot. I danced into the crowd and held her tight, and she was a lot of woman moving against me. What with the two quick drinks and our thin summer clothing, she felt very good. The crowd pressed in all around us, and it was as if we were alone. My hand moved from the middle of her back, lower, until I felt the generous swelling of flesh. She kept her head down and said nothing. We danced closer, rubbing against each other, and then she looked up at me, breathing harshly. 'I hope Leo isn't as good a dancer as you are, Harry.'

'Why not?' I said, my own breath coming fast.

She moved away from me. 'Because I don't approve of him having – such fun. Let's go back to the bar, huh?'

I nodded, but I wasn't happy about it. Not that I'd expected to make her, but it was a shame to end the excitement, the pleasure.

We threaded our way toward the bar. She must have thought I was insulted because she said, 'We'll have to dance a few more times before summer ends.'

'Dance?'

She laughed. 'Yes, dance.'

'Ah, me,' I said, making my voice mock-sorrowful.

She laughed again and shook her head. 'On second thought, we'll just talk from now on.'

I laughed too, envying her in a way – and Ellie. They both must have had occasional longings to experiment with other men, but the longings were never strong enough to overcome their resistance, their beliefs in the rules and regulations of marriage and society – their love for their husbands.

Love. I had to push my mind hard to recall what it was – the intense friendship, the desire to be with someone, the near-painful physical and mental need.

I remembered feeling that way about Ellie, and remembering made it all come back. I suddenly understood how much pleasure I was missing. I also understood that sick thoughts had driven love from my mind.

Ellie still had it. She loved me, and I felt it, and I envied her. She was lucky. She could enjoy me. And I could enjoy nothing.

I was immersed in fear and despair – and death.

Ellie and Leo were waiting for us near the bar. Ellie smiled a welcome to me that radiated warmth, that radiated love; and my own love awakened and I wanted to tell her about it. But then the noise and music and voices reached me, and so did awareness of how senseless everything was, and I lost the memory of love.

Leo Brun was just finishing another Manhattan. 'Now that's going too far,' Mirinda said sharply.

Leo put down his empty glass. 'Shut up.'

'Oops,' Mirinda said. 'Here we go again.'

'Listen,' Leo said thickly. 'You know what you can do if you don't like it.' He turned to Ellie, grabbing her arm. 'Let's dance again, Ellie.'

'No thanks,' Ellie said, and glanced down at the hand on her arm.

'Aw, c'mon,' Leo begged, thick face screwed up as if close to tears. 'Just once more.'

'I have this dance, Leo,' I said, then smiled and moved up to him.

He turned impatiently. 'Why don't you go dance with Mirinda?'

He was really stewed, and he'd done it in record time. Ellie tugged her arm, but couldn't free it from his grasp.

'Let go, Leo,' Mirinda said. She glanced at me and her eyes begged for good will and understanding. 'Please, Leo.'

Leo ignored her. 'It's a rumba, Ellie. I'm great at rumbas.'

Ellie sighed, about to give in to avoid trouble, but I'd had enough. I grabbed Leo's hand and pried open his fingers and Ellie moved away.

'Okay!' Leo said, and whirled on me. 'Okay, so you're asking for it!'

'Leo!' Mirinda said sharply. 'If you don't come with me right now you can forget about coming back to the cabin altogether! I mean it. I'll lock the door.'

He glared at me. 'Okay,' he said. 'Only first I want to show how I cut big jerks down to my size.' He drew back his right fist and let fly a roundhouse at my head.

It was child's play to step away from it. And now I was angry. I could easily have chopped him down, but I didn't. Leo would play where Curt and Stan and the bartender wouldn't. But Leo wouldn't offer any real competition – not in his present condition. So I swallowed my anger and walked away with Ellie.

Mirinda called after us, 'I'm terribly sorry. He drank too – '

'My God!' Ellie said as we began dancing. 'People were looking at us and everything! I'm so shocked. He seemed like such a quiet man – and then the way he danced with me – and then this.'

'Forget it,' I said. 'It didn't mean a thing.'

Ellie danced beautifully, even though she was unnerved. But there was little pleasure in it for me, outside of the pleasure of movement, of rhythm. We danced and talked, and after a while I saw Mirinda leading Leo outside. From that point on I was bored. Ellie introduced me to other women and their husbands, and I danced with a tall, thin blond who kept chattering about her winter vacation in Florida, and time passed. The management had set up a buffet table and an announcer made a great to-do about how it was free and represented the policy of the colony – 'Your pleasure is our greatest profit.'

Ellie and I both winced at that one, and then Ellie said she was hungry and wanted a sandwich. 'Afterwards, I'll check the baby,' she said.

135

'I'll check the baby,' I said. 'I'm not hungry and can do it while you're bucking the chow line.'

She nodded her agreement, and I went outside. The night was cooler now, the sky full of stars. I enjoyed the walk up the hill, but then had to stop and try to place myself. I couldn't find a light in the area where I thought our cabin was located, and Ellie had left the kitchen light burning. Stephanie and her friend must have decided that light cut down on their privacy. Well, I'd give them as rude a jolt as I could! Imagine making me stumble around in the dark –

I caught a bulky shadow ahead and to my left, and moved carefully, silently toward it. After a while, I could make out the cabin. I could also make out our chairs, and they were empty. I stood there and examined the nearby grounds, and then heard a sound – a kissing sound. Another minute of peering through the darkness, and I spotted Stephanie and her friend. They were lying on the grass about ten feet from the kitchen door. I came up softly, quickly, and by the time they were aware of me I'd managed to stumble over them and shout, 'What the devil's going on here!'

Stephanie squealed, and a boy's voice said, 'Hey!' and they jumped up.

'It's Stephanie, Mr Admer,' the girl said, her voice frightened. 'I – I was just sitting on the grass with my friend.'

Her 'friend' was wiping at his face, Stephanie was doing things to her clothing, and they both cleared their throats. Then the boy said, 'Guess I'll be heading back to the camp.'

'Yes,' Stephanie said, still shocked and frightened.

'Why'd you turn off the light?' I said, and I was still

angry. 'I could have stumbled around here for an hour without finding you.'

'Well,' she said. 'Well – '

'Light attracts mosquitoes,' the boy said, and now he sounded angry, sullen. He was a big kid, about six-two and husky from what I could see. 'Anyway, you should've called out.'

'Really?' I said. 'I think you'd better leave before I help you to leave.'

'And I think you'd better watch your mouth,' he snapped back.

'Wallace!' Stephanie said. 'Stop that! I'm sorry, Mr Admer. Honest, I didn't think – '

I moved closer to the big kid. 'Get out of here, you fresh punk. Get out before I take you apart.'

I thought he might play, but he wasn't the tough kid he'd tried to appear. He walked away fast, going down the hill toward the road. I went to the cabin and felt my way into the kitchen and put on the light. Stephanie stood outside while I checked Debbie. When I came back, she said, 'I'm sorry, Mr Admer. Please don't tell your wife. She'll tell my mother. Please, Mr Admer. We weren't doing anything bad. Honest. Just holding hands and talking.'

She'd fixed her face and clothing, and was looking at me with wide, pleading eyes. She was cute, all right, and I wanted to tell her I knew she'd been petting and that I felt she had every right to have fun while she was young. I nodded and said, 'Keep your ears open. Debbie gets up for a bottle around twelve or twelve-thirty.'

I walked past her and she said, 'Thanks, Mr Admer. You're swell.' The fright had left her voice; she sounded happy again. 'I'll sit inside until you come back. I'll read.'

I nodded and kept going. I went down the hill and into

the recreation hall, and the noise hit me all at once. I didn't want any more of it, but Ellie waved. She was with new people and she introduced me. In a minute we were dancing and she said, 'Isn't it fun, Harry? We haven't had an evening like this since your father – ' She stopped and looked up at me. 'Sorry I mentioned it.'

'Why?' I said. 'He's dead and we both know it.'

She said, 'Yes,' and dropped her eyes and we danced on. But a few minutes later she spotted another friend and stopped to introduce me, then chattered away about how nice the place was. Death didn't touch her. Death didn't touch any of these people. So they were healthy and I was sick. So I preferred being sick to being healthy, when health necessitated being blind to the truth . . .

We left the recreation hall a few minutes after one, and Ellie put her arm around my waist in the darkness and hugged me. 'I had a wonderful time, honey. Did you?'

I wanted to tell her I'd had a lousy time. I wanted her to know my bitterness and pain and boredom. I wanted her to draw away from me.

But she was happy so I held back, and we reached the cabin. Ellie paid Stephanie, and the girl said good night and left. We went to bed, and I made love to Ellie because it was the thing to do.

This place wasn't going to bring me any pleasure, any forgetfulness. I'd have to sweat out the next two days. Maybe I'd get an early start Monday afternoon – tell Ellie I had a few things to do at home – and so avoid staying until Tuesday morning.

But my two-week vacation would be coming up the beginning of August. Two full weeks here. What the hell would I do with myself?

The thought was actually terrifying, and I shut it out of

my mind and tossed around until I fell asleep. Since my father died I'd been dreaming a lot. Bad dreams, unhappy dreams. And it happened again tonight. I was coming up the hill from the recreation hall and it was dark, and I saw Stephanie and her boy friend lying on the grass. I went up to them, chased the boy away and turned back to Stephanie. I put my arms around her, kissed her and tore off her clothes. Her body was luscious, more that of a young, healthy woman than a teenager. She cowered on her knees before me as I ripped off my own clothes until I stood naked. She said, 'Mr Admer, what are you doing? Mr Admer, please!' And her voice was Louise's. I laughed and stepped closer to her, my erection on a level with her face. She stared at it with big eyes, her lips parted slightly. I looked down at her. I wanted her lips on me, to feel the moist warmth of her mouth around me. I took another step forwards, and she leant back. She said, 'I can't, Mr Admer!' Her eyes were huge and frightened. I laughed again and said, 'I can!' And I stepped around her, moving behind her to put my hands on her shoulders and push her forwards. She went down onto her hands, and I knelt quickly behind her. I put my hands on her hips and lifted her so that she balanced on outthrust hands and knees. The twin moons of her buttocks gleamed pale in the darkness. I put my hand on the cleft and slid my fingers slowly down until I felt the moist lips and the crinkly pubic hair. She said, 'Mr Admer, please!' And again her voice belonged to Louise, and I was unable to tell whether she pleaded for mercy, or begged me to go on. I didn't care. This time I would not be frustrated. I eased her lips apart and positioned myself to enter her. I placed both hands on her smooth hips and dragged her towards me as I thrust forwards, impaling her. I sank in deep, her buttocks pressing deliciously

139

against my stomach. She moaned, and I began to move urgently against her, ramming deep into her with each stroke. And then someone came along with a flashlight and put it on us, and a voice I knew said, 'You're destroying yourself, Harry. This is rape and they'll put you away and you'll die and that's what you want, what you want, what you want – ' I realized it was Moe Crown, and I couldn't say a word and just lay there, spotlighted for the world to see, wallowing in my sin and guilt and shame. And yet he was right – I was glad to be found, glad to be destroyed.

Early in the morning, with gray light just beginning to filter into the room, Debbie stood up in the crib, screaming for Grandma Admer. Ellie couldn't quiet her, and my promises to bring Grandma up next week did no good. Finally, I lost patience, jumped out of bed and smacked her across the bottom. That really upset the kid, and she threw up, and Ellie wailed, 'Why'd you have to do that, Harry? Are you trying to make your own child hate you?'

I guess the answer to that was yes, but I whirled on Ellie and shoved her halfway across the bedroom, then went outside in my pajamas. It was cold, and the grass was wet under my bare feet. I returned to the bedroom and got a blanket, and I didn't answer Ellie when she asked where I was going. I went outside again, opened the contour chair, lay down and covered myself. It was far from comfortable, but I preferred it to being inside with my family.

I started to think of the why's, and then said, 'To hell with it!'

I managed to sleep until eight-thirty, when kids started chasing each other around the cabins. Then I had breakfast and made up with Ellie and took Debbie down to the lake. I saw Leo Brun carrying his kid along the shore. He ducked his head, made believe he hadn't seen me, scurried away toward the road. I didn't blame him for being ashamed.

The long week end passed, and the days were far from uneventful. Leo Brun came to the cabin early Saturday night and apologized abjectly, saying he'd been crazy drunk. We went to the dance with him and his wife, but didn't stay long. We returned to the cabin at ten and checked on the sitter – a thin girl named Rena who wasn't nearly as attractive as Stephanie and who paid much more attention to her job. We took the car and went to a drive-in theatre that was showing a crummy double-feature – western and a horror film. I stopped paying attention to the screen after half the western.

Sunday morning I played a game of handball with three men whose names I forgot a moment after we were introduced. Later, I went swimming with Ellie and Debbie, playing with the baby close to shore. It was fun, and after lunch we rented a boat from the lifeguard, who'd been given the concession to pad his skimpy salary. We rowed around the lake, examining the boys' camp and many private homes. At dinner that night I drank two sixteen-ounce cans of beer and got drowsy, and Ellie said she didn't feel like going to the dance anyway. We sat outside the cabin, listening to music on the portable and looking up at the star-filled sky and talking. Then we went inside and played canasta until two A.M. I felt closer to her than I had for months.

Monday morning, while Ellie was cleaning the cabin, I took Debbie out in a rowboat, and she delighted me by sitting straight and still, singing song after song. Ellie had taught her quite a few, and hearing that sweet little voice piping over the water was enough to keep me happy for a year. Or so it seemed. After lunch, the three of us drove into Hopewell Junction, and then farther on into the country. We parked beside a field in which cows were grazing, and laughed at Debbie's remarks, and drove back to the cabin feeling good. We had steak for dinner, and I told Ellie I wanted to leave in a few hours because morning traffic was too tough to buck and I'd make better time driving at night. She was a little disappointed, but gave in with a smile. We were a happy family; but then I ruined everything. Debbie must have been overtired because she got wild and dumped her plate of carrots on the floor. Ellie scolded her gently, and then I heard myself shouting and felt myself growing terribly angry. I jumped up and spanked her, and she shrieked. Ellie snatched her away, put her into the crib and comforted her for a good half-hour. By the time she came out of the bedroom I was ready to leave, and I accusing her of undermining my authority, counteracting my disciplinary measures, spoiling the child. She argued the point bitterly, saying I was becoming a violent neurotic. I knew she was right, but it only made me angrier. I lost my temper completely and called her everything I could think of, and she lashed back at me. The final result was that I stamped out of the cabin with Ellie bawling in the kitchen and the kid whimpering in the crib.

I ran into plenty of traffic, the worst I'd ever experienced. But I smoked a cigar and put on the radio, and was thankful to be on my way.

At the Hawthorne Circle a lot of traffic dropped off, with the result that I was able to average about forty miles an hour on the Saw Mill River Parkway. Many drivers averaged thirty, or even less. A few cowboys cut back and forth between two southbound lanes to hit near seventy. It was one of these cowboys – an elderly man in a gray and black Chrysler hardtop – who put the icing on my week end. He began his dance of death by rocketing by on the right with a blare of horn, glaring at me as if to say that my forty-miles-per wasn't nearly fast enough for the left lane. I began to mouth an appropriate suggestion, but he was gone. He swung directly in front of me, hesitating as he sized up his chances of cutting back into the right lane before a black sedan blocked him. He decided he could make it and swung his Chrysler hard right and fast ahead. At the same time, the black sedan picked up a little speed. The black sedan's front met the Chrysler's rear right fender with a sharp sound, and the Chrysler's driver jerked around in his seat as if pulled by strings. He was no longer in control of his vehicle, and it was still doing close to seventy.

As soon as I saw what was happening I slammed on my brakes, gripped the steering wheel hard and began looking for a way past whatever would develop. I was lucky. The Chrysler bounced back in front of me, rear end swinging far left, teetering dangerously on the two left wheels. The black sedan went the other way, up on the grass of the shoulder, and came to a quick halt. I swung my wheel hard right, hearing brakes behind me screeching as traffic came to a stop. I went by the teetering Chrysler, watching it in my rear- and side-view mirrors. It seemed about to straighten, about to steady in the left lane – and then it swung farther left, directly across the line of cars coming from New York. A station wagon full of people hit it – squarely on the side.

The tremendous initial smash of metal was followed by several smaller sounds and by further screeching of brakes as traffic on the northbound lanes came to a halt. I pulled off the road onto the grassy shoulder and cut my ignition. I looked out the window.

The station wagon had stopped dead, folded like an accordian, and another car was just plowing into its taillights. The Chrysler was spinning across the road like a toy, and came to a stop just short of the shoulder. Then everything was still, everything quiet, and it stayed that way for a few seconds. I was about to start up again, about to get away from the change, when a voice screamed. It came from either the station wagon or the car that had piled into the rear of it, and it was so high and shrill and agonized there was no running away.

I got out, sprinted across the southbound lanes and reached the station wagon at about the same time that five or six other men got there. The front doors were sprung open, and everyone inside had been thrown into the front seat and partly out the open doors. Six or seven of them, all ripped up, and not a sound or movement or anything.

'Christ,' a tall guy said, turning away. 'Christ, they're all dead. Christ almighty – '

I knew I was going to step up to that open door and look in. I did. I looked at that twisted, crazy jumble of arms and legs and faces and blood and bones and intestines and God knows what else. It was ugly beyond belief.

I turned away, feeling my gorge rise, and tried to stop the nausea by breathing deeply.

'Mamma!' a tall man whispered, hanging his head and swallowing drily. 'It shouldn't be!' He looked up as I walked slowly toward the crowd gathering around the car that had smacked into the station wagon. 'It coulda been me,' he said. 'It coulda been you.'

I had news for him. It *was* him; it *was* me.

I stopped a guy walking away from the second car and questioned him.

'Two women,' he said. 'One of them has a broken

shoulder – painful as hell. The other, the driver, got away with just a few cuts and bruises.' He nodded at the station wagon. 'I don't see them doing anything there.'

'No,' I said, and suddenly the picture of that front seat became too much, and I turned toward the shoulder and the darkness.

'Not all of them?' he whispered.

I didn't answer. I went up on the grass and bent over and was sick. I wiped my mouth with a handkerchief and went back across the northbound lanes, then had to stop before I could cross the southbound lanes. Traffic to New York was already in full swing, with drivers merely slowing down for a quick look at the accident on the other side of the road. I saw some shake their heads and a few actually grin as they spoke to companions.

That was normalcy. That was looking at death and shaking your head, or smiling, and always thinking, 'Not me. It won't happen to me.'

That was what Moe wanted me to do. That was normalcy.

I crossed the lanes and got into my car and drove onto the road. I didn't do more than thirty-five miles an hour all the way back to the city. When I reached home, it was midnight. The first thing I did was to pour a glass full of Chablis and drop in an ice cube. I left it on the coffee table while I undressed and showered and got into pajama bottoms. By the time I was ready to drink the wine, it was cold. I raised the glass to my lips and didn't put it down until it was empty. Then I went to bed.

I got up at six-fifteen, unable to sleep any longer, and washed and dressed. I went down to the super market at seven and was the first customer. At the corner candy store, I picked up the *Times*. In the apartment, I made

145

breakfast and read the paper as I ate. I found the story of the accident on a back page.

Seven people had died – all in the station wagon. The two women who had smacked into the station wagon were recovering in a hospital. But what really got me was that the cowboy in the Chrysler – the man responsible for the whole thing – had come out of it with nothing more serious than a bruised mouth and a few cuts.

Since the story made no mention of the part he had played in the accident, it was possible that he would get off with nothing more than his few cuts. And seven people were dead.

I closed the paper, shrugging. So much for God and the rightness of things.

I washed the dishes and walked to the BMT. Going up the steps to the platform the man ahead of me stumbled, caught the railing, looked back at me with a shamed grin. 'If you fall down these steps it's good-by Charlie.'

'Yeah,' I said.

We got into the same car, and every time I happened to glance his way I could hear him saying, 'It's good-by Charlie.' I don't know why, but I finally had to walk to the other end.

I wasn't any happier at the other end of the car. I wouldn't be any happier at the other end of the world.

11

We didn't get too much work done in the morning. People kept wandering in and out of the bullpen, talking about the long week end – how nice the weather had been, all the fun they'd had, and so on.

Around eleven o'clock things settled down, and I got to work on the crossword layouts. Half an hour later, Louise Gorden came into the bullpen, carrying a big envelope. 'Louise,' I called.

She looked at me. 'In a minute,' she said, and she was cold, unfriendly. She went round the partition to Curt Sawyer's desk and gave him the envelope. They talked, and Curt grinned up at her, being cute. But his face was pale and drawn, his eyes tired. He looked ninety. It was tough playing man-about-town at his age.

Louise left him and came around to my desk. 'What is it?'

I spoke softly, shielding the conversation from Mary Braken. 'What was Sawyer jawing about?'

'None of your business,' she snapped. 'Anyway, it wasn't personal, and I wish you'd be the same.'

'When that happens,' I said, 'I'll be dead.'

She didn't accept the compliment. She merely waited.

'Have a nice week end?' I asked.

'Very.'

Somehow, I didn't believe her. There was a bleak look about her eyes.

'I'm busy, Harry. I've got correspondence to get out. What is it?'

Her attitude chilled me. It wasn't the right time to make a pitch, but I looked at her tan skirt-and-sweater outfit, at her hair and lips, and I just had to go ahead. 'How about dinner this week?'

She shook her head, emphatically.

'Any day at all,' I begged.

'No.'

She turned away, but I grabbed her hand, held it under the level of the desk-top so no one could see. A quick glance at Mary showed that she was reading proof.

'Harry!' Louise whispered, eyes traveling around the room. 'Let go!'

'Not until you say you'll see me.' I kept a smile on my lips, but I wasn't kidding.

'All right. Let go.'

Her capitulation was too sudden, and her voice hadn't lost its chill, but I let go.

She stepped back and glared at me. 'You do that again and I'll tell Mr Henrich!'

'What about our dinner date?' I said, still with my phony smile.

'Never,' she said, and walked out.

I got back to work, full of shame and anger and confusion. It was no good, no good at all.

And yet, the thought of giving up never even entered my mind.

At noon, Moe Crown came around to my desk. 'Lunch, kid?'

'No, thanks, I'm eating later.'

'I can wait.'

'Better not,' I said coldly. 'I might be meeting a friend.'

'Harry – ' he began, and I finally raised my eyes, ashamed of treating him so badly, angry at myself for being ashamed, angry at him for creating this trouble

148

with his insistence on friendship. We looked at each other, and Moe took the cigarette from his mouth. He killed it in my ashtray and said, 'Never mind. Why should I bother?'

'Thanks,' I said. 'That's the first sensible thing you've said in a week.'

He was turning away, but whirled on me. 'Watch your tongue, mister! I'm still running this division!'

I'd never seen him as angry before. I nodded. 'Sure you are. That's why you shouldn't consort with the hired help.'

He nodded grimly and stamped out of the bullpen. I lit my pipe and smoked while I worked. I felt lousy. Everything was going wrong. A man had so little time to enjoy life, and everything went wrong.

I got up and walked down the hall to Stan Henrich's office. Louise was sitting at her desk, eating a sandwich and reading a magazine. 'Where's Stan?' I asked, stepping inside.

'Out to lunch.'

I closed the door.

'Hey, leave that open!'

I wasn't worried about anything now. She would see me this week. I'd taken too much from her to drop the matter.

'Let's not play games,' I said, moving forward. 'When are we having dinner?'

'I told you before I wouldn't – '

I reached out and touched her hair. She jerked back.

'Harry, I'm not going to ask again! Open that door!'

'And if I don't?'

She stared at me. 'I'll raise the roof. I'll yell, Harry! I mean it!'

I nodded, and I wasn't afraid. I didn't care. I just

didn't. 'Fair enough.' I grabbed her chin with one hand and bent to kiss her. She twisted her head away, shoved back her chair and got up.

'You're crazy,' she said, but I caught the change in her voice. She'd been reached. 'Only a crazy man would do a thing like this!'

'Yes. But only for you. Just remember that. Only for you.'

I came toward her and she didn't back away, and I put my arms around her. She stiffened. 'For God's sake – if anyone comes in!'

'Screw 'em,' I said, and bent to her lips and found them while she struggled to get free. When I raised my head her eyes were on me, frightened and excited.

'When, Louise?'

'Friday,' she said, and wrenched away and walked around Stan Henrich's desk. She licked her lips and smiled. 'Friday or never, Harry.'

Just for a second, I was angry. I felt she was hurting Ellie and Debbie; hurting them deliberately. But then it passed and I said, 'Fine. Seal it with a kiss?'

She waved her hand angrily. 'Open the door, Harry! I'll get in trouble!'

I opened the door and went back to the bullpen. Mary Braken had gone out to lunch; so had the entire staff on the other side of the partition. That was what I wanted – to be alone to telephone Ellie.

I dialed the operator, got Long Distance and gave the number of the combination candy-drug-grocery store which was on the road near the cabin colony. They had a public address system to call people to the telephone. The proprietor answered, and I asked for Mrs Harry Admer. About five minutes later Ellie's voice said, 'Hello?'

'Hi, honey, it's Harry. How're you and the baby?'

'Fine,' she said. 'Weather's been perfect. How is it in the city?'

'Hot.' I paused, putting my story together.

'Is anything wrong, Harry?'

- 'In a way. I've got some rush work to get out before Monday. A deadline. A few of the other artists are on vacation, and they couldn't get the right free-lancer, so I'm stuck. I won't be able to finish by Friday.'

'But that means you'll have to work on your own time!'

'Yes. And I'm afraid I'll have to be in the city – where I can check with Stan Henrich Saturday or Sunday on some fine points. I won't be able to make it up to the lake this week end, honey.'

'Oh, Harry! The baby will be so disappointed and I – ' She stopped, then said, 'Of course, if you can't help it, you can't. But gee, it makes me mad to think of them doing this to you when they know you've got a cabin for the summer!'

'I know, Ellie. Makes me mad too. But what can I do – tell them to shove it?'

'No,' she said quickly. 'Of course not. One of these days you'll get a better job, but at the moment – ' She didn't finish.

'Yeah. Well, I've got to run down and get something to eat.' It was the first bit of truth I'd given her. 'Love to the baby. And I'm sorry.'

'I know, Harry. I'll miss you. '

'Good-by,' I said, and felt ashamed.

''By.'

I hung up, went downstairs and walked to the Automat on 42nd. I ate, killed time looking in store windows, then returned to the office. When I came into the bullpen I heard Moe coughing his guts out. Mary Braken looked

151

up from her desk and said, 'Lord, he's been coughing for more than ten minutes! I don't see how he goes on. Seems he'd have a stroke or something!'

I shrugged and went to my desk, and my phone rang. It was Stan Henrich; he wanted to know what I was working on. I told him, and he said, 'Hell, clean forgot about that lousy crossword stuff!' He paused. 'I don't suppose you'll have time to do a little homework tonight and tomorrow? As a favor, Harry.'

I almost laughed, thinking of what I'd told Ellie.

I knew it was a chance to get in good with him. He might go to bat for me the next time the question of raises came up. But I wasn't going to bother. It just didn't seem important.

'Sorry, Stan. Got a heavy social schedule lined up. Why not use a free-lancer?'

'Yeah,' he said flatly. 'Except that the old man checks outside expenses carefully. It doesn't make him happy when I run up bills. He figures we can do everything right here. Well, maybe I'll get one of the girls on the fifth to do it.' He hung up.

I was about to load my pipe when I heard Francine Loes say, 'Watch out!' Ramona gave a little scream, and chairs scraped. I looked up through the partition and couldn't figure it out for a second. Everyone was shouting and moving.

Everyone but Moe. I couldn't see Moe. And then I did. He was on the floor.

I got around that partition faster than ever before. I reached Moe at the same time as Curt Sawyer, and we both bent to him. Curt said, 'Moe! Moe, what's the matter?'

'Get him into the chair,' I said, and then wondered if we should. I'd read somewhere that the best thing to do

152

was let an accident victim lie still until a doctor could determine what was wrong. But Moe wasn't an accident victim . . . 'Wait, Curt. Let him lie.'

Curt turned his head and shouted, 'Someone, call a doctor!'

'An ambulance,' Francine said, standing nearby, hands clasped together. 'An ambulance. Look how white he is! God – '

I don't think I'd actually looked at Moe until that point. I'd been so stunned, so shocked and frightened, I hadn't had time to look. Now I saw how shallow his breathing was, how pale his face, how his eyelids were fluttering. A second later, he opened his eyes, moved his lips and said, 'What's – what's this?'

'You fell,' Curt said. 'Fell out of your chair, Moe. You all right now?'

Moe sat up, looked around and shook his head. 'Fainted. Just fainted. Coughed so damn much. Help me up.'

We got him to his feet and then into his chair. He leaned back and reached automatically for the pack of cigarettes lying on his desk. I slapped them to the floor.

'Hey,' he said, looking at me.

'Let 'em alone,' I said, angry. 'You can do without them a few minutes.'

'Sure. But they won't kill me. Not them. And not this little dizzy spell.'

'Maybe not,' Curt said. 'But he's right. You shouldn't smoke now.' He turned to Francine. 'Did you call the doctor?'

She shook her head, looked at Ramona.

'No,' Ramona said. 'I thought Francine did. I'll call now.'

'Forget it,' Moe said, voice stronger. 'I'm okay. I'll rest

a few minutes and be ready for work. Just a fainting spell.' He looked at me again. 'Hey, kid, you look worse than me.'

Maybe I did. I felt weak and sick. I'd thought he was a goner a few minutes ago. And how could we have an office without Moe Crown? He *was* the office. To me, at least.

We stood around and talked to him, and his color returned. Finally, he got up and said, 'Okay, back to work. I'll wash my face and take a drink and be right as rain.' He walked out of the bullpen.

I went back to my desk. Mary Braken was standing there, trembling. 'I couldn't help him,' she said, voice strained. 'I couldn't go over there. I thought he was dying and I couldn't – ' She shook her head. 'God, he isn't too much older than I am. And when he was lying there – ' She turned quickly, went to her desk and sat down.

I understood. She had seen herself lying there. She had caught a brief glimpse of her own mortality.

When Moe came back, he paused near me. 'Thanks for the concern, Harry.'

'Sure,' I said. 'Don't you think you oughta take off the rest of the day?'

'Hell, it's only two-thirty, and I feel fine. I got a mystery mag to paste up.'

I shrugged, and he went on to his desk. Everything settled down, and I got into those crossword layouts. Half an hour passed, and then Francine said, 'What is it, Moe?' her shrill, frightened voice carrying.

I looked up and saw Moe leaning back in his chair, eyes closed. He waved his hand as if to say it was nothing. But we kept watching him, and he didn't look well. Then he sighed, leaned forward and rubbed his chest and stomach with both hands.

Curt walked over to him and said something, and Moe shook his head. I wanted to go around there, drag Moe out of the chair and send him home in a cab, but I didn't move. He was a big boy; he'd take care of himself.

A minute or so later he stood up and got into his jacket. I didn't hear everything he said, but caught enough to understand that he was leaving. He came around the partition, gave me a nod and went out the door.

I went on working, but I could still see his face as he'd walked by. It had been gray. Dead and pasty and gray . . .

At four o'clock I felt thirsty and decided to have a Coke in the Woolworth's on Fifth. I caught an elevator down, and then decided a beer would taste better. I went into the bar on 40th and drank a bottle of Bud. I had another, and by the time I finished it was four-twenty. I walked out, passing a phone booth on the way, and wondered if I should give Moe a call. But I decided against it. He might take it to mean I wanted to get back on a close personal basis with him. Besides, he'd be okay tomorrow, or the day after, whether I called or not.

I crossed the street, walked into the lobby and then couldn't see myself working any more today. The hell with it. I'd go home right now.

I got to the office before nine the next morning. Mary was already there, and she said, 'I turned off your lamp yesterday, Picasso. What happened to you?'

'Decided to go home. Thanks for the assist.'

The rest of the crew drifted in during the next half-hour, except for Moe. Then Francine got a call and said something to Curt and Ramona, and came around to my desk. 'Moe's sister just called. Moe's not going to be in today.'

'Oh? She say what was wrong?'

'Not exactly. Seems he went to the doctor yesterday and got orders to stay in bed.' She went back to her desk.

A few minutes before noon I went into the hall and walked to Stan Henrich's office. Stan was at his desk, but Louise wasn't around. I went on to the stockroom and looked inside, and she was searching through the big closet. No one else was there.

'Need some help?' I said, coming over to her.

She glanced over her shoulder. 'No. I'll find it myself.'

I turned, so I could keep an eye on the hall, and put my hand on her arm. 'You look lovely today.' I meant it. She was wearing her pale-blue flare-skirted dress with the sweet-sixteen touch.

'Thanks, but please don't touch the merchandise!' She shook her arm free.

I laughed, glanced at the hall, then put my arm around her waist. She gasped, squirmed away and whispered, 'What's wrong with you! Someone could walk by and see! Even Mr Lobert himself!'

I was elated. She didn't show the slightest sign of that terrible unfriendliness I'd grown to expect of her at odd moments. She was frightened and angry, but not cold and contemptuous.

'Mr Lobert?' I said, leaning against the closet. 'He hasn't come up from the fifth floor in over two months. He probably won't until Christmas.'

'You know what I mean, Harry. Please move away and let me get my paper.'

I was trembling with excitement, my hands damp and my mouth dry. I felt I just had to put my hands on her – touch her, caress her, kiss her. But Gil came in and said, 'What'll it be?'

Louise told him what she wanted, and I stepped away

from the closet. 'How's the boy?' I said, wishing him in China.

'Okay,' Gil said. He gave Louise a package of paper and she left quickly.

'Nothing for me,' I said. 'Just killing a little time.'

He nodded. 'I think Vince wants to see you, Harry. Something about a party you wanted to go to.'

'The cellar club in New Lots?'

'Yeah.'

'When is it?'

Gil shrugged. 'You got me. I haven't been around there lately. My old man don't like the crowd, and I gotta play up to him if I wanna use the car.'

'Is the joint that rough?'

He shrugged. 'My old man just thinks so.'

'When will Vince be around?'

'Any time. He's on deliveries today. Checks in and out all the time.'

I went back down the hall and looked in Henrich's office. Both he and Louise were gone. I was disappointed; I'd wanted to ask her out to lunch. In her present frame of mind she might have accepted.

I went to the washroom, then came back along the hallway. I looked in Henrich's office again, and Louise was filing some stuff in a tall cabinet.

'Thought you went out already,' I said. 'Want a free lunch?'

She shook her head. 'I'm meeting my sister at one-thirty.'

I was about to walk away when I heard Vince's deep voice. 'Wanna see you, Harry. It's that party you asked about.'

'Party?' Louise said, closing the filing cabinet. She sounded playful. 'I like parties.'

Vince looked her up and down. 'You don't say? I must've asked you a dozen times the first couple weeks you was here. How come you didn't like 'em then?'

Louise gave me a quick wink and said, 'You've gotten so much more mature since then, Vince. You've become so smooth and debonair. What about that party?'

He didn't know quite how to take it. 'Aw,' he finally said, 'come off it.' He turned to me. 'This Saturday, Harry. Starts at eight-thirty or nine. They raised the ante to three bucks a head. Were you kidding about wanting to go?'

'No,' I said.

'Neither was I,' Louise said. 'Can I go too, Vince?'

He looked at her. 'I'd take you myself if I didn't already have a date.'

'Then Harry'll take me.'

'Sure, sure,' Vince said. 'Harry's married. He's coming alone – ain't you, Harry?'

I shrugged. 'I planned to come alone, but if Louise wants an escort – ' I let it hang there, praying she'd pick it up. If Vince thought of it as a harmless job of escorting, brought on by Louise herself, there'd be no talk in the office. Otherwise, I wouldn't be able to press the issue.

Vince glanced at me, surprised, and then helped things along. 'Yeah, why don't you do that, Harry? Just for laughs.'

Louise raised her eyebrows and smiled 'Sure, Harry, just for laughs.' But now the change I dreaded began to take place. She was needling me, and it wasn't nice. She was getting that cold, vicious tone of voice. 'Please, Harry. You wouldn't turn me down, would you? I know you'd never think of doing anything your wife wouldn't approve of, but I'm harmless.'

Vince hadn't helped, after all. He'd messed things up.

158

He'd reminded her that she was playing with a married man, a taken man – exactly what I'd fought to make her forget. But he wasn't attuned to subtleties.

'It's okay, Harry,' he said, his dark, lowering face split by an unaccustomed smile. 'No one'll think bad.'

'Of course not, Harry,' Louise said. 'No one could ever think bad of a man like you. It's just for laughs.'

'Okay,' I said, and I wanted to get away.

'That'll be six bucks,' Vince said. 'In advance.'

I gave him the money.

'C'mon in the stockroom,' he said. 'I'll write down the address.' He walked away.

I stepped further into Henrich's office. 'You've made me very happy, Louise.'

She was looking down at the floor, and answered without raising her eyes. 'And you've made me laugh, Harry. If they only knew the kind of man you are!'

It was time to get away. If she went on she'd talk herself out of both our dates. And yet, I had to establish the fact that both dates did exist. I forced a laugh and said, 'Friday and Saturday – I'm going to have to buy you flowers for *two* dates. So long.'

She was raising her head as I left, opening her mouth. But she didn't call me back. I'd avoid talking to her tomorrow and Friday. This was my big chance. If I didn't get her this week end I never would.

I picked up the address from Vince and went out to lunch. I came back and stayed at my desk the rest of the day. At four-thirty my mother called.

'When are you coming to visit me, Harry?'

'Well, Mom, I've been busy. Dinner dates with business people and all that.'

'Please, Harry, come over tonight. I've got your old

159

room all fixed up. I'll cook a good dinner and you'll relax.'

'You've got your hands full with the boarders – '

'That's not so, Harry. They're not any trouble at all. In fact, I think I'll be able to go up with you to the lake sooner than I told you. Maybe in two weeks. Come tonight, Harry.'

She sounded so anxious, so lonely. But I couldn't face the old place – not tonight. I didn't know what to say.

'Honest, Harry, you won't even know the boarders are there. They're quiet people.' She laughed nervously. 'You know how newly-weds are – they stick to themselves. Please, Harry, for my sake.'

'Not tonight,' I said, sweating. 'I've got work – '

'Then tomorrow.' She sounded like she was about to cry. 'You can't stay away forever. You've got to come sometime. You've got to forget sometime.'

It was too painful. I ended it the only way I could. 'Okay. Tomorrow. I'll go to my place first and drive over in the car. I'll be there about seven.'

'Wonderful, Harry! I'm so happy! What do you want me to make? *Fleishedika borscht?* Stuffed cabbage? *Helzle?*'

'Anything, Mom. I gotta finish some work now.'

'Good-by, Harry. *Zei gesundt.*'

'Good-by, Mom. You be healthy too.' I hung up.

I loaded a pipe, lit it, sat there smoking. So I'd be going back to the old place tomorrow – for the first time in over three months. Back home, where I'd lived most of my life, where the memories were.

It made me sick to think of it.

12

After work I ate in a cheap restaurant in Manhattan, then took the subway home. At seven o'clock I walked to the apartment house and moved past the mob of people sitting on chairs ranged along the sidewalk, nodding at those who spoke to me. When I entered the lobby I stopped. I didn't want to go upstairs and watch television. But what else could I do?

I could visit my mother or Ellie's parents.

I'd see my mother tomorrow, and I had no desire to see Ellie's folks.

I could call up Mort Brenner or Ellie's brother Lou. I hadn't treated either one of them nicely, but maybe if I told them I hadn't been feeling well . . .

No, I didn't want to see them. And I didn't want a movie or a bar or anything else.

So what the hell could I do?

Suddenly, I was full of panic. It seemed as if I were shut in a small closet, tied hand and foot, doomed to spend my life in complete immobility. I couldn't go any place, do anything, find any pleasure in life.

I shook my head, went out the back door and through the alley to the street. I walked to where my car was parked, got inside, drove toward the Belt Parkway. I'd take a long drive – all the way out to the Island.

Louise Gorden. If I could see Louise Gorden, I'd be all right . . .

I reached the new development above Roslyn at nine o'clock and drove slowly past Louise's house. The lights were on, people moved inside, someone was sitting in a chair on the lawn. I drove to the dark spot where we'd parked last week and stopped. I cut my lights and ignition and turned to look back at the house. Was it Louise out there on the lawn?

I opened the door, then closed it again. I couldn't take a chance of angering her. I had to wait until Friday night to see her. It was Wednesday. Only two more days. Only Thursday and Friday. Then things would happen. I'd make them happen!

I U-turned and drove back past the house, quickly this time, without taking my eyes from the road . . .

Thursday, I finished the crossword puzzle layouts before noon, put them in an envelope and brought them into the stockroom. Gil was there, and I told him to deliver them to the fifth floor right away. Then I went back along the hall to Stan Henrich's office. He was leaning over Louise's desk, pointing out something on a large illustration.

'I finished the crossword layouts,' I told him. 'Maybe I can help with that rush stuff you were talking about yesterday.'

'No, I already farmed it out. But wait here. I'll check with Seldon. We shuffled the schedule on the pulps. I want to know what comes first.' He walked past me and out of the office.

I was alone with Louise, and from the cold look she gave me I knew I'd better play it safe. 'Tell Stan I'll be back in five minutes.'

'What were you doing near my home last night, Harry?'

'What?'

She glared at me. 'I won't have you sneaking around – '

I laughed. 'Me? I wasn't anywhere near your place last night.'

162

Her hard stare wavered. 'I thought it was your car. I was on the lawn – '

'Lots of Dodges like mine around, honey. I'll be back in a few minutes.' I went to the washroom, thinking she must have eyes like an eagle. Imagine spotting me like that!

I killed some time and returned to Stan Henrich's office. Stan was there. He gave me my new assignment – at least a week's work – and I went back to my desk. It was one-fifteen before I decided to eat, and then I realized Moe Crown hadn't come in. Ramona was back from lunch, so I walked around the partition and asked her about Moe.

'His sister called in again, Harry. He's still in bed.'

'But what's wrong?'

'She didn't say.'

I ate at the Automat. I wondered about Moe, and wanted to call and speak to him. But I didn't. I went back to the office and worked.

At three-thirty my stomach suddenly tied itself into knots and I couldn't go on working. I called Stan Henrich on the phone and told him I felt ill and was going home.

'Sure,' he said. 'Take care of yourself, Harry. Hope you'll feel well enough to come in tomorrow.'

As soon as he said that – established an alibi for my being out Friday – I knew I *wouldn't* come in. I'd take tomorrow off, stuff myself with Mom's good cooking, look around the old neighborhood. I'd enjoy myself.

The cramps went away when I got off the BMT in Brooklyn. I walked to the apartment house but didn't go upstairs. I had a toothbrush, shaving material and some clothing at Mom's place. I got in my car and drove toward East Flatbush . . .

The four-family house was on East 93rd Street, half a

163

block off Linden Boulevard. Mom's apartment was on the top floor front, five big rooms. She and Dad had lived there since I was six and my sister Helen four. It was home, and the long, tree-shaded street lined with two- and four-family houses was the old neighborhood. It was a good neighborhood, for Brooklyn. All the kids had gone to Tilden High, and most had graduated, and more than a few had gone on to college or business school.

I parked in front of the house and got out. Mrs Loew, the landlady, called to me from the raised porch.

'Hello, Harry. My, but it's been a long time since you've been around!'

I nodded, walked up the six stone steps and opened the hall door. She said, 'Your mother has two such nice boarders. Really nice young people. You'll like them. How's your wife and baby?'

'Fine,' I said, turning to her. She was sitting on the green wooden bench, her enormous body covering almost all of it, her huge arms hanging down on either side. She'd always been fat – at least as far as I could remember. And I'd never liked her. She'd chased my sister Helen and me and our friends off the porch when we were kids. I disliked her with the feelings of childhood. Here, in the old neighborhood, I reacted to everything with the feelings of childhood.

I went into the hall, and a tightness gripped my chest. I was home, the home was where Mom and Dad lived, and where was Dad?

I went up the long flight of stairs, turned left, toward the front apartment, and tried the door. Before Dad died, it had always been open, but now it was locked. I rang the bell.

Mom opened the door. She stood there, looking at me, and I looked at her. She was tall, slim and gray-haired;

she had a good face and good figure, only now she looked old and tired. 'Harry,' she said, and it was almost a whisper. Her eyes filled and she half turned away from me and said, 'I'm being silly. The first time you're here since it happened, so I'm being silly.'

I came inside the small foyer, and we kissed. To my right was the bathroom; behind me was the back bedroom; in front of me was the kitchen, the living room, and then the two bedrooms branching off the living room. One of them had been my bedroom, the other Mom and Dad's.

We went into the kitchen and sat down at the table, and I spoke quickly in order to stop the sickness growing inside me. 'What room do the boarders use?'

'Didn't I tell you on the phone? The back bedroom. It was always a spare room since Helen got married, so nothing's changed.' She jumped up, hurried to the stove near the window and raised the lid on a big pot. 'Another fifteen, twenty minutes, Harry; and the stuffed cabbage will be ready. I didn't expect you so soon. But you can start on your appetizer if you want. I got cantaloupe and watermelon.'

'Okay. Watermelon.'

She served me a huge slice and sat down to watch me eat it. I took a bite, and it was cold and sweet. When I finished I wanted to say I'd had my dinner. But how could I? She'd been waiting three months to feed me.

'Maybe another slice, Harry? I want the *holuptchis* to cook ten more minutes.'

'No, Mom. Guess I'll go into my room and lie down a while.'

Quick concern darkened her face. 'You're sick? You want something – an aspirin or something?'

I got up. 'No. Just a little tired. Had a hard day.'

165

I went through the living room to my bedroom and closed the door. It was small, square, with two windows facing the street, overlooking the porch. It hadn't been changed. My old metal bed was still there, and my dark mahogany chest of drawers and matching writing table. I'd slept here, done my homework here, dreamt of the future here. And in the week after Dad had died, I'd returned to face horror here.

But now I was tired. I lay down, closed my eyes and didn't think. It was good lying quietly, listening to the sounds from outside. Kids were playing down the block; I could hear their voices, but no words. And someone was coughing – not like Moe Crown, just a momentary thing. And a woman was shouting across the street, probably at her child. All normal sounds, sounds that wouldn't change much in a thousand years . . .

The next thing I knew Mom was shaking me gently. 'Harry. Harry, wake up. It's six-thirty.'

I sat up and rubbed my eyes. 'Six-thirty?'

'Yes. I came in twice, but you looked so comfortable I just couldn't bother you.' She paused. 'The boarders are already eating.'

I got off the bed. 'Think I'll shower before dinner.'

'You're not happy about them being here. The extra money comes in handy, but if you're not happy – '

'Don't be silly,' I interrupted, put my arm around her shoulder and kissed her cheek. 'C'mon, let's go meet the newly-weds.' I kept the smile on my face as we left the bedroom, but she was right – I didn't like the idea of strangers living here.

When we came into the kitchen the young couple seated at the table looked up and stopped eating. The girl was pretty, with a plump face and blond hair and a sweet timorous smile. She was well-stacked, but I couldn't see the rest of her figure. The boy was dark-haired, dark-skinned, nice-looking in a heavy-shouldered, round-cheeked way. He stood up, and I saw he was short and stocky. He cleared his throat and then glanced at his wife. 'Uh – ' he said, as if about to make a speech, but then he stopped. He cleared his throat again and glanced at my mother.

'I'm Harry Admer,' I said, their discomfort reaching me, embarrassing me.

'My son,' Mom said proudly. 'He's an artist, like I told you. I showed you his pictures in the magazines – the cowboys and other things.'

'Yes,' the boy said, and his voice was surprisingly deep. He nodded at me, eyes jumpy. 'Yes, she did show us. They were good pictures, Mr – ' He stopped, as if wondering what to call me.

'Harry,' I said, and decided to end this farce and get into the shower. 'I hope you and your wife like it here. Now, if you'll excuse me – '

'This is my wife,' the boy said, his mouth spreading in a wide smile. He looked at the girl, and she stood up. She had a good figure. 'Her name's Frances. Everybody calls her Frannie.'

I said, 'Nice to meet you,' and felt stiff and stilted.

'Tell Mr Admer *your* name,' Frances murmured, and laughed nervously.

'Oh, yeah. Didn't I say it? Carl. Carl Straus.'

I smiled, and my mother nodded at them and said, 'Go on eating, children. Go on.' She looked at me. 'Aren't they nice?'

I said, 'Yes,' and excused myself.

I showered for twenty minutes, making the water progressively colder, trying to work up a brisk, alive feeling. I dried myself, got back into my clothes and went to the medicine chest for some hair cream. I opened the mirror door and saw the injector razor in its transparent plastic case. Dad's razor.

I closed the door, looked at myself in the mirror, told myself I was being foolish. But the blood pounded in my ears, and I got a thousand sick, crazy thoughts. Was the blade in that razor the one he'd used the morning of the day he'd died? Was there still some trace of his beard or skin on it? If I took it out would I be holding some part of my father, some little part of his body? What had he been thinking when he'd looked in this mirror that morning? Of me, or Ellie, or Debbie, or Mom? Of death? Had he felt any premonition, any weakening?

Thousands of thoughts, most of them ephemeral I couldn't pin them down. Flashes of feeling. Cold, terrifying flashes.

I stared into the mirror, at my eyes. Wild eyes. Deep-sunken, sick eyes, bloodshot in the corners. No, not really. But they made me feel something. Fear? But what can a dead man fear?

I wasn't dead. I wouldn't die.

Someday.

But that was far off.

Dad must have thought the same thing – that death was far off. And he died a few hours later.

But I was young. Death had to be far off.

I left the bathroom. The door to the back bedroom was closed, and I heard the girl giggling. I went into the kitchen, and my mother was at the stove. She smiled at me and said, 'I'm so glad you liked them. They think you're wonderful. They said you were impressive. That's the word Frannie used. Impressive, she – '

'Okay,' I said, and sat down at the table. 'Let's eat, Mom.'

We ate, and she told me the local gossip.

'What about Mr Giannelli?' I asked. He was a coal distributor who lived in a two-family house at the end of the block. He'd been very sick the last time I'd heard of him – about a week before Dad died. 'Someone told me he had cancer. Was that just a rumor?'

Mom fiddled with her cup and sighed.

'Did he die?'

She nodded, looking at the table. 'Too young to go like that.'

'He was sixty, wasn't he?'

'Fifty-eight. Isn't that young, Harry?'

'Not really.'

'I'm sixty-one.'

My stomach jumped. I hadn't been thinking of her. 'But you're healthy,' I said, and finished my cup of tea. Suddenly, I was angry at her. 'Why the hell do you have to bring yourself into every conversation about sickness or – ' I choked back the words, but I was raging inside. I wanted to shout, hurt my mother, push her away from me. She was sixty-one, and I was afraid for her, and I didn't want to be afraid for anyone. I wanted to be free of fear.

'I'm going down,' I said.

'You'll be back?' she asked, puzzled and hurt by my explosion.

I nodded and left the apartment.

Downstairs the porch was empty, but I didn't feel like sitting. It was a warm, clear night. I'd walk. I'd look at the houses where my friends had lived, where their parents still lived, and I'd remember the old days. Time would pass, and I'd grow tired and go to bed early.

That seemed about all I could look forward to – going to bed early.

169

I walked up the block, away from Linden Boulevard, and came to the next four-family house. Irv Bellish had lived here. Irv had been my closest friend during grammar-school and high-school days. And we'd stayed friends through college. Then he married and moved from the neighborhood, and we saw each other only once in a very long while. The same went for my other two friends, Joe Crell and Warren Frankel.

I looked at the house and remembered the old days and felt nostalgic sadness. There'd been lots of good times. My childhood had been happy. And my adolescence. God, the things we'd done!

Like Halloween. We were sixteen and threw a party in Old Man Cohen's basement – just the four of us. But we sent out invitations to ten girls. They all came, and we told them the other boys had been unable to make it due to a strange streak of sicknesses and conflicting parties and last-minute crises. The girls had been angry, and four had walked out, but the others felt they might as well remain. After all, it was too late to line up another party. And so Irv, Warren, Joe and I danced with six girls, ate with six girls, tried to pet with six girls. We flopped on the last point, but did end up with the four prettiest. And we'd laughed ourselves silly all evening long.

Even now, thinking of it made me smile.

There were some people sitting on Irv's porch, and one of them was Irv's father. But he didn't notice me, and I didn't care to bring myself to his attention. I walked on. The next house meant nothing to me, and the one after that the same. The third was where Dora Lorsh had lived, and it was full of memories. Dora had been my big moment from my seventeenth birthday until after my nineteenth – my childhood sweetheart, and not in a childish way. We'd gone steady for over a year, had planned on marriage, had finally quarreled over her dating another guy. The other guy turned out to be nothing at all, but by then we'd both looked around and Dora had met a boy whose father owned a busy cafeteria on Pitkin Avenue. She married him about the time I was finishing basic training in the Army, and he never did go into service. She lived in Westchester now, had two children and was still very pretty – or so my mother had told me.

How I'd loved that girl! I'd dreamed of her at night, thought of her throughout my Army service, told myself I'd get revenge by seducing her some day. I'd been such a gentleman with Dora, such a damn fool. She'd always been willing to give in, and it was a sure bet her husband had tried her out long before marrying her. But not Little Lord Fauntleroy Admer. I'd wanted to save everything for the honeymoon, wanted everything to be perfect between us. By refusing to take her I thought I was proving the depth of my love. And by the time I wised up she was married. But I'd decided to get her anyway. Many a night in an Army barracks I'd figured on ways and means of visiting her when her husband was at work, making my pitch, having her, and then laughing and walking out with a few choice insults. And I might have tried it if I hadn't met Ellie right after leaving the service.

Thinking of Ellie made me think of the candy store where I'd first met her. It was on Church, two blocks from East 93rd. I'd come in to buy a pack of cigarettes, and she'd been sitting at the counter with a friend, drinking hot chocolate. It was a brutally cold winter night, and the friend, a flirty little redhead, remarked about my frost-touched cheeks with a saucy poem. 'Little boy with cheeks of red, cheeks that match my flaming head.' And she grinned and gave me sidelong glances. I responded with something like, 'Too bad my red cheeks are natural, because that kills the match.' Ellie laughed, and her friend grew angry. A minute later the friend said she was leaving. Ellie shrugged and said she wanted to finish her drink. When the friend left I sat down next to Ellie and said she should beware of friends with flaming hair and matching tempers. Ellie answered that her friend was all right, most of the time, and we began to talk. After that, I walked her home. She lived across Kings Highway, on East 58th, which wasn't as far from 93rd as it would seem. The streets didn't go in consecutive order of number, and it was only five or six blocks from my home. I asked for a date, got it and from then on I was dead. We didn't go steady at first; in fact, we knew each other three years before becoming engaged, and it was another year before we married. But it was the real thing all the way.

I'd been happy then. Life had been a lark. Like the kids in Mom's house. A never-ending adventure.

I walked past Dora's house, and then someone called my name and I turned. The tall, slim woman was coming down the porch steps, smiling. Her hair was blond, and its natural shade had been brown. Her nose was straight, and I remembered it having a tiny bend at the bridge. Her face was fuller, carefully made up. She wore a brown print dress, in very good taste and obviously expensive. She looked different, but I knew her right away. Dora.

'Harry!' she said, and held out her hand. 'My it's been years and years! How long *has* it been?'

I didn't know, but I decided to answer as if I did, as if I had counted the years and months, as if it had been something important to me.

'Six years, three months, Dora. Or maybe four months.'

172

She squeezed my hand, and then her eyes flickered away from mine and she tried to let go. I held on.

'You look wonderful,' I said, and put feeling into my voice. 'You – you don't look like the mother of two children.'

She flushed, and I let go of her hand. Then she said, 'Going any place in particular?'

'No,' I said, making my eyes move hungrily. I was acting, building this thing to the limit. It was something to do, something to fill time, something to chase other things from my mind. 'Want to walk along with me? I'm taking a sentimental journey, looking over the houses where friends used to live.'

'All right.' She ran back to the house and inside. A moment later she came out and over to me. 'Mother gave me a funny look,' she said, laughing. 'She saw us through the window and remembered how much I used to – ' She laughed again. 'You're handsome, Harry. You've gained weight and lost hair, and it suits you.'

We walked past Joe's house and crossed the street to Warren's. We talked about them, and then we'd reached the end of the block.

'You're married too, aren't you, Harry?'

I took her arm and began to cross the street. 'Yes.'

'You have a little girl?'

'You're well informed.'

She laughed. 'I – I was always interested in you.'

We'd reached the other side of the street, but I didn't let go of her arm. 'And I in you. Still am.'

'Why, Harry! And you an old patriarch!'

'And you an old matriarch. No, that doesn't fit you, even as a gag. Even young matron doesn't fit you. You're still a girl, Dora. A beautiful girl.' I smiled to give myself a way out in case she scared easily. But she didn't scare

173

at all. She began to talk about her husband, about the trouble they'd had the last two years, about how she and her kids had been spending days at her mother's place to ease the tension.

'It's not going too well,' she said, and her arm rested pliably in my hand. 'I – I sometimes wonder what it would have been like if I'd married you.'

'Always time to find out, even without a rabbi.'

'Now, don't be fresh, Harry.' But she smiled at me, and her eyes glittered. 'You're probably the most adoring husband and father around.'

It was a question. I gave her the answer she wanted. 'Sure, but I'd never say it under oath.'

She laughed and I laughed, and we walked closer together. It was getting dark. We walked to Rockaway Parkway and up toward Eastern Parkway. It was completely dark by the time we turned back, and she was walking very close to me and we were holding hands.

'I feel wicked,' she said, and her laugh was unnatural now, excited now. 'Imagine, we're both married and here we are, holding hands. Don't you feel wicked too?'

I felt tired. I didn't want Dora. She was another Terry Drego. She would use me for her own purposes – to bring back the old days, to prove she could seduce an old flame, to strike out at her husband. Like Terry would have used me to sell her stories, to sustain the constant reassurance she needed as to her beauty and desirability.

I didn't want that type of woman. I wanted Louise Gorden, who didn't really want me, who fought me all the way, who probably hated me.

We turned down Wilmohr Street and came to an empty lot. It was a dark, deserted spot, and Dora stopped. 'Wait a minute, Harry.' She sounded tense and nervous. She bent and fiddled with her shoe, then straightened.

We were suddenly very close. 'You'd never have passed up an opportunity like this in the old days,' she whispered.

I took her in my arms and she pressed against me hungrily, body rubbing mine, lips open and demanding. I reacted to her hunger, but it wasn't anything I couldn't control. She must have thought I was on fire.

'Harry, be careful!' And she came in for more.

We moved deeper into the shadows of the empty lot. It was really dark back there, and I was pretty certain we could not be seen from the street. Dora came back into my arms in a hurry, her mouth hot and urgent on mine. I used both hands on her, caressing her breasts and hips and buttocks. She pressed harder against me, her hands reaching under my coat to tug my shirt loose and clutch at my bare skin. She was grinding her hips against me, and although I still felt totally in control, I also began to feel an instinctive reaction. I eased her skirt up and shifted one hand round between us. She wore no girdle, and the flesh of her stomach was smooth and hot under my palm. I slid my hand down inside her panties and began to touch her. I put my left hand under her panties at the back, squeezing hard on the firm flesh of her buttock. She gasped, moving her hips in time with my probing fingers. I began to kiss her neck. Her movements became more urgent, and I felt her juices slick on my fingers. Then she let out a little scream and shuddered, her nails digging into my back. Her body went rigid, and she let out a long, slow sigh.

'Oh, Harry. That felt so good.' She moved away from me, and I thought it was over. But she smiled seductively and said, 'Now it's your turn.'

She settled her rumpled clothes back in place and went down on her knees. I stood numbly as she tugged my belt loose and drew the zip of my fly down. In one movement, she pulled my pants and shorts down to my ankles. It was like the time on the couch with Louise, when she had masturbated me. I wanted what Dora was offering, but at the same time, I didn't. I wanted to pull away. Leave her there, on her knees, with her mouth open. But I couldn't make myself do it. My legs were locked, my feet anchored. My erection strained to sink into the promise of her mouth.

She said, 'Oh, Harry.' And licked her lips, rounding them into an O shape.

She reached out, cupping my buttocks in her hands and drawing me towards her. I shuffled a step forwards, looking down at her blonde head. Her eyes were fastened on my penis, her mouth opening to take it in. She closed her eyes as her lips touched the head, and she moaned deep in her throat. I gasped, fire igniting in my belly as her tongue lapped the tip. She slid her head forwards, taking me all the way in, until her face touched my pubic hair. Then she withdrew slowly, and began to slide her lips rhythmically over the head. I stiffened until the pressure was almost painful. Instead, it was exquisite. Her mouth was warm and wet, her lips slick. They slid again down the length of my shaft, Dora's fingers digging into my buttocks as she drew me hard against her face. She did this several times, the ecstatic agony filling me almost to bursting point. Then she returned to the head, teasing with her tongue, sliding her lips faster and faster, back and forth over the swelling, sensitive tip. I shuddered as I felt my climax approaching, and she slowed her sucking, stroking movements, taking more of me into her mouth so that I trembled on the very edge of release. She made that little moaning sound again and began to stroke faster at the head. I put my hands down, twining my fingers in her hair as I felt my orgasm reach bursting

176

point and explode into her mouth. I cried out, shuddering as her fingers tightened on my buttocks, holding me still as her mouth worked furiously, drinking me with an abandoned thirst.

Finally she pulled away, swallowing. She licked her lips. She was smiling. I passed her my handkerchief, and she wiped her mouth as I fastened my pants. I helped her to her feet, and she smoothed her clothes into place.

'I have to get back,' she murmured. 'You going to be at your mother's for a while?'

'Yes,' I said, and now the old dream of seducing her was gone. But the part about walking out on her with a crushing insult still lingered. I wondered if it was worth the trouble. 'I'll probably be around a few days each week for the rest of the summer.'

'Then I'll see you. I – I'll let you know how to – how to see me alone.'

I could have told her she wasn't worth it, or that I preferred being with my mother, or any one of a dozen vicious little things that would make my dream of vengeance come true. But it wasn't worth it. I didn't dislike her, I just didn't feel anything for her one way or the other. I would have made love to her if we'd met in the right place, but I wouldn't go one step out of my way to effect such a meeting.

'Okay,' I said, already dismissing her from my thoughts.

We reached her house, and said loud, sterile good-bys because her mother was sitting on the porch. I went to Church Avenue, to the candy store where Ellie and I had met, and bought a package of cigarillos. I walked to a little bar near Linden and had a Scotch and beer chaser. That was to make me sleepy. I walked back to the house, and Mom was on the porch with Mr and Mrs Gernstein, the ground-floor-back neighbors. I told her I was going to get a good night's sleep, and she said, 'That's fine, Harry. Anyway, it's almost ten. Uh – the young couple is there – ' She stopped, and I waited.

Mr Gernstein, a dried-out little man with bald head and thick glasses, laughed. 'She means you should be careful not to bother them, Harry. Newly-weds, you know.' He guffawed and his wife shushed him, and my mother showed her disapproval by silence.

Finally Mom said, 'I meant you should keep the television low if you decide to watch, Harry. The boy works in a fruit market and gets up very early – five-thirty, most mornings.'

Mr Gernstein guffawed again, and started to say something. His wife cut him short with, 'Morris! No more beer for you at supper!'

That made me grin, and I went upstairs. The apartment was dark; the back-bedroom door closed. I put on the light in the kitchen, glanced through Mom's *Daily News*, and went into the bathroom to brush my teeth. Then I got into pajamas and returned to the kitchen to turn out the light.

Just as the kitchen went dark, I heard bedsprings creak in the back bedroom. I wanted to turn away, go to my room where I wouldn't be able to hear them, but I stood rooted to the spot. The squeaking stopped, started, stopped, and then hit a steady, rhythmic pace. I heard other sounds, or imagined I did. I heard the boy grunting; the girl moaning.

I was barefooted, and moved softly toward their door. I stopped, and the squeakings were clear, and the tiny voice-sounds were, too.

And suddenly I wanted to stop them, to chase them from my house. This was a place of death, not life! They had no right to make love here, to be happy and believe in life here!

I went to my room, got into bed and closed my eyes. The Scotch with beer chaser was a dud; I was wide-awake. And I felt twisted with fear and hate and confusion.

I couldn't hear the newly-weds now, but every sound from the street seemed to be part of their love-making.

I did something I hadn't done in years, something I didn't understand. I rolled over on my stomach and put my face in the pillow and cried. I stopped in a few minutes and felt like an idiot. I fell asleep soon after.

13

Mom woke me at seven-fifteen the next morning – Friday – thinking I was going to work. I wanted to sleep a little longer but couldn't take the chance that she'd suspect something.

'Same old *Hershela*,' she said, smiling as I groaned my way out of bed. 'You always hated to get up in the mornings. From kindergarten on you hated – '

I went into the bathroom, wondering what I'd do with myself today. Maybe I'd go swimming. But that was too much trouble. All I actually wanted to do was kill time until tonight – until I picked up Louise.

Which reminded me – I'd have to call the office and say I was sick, and then speak to Louise and tell her our date was still on.

I shaved and washed and had breakfast. Then I kissed Mom good-by and she told me to give her love to Ellie and the baby. She added that she expected me back at her place on Monday. I nodded at everything, figuring it would be easier to explain some other time. And I didn't intend to come back here . . .

I drove down Linden until I saw a candy store. I went inside, called the office and asked for Moe Crown. Ramona answered his phone, saying that Moe was still out. I told her I wasn't well, and then asked her to switch my call to Louise Gorden. When Louise answered, I said, 'I've got a bad case of lazy-bonitis, honey. But I'll recover in time for our date. Where should we meet?'

'As long as you're not coming in to Manhattan, you

might as well pick me up at my home. Park at the corner. I'll be waiting there.'

'Seven o'clock okay?'

'Eight-thirty,' she said. 'And even that'll make the evening too long.'

I laughed, trying to get her to do the same, but she said, 'The more I think of this date, the more I'd like to forget it.'

'I've got to hang up,' I said, getting angry. 'See you.' I slammed the handset on the hook, sweating in the tiny booth. I was running out of patience with her; I was beginning to tire of the game. If she didn't come through this week end, I'd boot her in the can!

Or maybe I'd *make* her come through!

I got back in my car and drove toward Boro Park. The thought of taking Louise by force lingered in my mind. Not that I would ever do such a thing. Of course not. That could lead to all sorts of trouble – loss of family and freedom.

I laughed at myself, and drove faster, and still the thought lingered. If Moe Crown had been around he'd have said rape was one of several logical conclusions to my affair with Louise. It would bring the self-destruction I wanted. According to him.

I laughed out loud, and the thought stuck, and I stopped laughing.

I reached the apartment at nine, decided it could use a good cleaning, and got to work. I vacuumed the living room rug, dusted all the furniture, and started on the bedroom windows. But I ran out of steam. I put everything away and hopped into the shower. By the time I'd dressed in slacks and a sport shirt it was almost one, and I was hungry.

I drove to a delicatessen on 16th Avenue and had a

181

pastrami sandwich, French fries and a bottle of beer. I finished at one-thirty, and sat fiddling with my empty glass, thinking of all the things I could do on this summer day. Go to the beach, or an air-conditioned movie, or the Brooklyn Museum of Art.

Plenty of things to do. Only I didn't want to do any of them.

I paid and walked out to my car. It was really hot now, really uncomfortable. I couldn't just stand around and wonder what to do and do nothing.

I drove to Coney Island Avenue, turned right and passed a small movie house, air-conditioned. I parked, walked to the marquee and looked at the showcase photographs. *Two action-packed adventure yarns!* a billboard proclaimed.

I hesitated, and glanced at the ticket booth. A tired-looking redhead with sullen, drooping lips flicked her eyes at me. She wasn't bad in a cheap way, a burlicue way. I walked to the booth and smiled. 'Good double feature?'

She had a magazine on her lap, and flipped over a page. 'Very good.'

I examined her tight white sweater. 'Hot, isn't it?'

She nodded disinterestedly. 'One?'

'Well,' I said, and kept looking at her sweater, 'I don't know.'

'Listen, mister,' she said, 'the show's *inside*. I wish I could go inside. It's cool there. And I wouldn't have to sit in this fish bowl.'

I laughed. 'I'm considering it.'

'Yeah? Then consider it some place else. Walk around the block or something. You're blocking the view.'

'And a very good view it is,' I said. 'Inside the fish bowl, that is.'

She finally cracked a smile. 'Be a good guy,' she said, and patted her hair. 'Buy a ticket or move away. The manager might come out and think I was playing during working hours.'

'When are working hours over?'

She smiled again. 'Go on, Romeo. You don't really – ' She stopped as a tall, heavy man came out of the theatre and up behind the cage. 'One, sir?' she said.

I shook my head. 'No. Maybe I'll drop around later and walk you home.'

'All right,' the heavy-set man snapped. 'None of that, bud.'

'None of what?' I said, and turned as he came around the booth to face me.

'Don't get wise with me,' he said, sticking out his chest. He had plenty of chest to stick out, but it seemed mostly fat. He was about forty, big all over, but definitely soft. 'I know your kind. Move on.'

I laughed. 'Make me.'

His face hardened, his eyes narrowed, and suddenly I was glad. He wanted to play. Curt Sawyer hadn't wanted to, and neither had Stan Henrich, the bartender in that gas-station restaurant or the baby-sitter's boy friend up at the lake. But this man was dying to maul me.

'Listen,' he said, voice thickening. 'Listen, I'll tell you just once more – '

It was a lovely red haze. It drifted across my eyes and blotted out thought and blotted out boredom. I slapped him hard, grabbed him by the shirtfront, ran him back toward the lobby doors.

And then he was yelling for help, and the girl was out of the booth and pulling at my arm. And it wasn't a fight any more, it was an assault. I let him go, and he and the girl stopped yelling. I stood there and said, 'What's the matter with you?'

He straightened his shirt with trembling hands, and the girl said, 'Go away. I'll call the police if you don't go away!'

'What's the matter with you?' I said to the man. 'Why do you let me push you around? What're you waiting for? What's happened to people in this lousy city?'

He didn't know what I meant, and the girl said, 'Go away, *please!*' They thought I was nuts, and I couldn't explain, and I turned and walked back to my car. I felt ashamed, and yet why should I? He'd wanted to fight at first. What the hell was wrong with him, with Sawyer and Henrich and the others? Why didn't they stand up and fight?

Was the answer in *me?* Did they see something that scared them? Did I show something besides anger – normal anger?

I drove back toward the apartment house, and I felt sick. The answer had to be in me. They saw something unnatural.

Wasn't that what Moe had said? Hadn't he seen death in me?

When I reached 16th Avenue, I lit a cigarillo and smoked it and wondered why I'd wanted to fight.

Screw Moe and his psychology! I'd just blown a fuse, lost my temper. That's all it was.

Sure. And I had run into a few nonviolent men, nonfighting men in the last two weeks. That's all it was. No one saw anything frightening in me. Of course not. If I wanted a brawl, I'd find it easy enough at that cellar club party. Vince's friends wouldn't hesitate a second. A fight was the cheapest commodity in New Lots.

Not that I'd want it. I'd be with Louise and have fun, and everything would be fine.

I went up to my apartment . . .

At six-forty I dressed and drove to a florist on New Utrecht Avenue. I bought an orchid corsage and wrote a note to go with it. But I tore up the first white card, and a second, and a third. The fourth turned out okay, and I put it in the transparent plastic box. It read:

If only for tonight, be kind to me.

In her present mood, the best way to approach Louise was with an abject plea.

I reached our meeting spot a few minutes before eight-thirty, and pulled to the curb. She wasn't there, but a moment later I saw her walking quickly down the street. She came to the car and got in.

'Hi,' I said, and gave her the plastic box. 'A little – '

'Let's go, Harry. I don't want my mother or father to see you.'

There was no arguing with that chill, peremptory tone. I drove off, and then said, 'I missed you today.'

She'd opened the box and taken out the corsage. She was looking at it. 'Thank you. I'm not dressed for an orchid, but it's nice anyway, Harry.'

'You're always dressed for an orchid,' I said, but she was right. She was wearing a simple gray skirt and white blouse. She wasn't trying to impress me tonight, as she had on our other dates. 'What would you like to do?'

She pinned the corsage to her blouse before answering. 'A movie, Harry. That's why I dressed this way. Just a movie.' The chill tone was gone, but the weariness that had taken its place discouraged me even more. It made me feel that she'd reached a decision, that she was merely playing out our two dates.

185

'We can do better than that, honey. How about trying one of those small clubs along – '

'A movie, Harry.'

The anger rose in me, and I fought it, but it wouldn't go away. I thought of driving to some dark spot and talking to her. And if she wouldn't understand how much I needed her I'd take her anyway!

But that was a crazy thought, and I shook it off. At least I tried to shake it off.

'All right,' I said. 'Let's go to the drive-in on Sunrise Highway.'

She didn't answer, and I glanced at her. She was staring straight ahead, a stony expression on her face.

'The card,' I said quickly. 'Did you read the card I put in with the corsage?'

'Card?' She searched through the box and found it. I flicked on the roof light. She moved her lips as she read, and then put the card back in the box and the box on the seat.

I turned off the light and said, 'I need you.' I wasn't lying. The last few days had built up my need, and I felt sure she could hear it in my voice. 'Please, honey.' I let it go at that, and waited.

'It's so stupid,' she finally said, but she wasn't angry. 'How can you need me?'

'I do. I don't know how, or why, but I do.'

'What good can come of it?'

'The pleasure of the moment. The pleasure of being together, of making love – '

'Never! And if you're going to talk like that I want you to take me home. The corsage was lovely and – and the card was sweet. But if you're going to talk about – about things like that I want to go home.'

'Okay, no more talk.' I wanted her. I had to have her.

186

I couldn't hold back much longer. It would be so easy to reach out and use my strength on her and satisfy the longings . . . I was helpless to prevent the jumble of thoughts that tumbled into my mind. I could reach out and tear that white blouse off her. Rip her brassiere loose to expose the breasts I had imagined so avidly. She might scream. Or she might be too frightened to do anything other than allow me to proceed. Only I knew somehow that she wouldn't be afraid. I had put myself in her power that evening in the apartment. Masturbating me, she had gained a hold on me. Oh, I could use my strength on her. I could drag her panties down and force her back on the seat. Take her there, in the car, on the street. But I'd feel that cold anger, and the thought of that dampened my angry excitement. Besides, what about after? If she cried rape, I could end up in jail. I could lose my job, my wife, everything. And at the end, I wouldn't have Louise, either. I'd have nothing.

I ached to do something, and I was afraid of the wildness, the intensity of my feelings. My stomach twisted, my throat and chest constricted, I wanted to cry.

I reminded myself that I was a married man on a lark. Just a lark. I was out for kicks. I didn't love the girl, so there was no reason for this mind-breaking, agonizing desire. No reason at all. It had to go away.

It didn't go away. And I remembered what Moe had said. If he was right my desire was based on something stronger than love.

Everything I was doing was based on the will to die. If Moe was right. Which he wasn't.

'We'll go to a movie,' I said. 'The drive-in.'

She sighed. 'What's playing?'

I didn't have the slightest idea. 'A good show. I forget at the moment, but it's a good double-feature.'

'Maybe I saw – '

'We'll check, anyway. Put on the radio and get some music, huh?'

She didn't argue any more, and I had nothing to say. The longing, confusion and repressed tears were swirling inside me. There was only one way to ease them, and it wasn't by talking. I'd get her in that open-air theatre and we'd have the privacy of my car. Even if nothing worked out tonight I might be able to change her attitude enough to make tomorrow night fruitful. Tomorrow night, with the drinking and the music and the slum kids loving it up in every corner . . .

I glanced at her as we sped along the highway, at the taut lines of her breasts pushing against the blouse, at the curve of her thighs filling the tight skirt, at the whiteness of her bare legs running down to high-heeled shoes. I couldn't believe she was made of the same stuff as Ellie, the same stuff as Terry Drego and any other woman I could get. Logic was no longer worth a damn. I wanted her, and she was unique, and she was worth any risk.

We reached the drive-in. She hadn't seen either of the pictures, and neither had I. The main feature was a technicolor musical, and she was pleased.

It was completely dark when we drove down the aisle-road, glancing in toward the rows of cars facing the huge screen. About the twelfth row I began to see empty spots. But I wanted to get further back, away from the mass of cars.

'You're going too far,' Louise said. 'I think I saw – '

'Next row,' I said quickly, and then we were at the next row. 'No, one more. It's better back here. Less noise from other cars.'

She didn't answer, and I went another two rows before turning in. I found a spot slightly left of center and jockeyed back and forth until the car was pointing directly at the screen, front wheels up on the cinder slope, right window close to the pole, on which hung two speakers. I cut engine and lights, and Louise reached through the window and got a speaker. She hooked it onto the window ledge, turned up the volume and leaned back.

'Pretty far,' she said, but she didn't seem to mind.

I glanced right and left. We had open space on both sides, and it was dark, and we were alone. The speaker blared gunshots, a voice yelled, 'Dirty coppers!' and gangsters fought guards on the screen. It was the second feature – a prison movie.

I slid a few inches closer to Louise, found her left hand and held it. She said, 'Harry, don't,' but didn't take her hand away. I stroked the palm, the back and the fingers. I rubbed the wrist and felt the tiny pulse beating, beating. I raised her hand, held it open and kissed the palm, kissed it long.

She turned to me. 'Harry, please don't spoil things. Can't we watch the picture?'

There was no anger in her voice, and the weariness was gone. But the change I was hoping for hadn't taken place. She sounded as if she meant what she said, as if she wanted to enjoy the movie.

I drew her close, and she said, 'Now listen!'

'Make believe I'm single,' I said, voice shaking. 'Just a boy and girl on a date.'

'Sure,' she said sarcastically. 'And you think I do things with every boy I date?'

'I'm not trying to do things, whatever you mean. I just want to have my arm around you, hold your hand, sit comfortably and watch the picture. I just want to feel close to you.' I pulled her against me, and I was trembling. I don't know what I'd have done if she'd refused. But she didn't refuse. She sighed and leaned against me and the stiffness went out of her body.

We sat there, and I began to watch the picture. I stroked her arm with my right hand, and after a while her head rested on my shoulder. Her hair was under my chin, and every so often I put my lips in it. Our left hands moved together, and the intimacy grew. It was wonderful. We were closer than we'd ever been, far closer than that time in my apartment.

I wanted to pull her around, kiss her lips, caress her body. But I didn't dare. That would come tomorrow. I'd have to wait until tomorrow. Tonight she would learn to like me.

At the end of the prison movie, I left the car and went to the refreshment stand. I brought back hotdogs and Cokes and a bag of popcorn. The musical started, and we sat apart, eating and drinking. I finished first and waited for her to finish, then put my arm back around her. She snuggled up against me, gave me her hand, said, 'It's nice here, Harry. It's cooler than I thought it would be. And not crowded.'

She sounded relaxed and pleased – almost happy. I couldn't resist the opening. I bent and kissed her lightly on the cheek. She said, 'Now, Harry,' and giggled. I had to fight hard to keep from going further. I must have trembled, because she said, 'Are you chilly?'

'No,' I said, voice thick, 'As far from chilly as possible.'

She glanced at me, and her lips curved upward in a little smile. 'Behave.'

I behaved. The musical was lousy, but she liked it. She hummed along with the songs and murmured appreciatively at the dance routines, and was still and attentive during the love scenes. Once, she drew away and said, 'Excuse me.' She headed for the lighted refreshment stand, which also housed the rest rooms. When she returned, she slid across the seat, right up against me, and took my hand. Again I controlled myself, thinking of tomorrow night – of the drinking and dancing and better opportunities.

But she spoiled my plan just before we left. The prison film had reached the part where we'd come in, and she drew away from me. 'Turn your head for a second, Harry.'

'What?'

'Something needs adjusting,' she said primly. 'Turn your head.'

I did, but I shifted in such a way that I was able to glimpse her for a second. She had raised her dress and was doing something to her underclothing. The smooth expanse of her thighs gleamed whitely, and my heart began to pound. The ache rushed in; the desire that was crazy-strong.

She looked up, and I jerked my eyes front and center. But I could still visualize those swelling thighs and her hand moving between them and her legs twisting. I cleared my throat and tried to shrug off the picture, put it into sterile words. Provocative, I told myself.

But 'provocative' meant nothing. I was filled with a longing and lust I'd never known.

She finished and said, 'Okay.' I backed off the incline and drove out to the highway. I put on the radio and we talked about the picture. And all the time I wanted to beg her to give herself to me, wanted to grovel for release from the terrible desire.

When we reached her home, it was one A.M., and the entire street was black. I shut the ignition and turned to her. She had taken off the orchid and placed it on the seat.

191

'I told my parents I was seeing a girl friend,' she said apologetically. 'Save it for tomorrow, Harry. It'll hold up well if you put it in the refrigerator.'

I nodded and reached for her, and she said, 'You're not going to spoil it, are you, Harry?'

'Just a good-night kiss,' I said, and my voice was a ridiculous croak.

She surprised me. 'All right. It's silly, but all right.'

She leaned forward, stretching her neck. She wanted a brief touching of lips, a sterile, adolescent kiss. I slid across the seat, grabbed her, mashed my mouth against hers. She made a sound of protest, and shoved at me with both hands. My own hands were moving over her body; and then I realized that her resistance wouldn't end. She was fighting hard.

It frightened me, made me understand that I could lose tomorrow night. I let go and slid away.

'I'm sorry,' I said, before she could open her mouth. 'I lost my head. Please, honey, don't be angry.' I was talking as fast as I could, frantic to stop her from saying anything that would break our Saturday-night date. 'I'm in love with you. I can't always control myself. But it won't happen – '

She finally broke in, saying, 'You're a nut!'

I laughed weakly. 'You're right.' There wasn't an ounce of pride left in me. I listened to myself cringing and begging, and didn't even wonder at it. ' – what I need is a good night's sleep. See you tomorrow. Shall I pick you up at the same place? Eight-thirty will be just about right. We'll reach New Lots – '

She was breathing heavily, touching her mouth, staring at me. Then she opened the door and got out.

'Okay,' I said. 'Same time, same place. Okay?'

She looked in through the open window. 'If I didn't

192

want to see what a cellar club was like I'd call the whole thing off right now.' The ice was back in her voice.

'So long,' I said, and pulled away.

When I reached the Belt, I began cursing her. I called her everything I could think of, and then went over the list again. I did it aloud, gripping the wheel hard, hitting eighty on the straightaways.

Bitch! I'd teach her the facts of life tomorrow night, come hell or prison!

It was after two when I got to bed, but I didn't sleep peacefully. I had nightmares. They were funeral scenes, one after another, and everyone I knew was being buried. I kept coming awake and going back to sleep, over and over and over, until it seemed as if the few hours to dawn had stretched into thousands. But life's thousands had shrunk to nothing.

At daybreak I got up and drank a water-glass full of straight whisky. It turned my stomach, but a few minutes later I felt warm and drowsy. I went back to bed and slept soundly . . .

When I came down at seven-fifteen Saturday evening a hot damp wind was whipping through the streets. It was already dark because of black, low-hanging clouds. I got in the car and headed for the Belt. It began to pour before I'd reached the broad highway.

I thought of Louise and hoped the rain would stop by eight-thirty. The way it was coming down now, her parents wouldn't let her step out of the house.

I drove onto the parkway, doing between thirty and thirty-five miles an hour. Visibility was lousy, even with my wipers in perfect condition. And the rain kept falling, harder and harder.

22

I reached the corner at exactly eight-thirty. Louise wasn't there, and it was still pouring.

I waited. I waited until eight-forty, and then began to worry. I put on the radio and tried to relax. At nine o'clock, the rain let up and I tensed, expecting to see her run down the street. But five minutes passed and it began pouring again, and I knew she wasn't coming.

There was only one sensible thing to do – go home. Or go to the party alone. But I wasn't sensible now. I'd looked forward to this too long. Tonight would be the culmination of the entire affair – one way or another.

I started up and drove slowly down the street. I parked in front of Louise's house and leaned across the seat and tried to see if anyone was standing near the big picture window facing the front yard. But with the rain, and drapes, I couldn't see a thing.

I straightened and felt the sweat begin trickling down my sides. I wouldn't give up this way!

I tapped the horn twice and looked at the house. I waited a few minutes and did it again; longer taps this time. Then I really leaned on the horn, and someone came out of the house and ran to the car. I opened the door and Louise jumped in. She was wearing a transparent plastic raincoat over a beautiful gray dress. She pushed the hood off her head. 'I never thought you'd come in a storm like this,' she said. 'I was sure you'd telephone and call it off. You should have.'

She was angry. And that made me angry.

'You're dressed, aren't you?' I said.

She was opening the snaps on her raincoat, and turned to glare at me. 'Sure I'm dressed! My parents are having relatives over tonight. My cousin Barrie is coming. That's why I'm dressed.'

I pulled away from the house. 'Your cousin Barrie must be quite the boy to rate that low-cut, figure-hugging number and spike heels. Where do you entertain him, in the bedroom?'

'How dare – ' She jerked her head away and stared out her window.

We reached the parkway, and I cursed the rain and cousin Barrie and my own stupid temper. Louise looked so damned attractive, so damned desirable.

'I'm sorry,' I said.

She didn't answer, didn't turn.

'I brought your corsage,' I said.

'Give it to your wife,' she snapped.

I wanted to use my free hand on the back of her head. I wanted to slug her, make her scream and cry and beg for mercy. I drove faster.

Later, I calmed down and said, 'Please, honey, put on the corsage.'

She was silent.

'After all, we're going to be together the whole evening.'

She turned and picked up the box. She opened the window and threw the box out, faced me. 'Now do you understand?' she said. 'Now do you see what I think of you and your corsages and your dirty mind and dirty plans – ' She paused for breath. 'Now do you understand that I don't want to see you?'

I wasn't angry any more. I knew something would happen tonight, that I'd get satisfaction, forgetfulness, completion in some way. 'I understand,' I said. 'You went out with me five times. I understand much more than you do.'

'We'll see!' Her voice climbed. 'We'll see at the party!'

'At the party, or after the party.'

'What?' she shouted, leaning over to bring her face close to mine.

'At the party, or after the party.'

She laughed – a loud, raging, braying sound. 'Sure!'

I didn't give a damn now. 'You'll love it,' I said, enjoying freedom of speech with her for the first time. 'You've been waiting for it since I took you to lunch. Maybe it isn't a conscious waiting, but it's there. You'll love it.'

'Crazy! You're crazy! Vince will take me home, or someone else. I'll go home with anyone but you!'

I slowed down and turned to look at her and smiled. I ran my eyes over the tight sheath of her gray dress, over her breasts and stomach and legs. I said, 'I've wanted you so long, so much. I'd have died for you, I think. Maybe I still would. Maybe I actually will.' I ached for her and thought of her resisting me, and knew I couldn't tolerate any more resistance. I nodded. 'Yeah, maybe I actually will.'

'Harry, take me home!' She was frightened. 'You're a married man, and I don't want anything to do with married men. Please, Harry.'

'I don't believe you,' I said. 'Think back, honey. Think back and you won't believe yourself.'

'Harmless,' she said. 'It was all harmless and I thought – ' She didn't tell me what she'd thought. She sat there, biting her lip, close to tears.

'I love you,' I said, and it was true. It would remain true until the game was finished. I didn't want to frighten

196

her, hurt her, but I would if it was the only way. 'I love you, Louise.'

She shook her head violently. 'Liar.'

'So help me,' I said.

'Liar!'

'I need you.'

She put on the radio, found music, turned the volume up high. We rode toward New Lots . . .

New Lots Avenue, between the old Rockaway Avenue trolley depot, now a razzle-dazzle farmer's market, and the Belt Parkway discharge artery of Pennsylvania Avenue, was one of Brooklyn's changing areas. The old European-Jewish, Spanish-Jewish and Italian population had begun to feel the squeeze of Negro and Puerto Rican elements moving in on two sides – from Pitkin Avenue on the north and Rockaway Avenue on the west. And within the predominantly Jewish and stubbornly entrenched Italian groups the dry rot of poverty had worked changes – evil changes. New Lots was fast becoming a battle-ground. And the kids had more to fight, more to hate than when I was a boy. There were shines and spics to fight, to hate. And that required greater proficiency in battle – gangs instead of individuals, weapons instead of fists. So the zip guns were manufactured in grammar, junior-high and high-school shop classes. And Sneaky Pete, marijuana and heroin were available for high kicks and Dutch courage.

Still, there were the good kids, and Thomas Jefferson High continued to turn out its quota of top-notch students and athletes. So New Lots wasn't all bad, or all good. But neither was it the place to seek safe and innocent entertainment on a Saturday night – not for a married man and a girl from an exclusive Roslyn Heights area. At least not in a cellar club.

And that's where we were going. I'd made my turn from the sleazy brightness of New Lots into the darkness of a tenement-lined street, peering through the rain in an attempt to spot house numbers and find the address Vince had given me. Louise made a little sound of revulsion as I slowed down. I felt no revulsion, but there was a tightness in my chest, a dampness in my palms. The old enemy – senseless violence – lived here.

But was it my enemy *now?*

I saw the glare of an unshaded bulb over a street-level doorway. I pulled to the curb on the other side of the street and said, 'Read it and weep, honey.' I glanced at her. She was staring at the hand-painted, red-lettered sign under the bulb. I read it aloud for her. 'Happy Warriors.' I waited for her to say something. She didn't. 'Want to go home instead?'

'Not with you,' she said, trying to sound cold, sure of herself. It didn't come off. She was scared. 'I'll speak to Vince and – ' Her voice died as three boys ran past us, crouching low against the driving rain as they crossed the street to the club. They yelled obscenities at each other, pushed for first crack at the door, opened it and lunged inside. No clean white light came from that doorway; only a dim, blue fog. Then the door closed and we were looking at each other. I smiled.

'Sure, honey. You'll speak to Vince, and he'll get a friend to take you home. Maybe one of those three defenders of clean-living will volunteer.'

She suddenly laughed. 'I think you're afraid, Harry. I really do! You know as well as I do that there are nice boys in every crowd. There are nice boys down in that club.'

She was right about my being afraid, and right about there being nice boys in every crowd. But she didn't know *why* I was afraid, and that the nice boys wouldn't enter into the picture. It wasn't the nice boys who would try to 'rescue' Louise, who would play with me when the red haze drifted across my eyes.

I got out of the car, walked around to her side and opened the door. I stood in the rain, waiting for her to step out. 'Let's go.'

She let me wait a few seconds longer, let the rain soak my hair and trickle down my face and neck. 'Of course, Harry.' She was still nervous, still scared, but there was a wildness entering her voice, an angry go-to-hell note. 'It's going to be fun!'

She got out, and we ran to the street-level door near the concrete base of a tall stoop. I opened the door, and the smoke and noise and thick blue light was a few steps down and ahead of us. Louise went first, down the steps to the long, narrow basement room, and someone whistled and someone else said, '*Marron!*' and then I closed the door and followed. 'Too bad,' a deep, hoarse voice bellowed, 'she's got a friend.' Another voice laughed senselessly, and another said, 'Maybe we can fix the friend.' More laughter, and I couldn't see anything but a press of bodies and smoke and streamers and blue fog. There must've been fifty people in that cellar.

And then the pressure flowed out of me, and I was ready for whatever kicks came my way, and I was wild and happy and strong. I stepped up beside Louise and took her arm. 'Let's find a hole in that mob and get ourselves a drink.'

She kept staring around the club, as if hypnotized by the mass of straining, writhing bodies on dance-floor and shabby armchairs and shabbier couches. Every inch of space was taken, and the air was thick with perfume and liquor and smoke and, in brief flashes, sharp with spicy food-aromas like salami, bologna, pickle, mustard. The music shifted from a brassy mambo to a dirty, low-down rock 'n roll number.

Look, look, look, what yo' daddy's got fo' you!
Look, look, look at his present, *baiiby!*
Look, look, look what yo' daddy's got fo' you!
It's the kinda love that don't 'low for no maybe!
Look, look, look, and make up yo' mind!
Look, look, look 'fore some other starts a-lookin'!
Look, look, look, 'cause no better love you'll find!
Reach out *baiiby*, and let's start cookin'!

The piano pounded incessantly in high flats; the drums – bongo and traps – explored every combination of jungle rhythm; the bass fiddle found variations on the drumbeats; the tenor sax slid in and out of the entire primitive fabric; and a trumpet blasted brief, independent calls to psychosis. The dancers and drinkers and petters around the dimly lighted room were answering the call, and so was I. I took Louise's hand and pulled her to the side, planning to skirt the crowd and find a place where we could dump her raincoat and have a drink. Then we'd dance. Then we'd let that sick music take us.

Look, look, look how I'm goin' to the moon!
Look, look, look, don't you wanna come along?
Look, look, look, you don't need a gas balloon!
Reach out *baiiby*, and use my song!

The silly repetitive, hypnotic lyrics kept coming, and the music kept riding, and I pulled Louise along, frantic to join the crush of dancing couples. Here was quick, cheap loss of self!

But two squat, stocky, muscular boys were blocking our path, their faces set in the tough-guy's inevitable sullen cast. 'You crashing, feller?' the one on my right said. He was twenty-two or -three, and his friend a year or two younger. 'You don't look like no paying member to me.'

The younger one was moving to my left, getting ready to slip around behind me, getting ready to grab my arms and hold me for a working-over. Just like that. No questions. Violence was cheaper than questions.

But I wasn't ready for violence – yet.

'Vince invited me,' I said quickly. 'I paid him. I paid for this girl too. You get Vince and he'll tell you.'

'Oh,' the younger one said. He stopped moving. 'Oh, you're the guy from Vince's office.' He turned his head to the crowd, craned his neck and shrugged. 'We'll never – '

'There he is,' the older one said. 'Hey, Vince! Hey! Vince baby!'

Vince came up to me, stuck out his hand and grinned. He looked at Louise and whistled. 'Mamma! We gotta have a dance, you and me!'

Louise giggled. She freed her arm from my hand and slipped out of her raincoat. 'Tell me where to put this and I'm ready.'

'After we have a drink,' I said, keeping a big smile on my face.

'I don't need a drink,' Louise said, stepping away from me. 'The music's enough, Vince. You'll look out for me, won't you?'

Vince put his hands on her neck and rubbed playfully. 'Mamma, if my date wouldn't split my head open I'd be with you all night!' Then he took his hand away, looked at me and said, 'Don't worry about her, Harry. I'll get her a guy. My cousin, maybe. He's the one I was telling

201

you about – twenty-eight. He's down here alone. So you go on and have your drink, and I'll watch out for Louise.'

He thought he was doing me a favor, relieving me of a burden and source of embarrassment. 'You think I'm going to sit around and drink all night?' I said, still smiling. 'I intend to practice my war dances on Louise. After all, I paid for her, didn't I?' I finished with a laugh.

He nodded. 'Yeah. That's right. Well, c'mon in back where we got the drinks and sandwiches. C'mon, this is a good party.' He leaned toward us and whispered, 'No trouble at all tonight. Good, clean crowd. We kept out everyone but Happy Warriors and their relatives – like brothers and cousins. Some friends, too. So it's a nice party, Harry. Nothing to worry about.'

I nodded, and Louise said, 'It looks wonderful!' The go-to-hell note in her voice had grown stronger. 'I want to dance with you, and your cousin, and all the Happy Warriors!'

'Hey,' Vince said, grinning at her. 'You been hitting the bottle? And you left out Harry.'

She shrugged. 'Should I worry about a married man?'

I laughed. 'That's just the kind to worry about.'

Vince roared his approval and led the way around the left side of the cellar. Louise followed, and I was right behind her. She didn't give me so much as a glance. Once a couple crossed in front of her and she had to stop suddenly, and I bumped into her. She moved away immediately, saying, 'That's the closest you'll get to me, ever again!'

The music rocked, and my blood answered the beat, and I reached out and slapped her bottom. She whirled around, red-faced, and I thought she was going to swing at me. But then she forced a smile and said, voice thick, 'You'll regret that, Harry. I'll see to it – tonight.'

I believed her. We followed Vince again, and someone put that wild record back on the machine.

> Look, look, look what yo' daddy's got fo' you!
> Look, look, look at his present, *baiiby!*

We'd stopped at a huge wooden table loaded with bottles, glasses and plates. There was beer, wine, gin, whisky, food and soft drinks. Vince took Louise's coat and hung it on a peg-board nailed into the wall behind the table. He came back to us, rubbing his hands together. 'Whad'ya think of the spread? Pretty good, eh? Try some of the solid potato salad, Harry. Real gone stuff.'

'I'll have a drink,' I said. I watched the way his eyes moved over Louise and added, 'Whatever you've been drinking.'

He stuck out his barrel chest, laughed and shook his head. 'I dunno, Harry. I been on super-Pete. I been mixing wine and gin, half and half.'

I took a closer look at him; he wasn't drunk enough to have had too many of those. 'Okay,' I said. 'Mix me one, buddy, and we'll be even.'

'One's all it takes, Harry.' He licked his lips and stared at Louise's tight, low-cut, figure-hugging dress. That gray sheath must have cost fifty dollars or more, and it was reaching Vince. I knew that the dress, and what was inside it, would reach others before this evening was over.

I didn't have to wait long for confirmation of that thought. A tall, well-built man, older than anyone else I'd seen down here, swaggered up to us just as Vince handed me a large glass of smoky liquid – a poor man's Martini, or half a dozen Martinis rolled into one.

'Hi, Vince,' he said, his voice soft and low, his face

tough-guy impassive. He gave me a brief flick of small brown eyes, then turned his attention to Louise. He went over her carefully, intensively, without bothering to mask it. 'You're hiding all the good stuff at this party, Vince. How 'bout that, cousin? That ain't right.'

Vince laughed nervously, like a kid with a feared, perhaps hated older brother. 'This is Louise Gorden. She's from my office. This is Carmine.'

Louise glanced at me for a second before smiling and putting out her hand. And in that second I understood what would happen tonight. She didn't like Vince, or Carmine, or any of these slum boys. But she'd play them along for my benefit. And if I didn't make the right countermoves I'd lose my last chance with her. Tonight *was* my last chance.

'Glad to meet you, Carmine,' Louise said.

The tall, dark, lean-muscled man held onto her hand and showed his teeth in a cocky smile, then went back to his tough-guy sullenness. 'Yeah,' he said. 'Same here.'

'And this is Harry,' Vince said. 'From my office, too. Carmine's my cousin, Harry. I told you about him.'

Carmine finally let go of Louise's hand. He turned his head and nodded at me. I nodded back at him. Carmine was twenty-eight, a man, but still a Happy Warrior at heart. He looked like he spent his time in a poolroom or studying old Humphrey Bogart movies.

'So you told Harry 'bout me,' Carmine said, voice ever so low, ever so bland. 'Well, you also told me 'bout him.' He glanced at me, a contemptuous flick of the eyes. 'You're married, ain't you?'

I took a long pull at my drink; the raw stuff hit hard and fast. In the few seconds before I answered Carmine I began to feel heat racing through my stomach. 'Yes,' I said. 'To a woman. Want me to explain how it works?'

Carmine's face showed surprise, then anger. Vince said quickly, 'Hey, that Harry's got a sense of humor! You gotta understand that Harry's always kidding, ain't you, Harry?'

I drank again, shrugged, turned my back on the three of them and got a slice of pickle. When I turned back Carmine was glaring at me. I bit into the pickle, chewed, drank again. I finished the whole glass of super-Pete and felt half plastered. I walked to Louise, brushing past Carmine. 'Let's dance, honey.'

Before she could answer, Carmine said, 'I thought you told me the girl he was bringing was single, Vince?'

'She is,' Vince said, and I recognized fear in his voice. He seemed worried about Carmine's reactions. 'But Harry's watching out for – '

'Harry maybe don't remember some rules.'

I turned to Carmine and grinned. The red haze didn't come. I wasn't really angry. I wanted to dance and drink. That wild, low-down music was hitting my guts now, sending me, rocking me. I wanted to shift into high and float away with Louise. 'Down boy,' I said, still grinning. 'There's enough for everybody. And you're right about my not remembering some rules. Fact is, it'll take you years to learn those I forgot.'

'Hey,' Carmine said quietly. 'Hey, you better – '

'Lemme mix you a super-Pete,' Vince interrupted, taking Carmine's arm. 'You ain't tried one yet, have you?'

'Leggo, stupid,' Carmine said, still quiet, still angry. He shook Vince off. He looked at me, eyes narrowed, and spoke to Louise. 'Wanna dance, kid?'

'Yes,' Louise said, and stepped forward.

I grabbed her arm. 'You're taken, honey. At least for the first dance.'

She turned and looked full into my eyes and smiled, giving me every ounce of charm and sex appeal she could muster. And with the wine and gin heating my blood the effect was instantaneous. I wanted her, and she could see it, and she said, 'I'd rather dance with Carmine, Harry. After all, a girl has to keep her eyes open for eligible males. And, as we all know, you're not eligible. Or are you?'

She'd promised to get back at me tonight; she'd said it in the car, and again when I'd slapped her bottom. She was doing it. I managed to shrug, and turned away from her, then saw Carmine's vicious face made even more vicious by a triumphant sneer. The red haze began to form, but Carmine and Louise moved away together and began to dance. Carmine held her tight right from the beginning. Everyone was grinding away to that music. He wasn't going to be an exception, and Louise couldn't stop him. She tried for a few seconds, smiling uncomfortably and saying something, and then gave up when he tightened his grip without answering.

'How about another drink?' Vince said, touching my arm. 'Hey?'

'A small one,' I said, and looked at him. He was worried. 'What's the matter, Vince? Carmine scare you?'

He glanced around and moved me away from some people who'd come up to the table. 'Don't mess with him,' he whispered. 'He's my cousin, but I don't like him. He's a bad guy. Honest, Harry, he's real bad. He don't work, and he takes money from a girl he goes with, and he takes money from his mother, too. He makes something on cards, but he don't work. That kind of guy is always bad. And Carmine's got a crazy streak.'

'I see,' I said.

Vince saw I hadn't been scared off. 'Listen, Harry, he

used a knife once in a fight with a guy. He got three months for that. But he'd use it again. I know it. If he was losing with his fists he'd use his knife.'

'Forget it,' I said, slapping him on the shoulder. He was a coarse, uneducated kid, but there wasn't a thing wrong with him. I could see it now, here, where he was in his element. In the stockroom he showed to poorest advantage. 'There's not going to be any fight. He'll dance with Louise, and then I will, and I'll watch out for her.'

'Yeah,' Vince said, still worried. 'But she acts sorta – Well, she don't seem to want to be watched out for.' He shook his head. 'She's a good-looking piece, Harry, but I'm sorry she was around when I told you about the party. I mean, she's acting funny. I mean, it ain't all Carmine's fault. You know what I mean?'

'Yeah. Let's have that drink. I'll mix it this time.'

I made two small gin-and-wines. We drank and put down our empty glasses. Vince led me to an armchair and said he'd be right back with his girl, Roberta. 'Unless she got mad because I was gone so long,' he said, laughing. 'She gets mad real easy. Boy, she's a hot-tempered redhead. Wait'll you see her!' He went on to say she'd dance with me all I wanted. He said he could never dance enough for her – she was a real cat, gone all the way.

He walked into the crowd, and I searched the dance floor for Louise and Carmine. I couldn't find them in the pulsing mass of bodies and dim lights and streamers and smoke. The music kept rocking, and I wanted to dance, and I wanted my partner to be Louise and only Louise.

Vince must have had trouble locating his redhead. I was left to myself a quarter of an hour, and in that time I spotted Carmine and Louise for a brief instant. He was really socking it into her, and her face had begun to take on the slack, heavy lines of desire. I got to my feet, but by that time they'd disappeared in the crowd. I could have gone after them, but I didn't. I wasn't ready yet. Let Carmine get his hopes up; let Louise want a man. I'd step in soon enough. Louise wouldn't leave with him; and even if she tried to she'd come for her raincoat. I'd keep my eye on that pegboard.

For the first time, I really looked at the other people. They were all pretty much of a type. The boys with their long-jacketed, loungy suits – some wearing one-button rolls. Blue and brown suede shoes were common, and so were pegged pants and spread collars with huge, loose Windsor knots. The girls wore bright print dresses, cheap costume jewelry, strong perfume, plenty of make-up. There were an amazingly high percentage of redheads, a popular color in Brooklyn, and easily obtainable in liquid or powder form.

An explosion of male voices grabbed my attention. Two boys had squared off against each other near the refreshment table. They were fighting over a girl, and the girl stood nearby, hand to mouth, taking it all in with avid eyes. The shorter, heavier boy threw two punches. Both landed on the taller, slimmer boy's face, and the taller boy went down. He got up, swinging from the floor, and missed. He got hit three times in succession – right, left, right – all in the body. He bent over, began to retch, was hurried out through a door to the left of the coat pegs.

It was all over. The shorter boy went up to the girl and grabbed her arm. He shook her and she said something, and he shook her harder. Then she melted against him. He tried to stay angry, and she wiggled a little. A moment later they were tied up in an armchair, hugging and kissing. The tall, slim boy didn't come back.

I smiled to myself. If I wanted to play, this was the place. The slum kids rushed toward violence. They lived by the cult of the tough-guy. To chicken out was the only cardinal sin, to show guts the only virtue.

I began to feel the heat. It was broiling in this over-crowded, smoky basement. I wiped my face and neck with a handkerchief and wondered where the hell Vince was, then saw him pushing through the crowd, leading a girl by the hand. She was short, beautifully built, with a round, Latin-type face crowned by a head of hair that should have been jet black but which had been dyed a flaming red. She wore a blue-and-white print dress that accented her jutting breasts, full hips and swelling but-tocks. She had no facial feature that could be called beautiful, nor any that could be called ugly. She was what I thought of as a 'pretty' girl. She looked good, but there was nothing compelling, nothing to remember about her. Louise, on the other hand, with her huge golden eyes and lustrous black hair and catlike figure . . .

I stood up as Vince and his girl approached. He introduced her as Roberta. We shook hands, and she smiled. Then she looked at Vince and frowned. 'But why didn't you come over and tell me?' she said, as if continuing an argument. 'I didn't know what happened to you. I waited and waited, and there I was all alone. I couldn't see you from the other end of the place. Why didn't you at least come over and tell me that your friends from the office was here and you was making them at home so I could've known what was going on?'

Vince rolled his eyes ceilingward. 'Mamma,' he said. 'This girl don't stop talking, nagging – '

'If you're gonna act like that,' she interrupted sharply, 'I can find someone else to dance with me. Lou and Tony

209

were hanging around. You know how Tony likes me. You know he'd kiss my foot if I let him.'

'Yeah. So maybe you should let him.'

Roberta switched her plump tail and turned to leave us.

'Aw,' Vince said. 'Aw, c'mon, 'Berta, I was only fooling. Don't act that way in front of Harry.'

She turned again and shrugged, and then smiled. 'We go steady,' she said to me. 'You wouldn't know it to hear us fight, but we been going steady four, no, five months.'

Vince winked at me. I didn't know what he meant, nor did I care. I was trying to find Louise on the mobbed dance floor. And I wasn't having any luck. I'd have to go out there and look for her.

Vince made it easy. 'Why don't you dance with Harry a few times, 'Berta? I'm beat, and he likes to dance. Don't you, Harry?'

'Sure thing.' I moved to her. 'May I?'

She nodded. 'I think I'm gonna like your friend, Vince. Maybe I won't dance with you at all tonight. So long, Vince baby.'

Vince laughed, but gave me a questioning look. I smiled reassuringly, and he relaxed. I took Roberta's arm, led her two steps away from the couch, and we were on the dance floor. She turned, came into my arms, and we were dancing. I did a slow fox trot, with frequent dips, to a blues number. Roberta snuggled tight against me, looking up, smiling with full, wet lips. She said, 'You remind me of a teacher I had in high school, Harry. Gee, I had a crush on him.'

'Thanks. I hope that means what I think it means.' But I was only making talk. My eyes were busy probing the crowd, trying to find Louise and Carmine.

Roberta laughed. 'Maybe it does and maybe it don't.

210

That's up to you to find out.' She snuggled even closer, fitting every fleshy curve to my body. A man of eighty would have responded.

'Mmmm,' she said, 'teacher was never this good!'

I laughed and began to enjoy myself, and then I saw Louise and Carmine. Louise was flushed, breathing heavily, moving against Carmine with complete abandon. He had his dark, cruel face pressed into her hair. He was smiling, thin-lipped and confident.

The red haze began to form. Louise looked right at me, blinked her half-closed eyes, opened them wide. Then she turned her head away.

The red haze thickened. I stopped dancing, asked Roberta to excuse me, left her standing with indignant words forming on her lips. I squeezed past one couple, circled another, came up behind Carmine. I tapped him on the shoulder. 'Mind if I cut in?'

'Aw, beat it,' he said, and tried to turn back to Louise. But the red haze was strong, and I was ready, and the blues gave way to a fast rock 'n roll number. I grabbed his shoulder.

'This is my dance,' I said.

He jerked free, faced me alongside of Louise, said, 'She ain't told me – '

'I don't care what she told you or didn't tell you. This is my dance.' I moved toward Louise, not really seeing her, and waited for Carmine to explode. But he merely stared at me, his face paling, his fists knotting at his sides. He kept staring as I reached Louise, took her in my arms and danced her away.

I turned and looked at him and laughed – laughed insultingly, telling him I thought he was yellow. He tensed but didn't move, and then I swung Louise into a Lindy-hop and lost sight of him.

211

We jitterbugged. She was still breathing hard, only now it was from exertion, movement, fast rhythm. I was really going, the liquor and music and heat and smoke setting me wild. I was dancing as I hadn't danced since I was a kid. And when I pulled Louise in after a break, I crushed her, bruised her, looked into her eyes and let her feel my strength and passion. The music changed and we went into a fast fox trot, and she said, 'Watch your step here, Harry. Carmine's no Stan Henrich. You'll get hurt.' She smiled as she said it, showing she would enjoy seeing me hurt. But she was frightened. She'd been frightened ever since we'd walked into this club. However Carmine affected her sexually, he hadn't been able to destroy her fear. He'd probably added to it.

'You really want me to get hurt?' I asked.

'Me? I don't care one way or the other. As soon as I see Vince I'll ask him to get a friend to take me home.'

I grinned. 'What about Carmine?'

She didn't answer. She danced with me and tried to stay away, and I pulled her tight and kissed her cheek and ear and hair. 'Stop it,' she said. 'Stop it, Harry. That Carmine is watching. He'll make trouble.' There was fear in her voice, but not for me. She was afraid of the entire place, of the entire atmosphere. 'Please, Harry!'

I kept dancing, kissing her, crushing her. I'd forgotten Carmine. Louise was in my arms and she was the only woman in the world and I wanted her, had to have her.

'I'll tell you what,' she whispered. 'I'll let you drive me home. Let's leave – ' Her voice died, and she made a small, sick sound. A hand came down on my shoulder, hard.

'Cutting in,' Carmine's quiet voice said. But it was different from before. He was primed for play.

I let Louise go and turned. The red haze was back, and

I hated him, and I wanted to rip him apart with my nails and teeth. I stepped up so that we were touching each other – face to face, chest to chest, knee to knee. I looked at him and noticed things I hadn't noticed before. He had oil on his thick black hair and perspiration on his upper lip, and a dark stubble of beard was beginning to form on his chin. He had a small round, white scar near his left ear, and his nose was thin on top, and he looked like a hatchet with a mouth. He was dark and strong and ugly – ugly to me. Hateful to me.

'You dirty punk bastard,' I whispered. 'You yellow punk bastard. You crawling – '

He was fast. He leaped back and swung in one lithe movement. His fist caught me high on the cheek, and a dullness invaded that area. I laughed. I kept laughing, even as I felt myself stagger sideways from the force of the blow. He was fast, and he was strong, but I was going to destroy him. There wasn't any doubt in my mind that I could do it. I'd been waiting to destroy, or be destroyed, for a long time. And Carmine couldn't destroy me – not tonight – not with Louise watching, her face strained and white, the fear gripping her. I would smash that fear by smashing Carmine, and so smash her resistance. It was all clear and simple to me, and logic didn't have a chance to pose questions.

I began to fight him. I fought him the way I'd fought as a kid, the way I'd fought as a soldier in Army-town barrooms on Saturday nights. I threw punches as fast and hard as I could, aiming for the body where I'd miss less often. I caught him half a dozen shots in the belly, and he yelled an obscenity and stepped back and then sat down. I wanted to finish him off on the floor, but that would turn the crowd against me. I stood there, breathing heavily, and glanced around to see Louise. She'd regained her color. She had her mouth open, her fists clenched. She said, 'Get him, Harry! Get him, Harry!'

I looked at the other people, and they were drawn back in a circle. 'Get up, Carmine,' one boy said. 'You can take the jerk.'

Carmine drew himself together and got up lithely, but he staggered a step to the side. I knew he was finished, and he knew it too. He was my height, my weight, but he'd been hit in the guts and he was outgunned by my rage, my urge to destroy. I stepped in for the kill, and he kicked out and caught me on the right knee. The pain was intense, and I almost fell. But then he made the mistake of rushing in to use his fists, and I let him have a stiff-fingered jab in the Adam's apple. He choked, coughed and bent over, held his throat and turned around and around, fighting for breath.

'Hey,' someone said, 'he shouldn't've done that. Hey, I think the guy fights dirty.'

'Carmine kicked him,' someone else said. 'So he had the right.'

A dozen small arguments broke out around me, but no one tried to do anything. I waited for Carmine to straighten so I could finish the job in true-blue American cowboy-picture fashion – with the opponent upright.

But the opponent had other ideas. He straightened, and he had something in his right hand. He moved his fingers, there was a snicking sound, and a six-inch blade leaped out and caught dim light. It was a thin, sharp, terrible piece of steel. It began to move, back and forth, and I couldn't take my eyes from it. I heard a girl scream and thought it was Louise, and heard voices break out in the crowd. Most shouted at Carmine to put the knife away, but a few said, 'Let 'em alone!' And the few seemed to carry more weight than the many; the few were Carmine's friends, the rocks of the neighborhood, the boys who would cow the rest of the group.

I finally raised my eyes to Carmine's face. He was moving his lips as if praying, still fighting for breath, and he was crazy mad. He wanted to kill. He *would* kill, if I didn't stop him.

And suddenly I was glad. I wasn't afraid. Why be afraid of something I'd been courting for weeks? It was out of my hands now. I would fight this man and his knife, and if I lost I would lose the boredom and fear and pain.

'C'mon you yellow bastard,' I said, raising my fists and leaning forward. 'Let's see you use that thing.'

He called me something I couldn't make out because his voice was so weak and thick and choked with pain. But it was filthy, and he was crazy, and he swung the knife in a wide circle. The blade flashed to my left, coming in toward my side and stomach, and I thought of my father and the man lying under the newspapers and the bodies in that station wagon.

I lunged forward to meet the bright steel, and the rock 'n roll played on, and I wondered if the darkness would come swiftly.

15

It wasn't anything I could control. It was movement without volition, defense without consciousness, survival on instinct. I fought the knife by rushing in close and using my nails and teeth and knees and elbows and head. I punched and clawed and bit and butted and kneed and jabbed. I fought without being afraid, without wanting to win, but I had to fight. I wasn't able to leave myself open to that searching blade.

And then I had my right hand on Carmine's throat and my left at his crotch. He was screaming, and something burned my left arm. I squeezed with both hands, and Carmine jerked and went limp, and the knife clattered to the floor. I let go and got up. My left arm felt wet, and I looked at it. The bright red ran in a thin trickle over the wrist to the hand and fell in quick drops to the polished-wood floor. I ripped open my shirt cuff, shoved up shirt and jacket sleeve, saw the small, bloody cut. I tied a handkerchief around my forearm, shoved down my sleeves, and then was afraid. I looked at Carmine, who was being helped into a sitting position by two tough kids, then turned to locate Louise. Another tough-guy was standing close to me, eyes narrowed on mine, stance pugnacious and ready.

'That was some fight, punk,' he murmured. 'That was the dirtiest ever.'

I wanted to get out. I was empty now. 'He pulled a knife,' I said in a loud voice. 'You saw him. Everybody saw him. I fought for my life.'

Someone came up beside me. 'Let him alone, Lou,' Vince was saying, and he put his hand on my shoulder. The hand trembled. 'I'm Carmine's cousin, but he was wrong. Hell, he pulled – '

'Some cousin!' the weak voice said.

We turned to Carmine. He was sitting on the floor, pale and sick-looking, scratched and bloodied, breathing heavily. 'Some cousin. You seen what he done. He comes in here and you seen what he done!'

Vince slid his hand to my arm and turned me around, and we walked toward Louise. She had a wild, disheveled glazed look about her. She seemed drunk and hypnotized, terrified and asleep. She was everything extreme. We went up to her and she took my other arm, and the three of us walked toward the refreshment table.

'Get your coat,' Vince whispered to Louise. 'Just grab it and we'll keep going, right out the back door. Don't stop or talk to anyone or answer anyone.'

He was scared, and now I was scared. I was scared of losing my chance with Louise.

'The bastard's running away,' someone yelled. 'You chickening out, bastard?'

'Don't answer,' Vince whispered as we went around the table. 'Don't turn or do nothing. Keep going!'

But we couldn't keep going. The two kids who'd been helping Carmine ran around the other side of the table and stopped in front of us. They looked past us to the crowd.

'C'mon, Tony,' Vince pleaded, letting go of my arm. 'C'mon, will ya?' There was no answer, and Vince said. 'Listen, Sid, you know this ain't my friend's fault. He and his girl are leaving now. We had enough trouble. C'mon.'

No answer. People were coming up behind us, and Louise whimpered. Vince suddenly stiffened, and his

217

voice got strong, harsh. 'Awright! I invited him, by Christ, and he's not getting leaned on by nobody!'

The two boys in front of us shifted their hard eyes to Vince. They didn't seem quite as sure of themselves now.

'That's telling 'em, Vince baby!' a girl shouted, and it sounded like Roberta.

Other voices murmured agreement, and the crowd pushed in on us, and they were divided. Vince murmured, 'It's gotta happen, Harry. It's gotta happen.'

It happened. The boys blocking our path moved in to grab me. Vince swung on the one he'd called Sid, and he and Sid went down in a tangle of fists and arms and legs. I shoved Louise toward the back door, past the boy Vince had called Tony, and then grabbed Tony. We wrestled, and I saw Louise stopping near the door. I yelled, 'Get out and find the car and stay there!' She opened the door and ran out, and the kid I was holding wasn't big enough to handle me. I shoved him to the floor and broke for the door, stepping on his hand in passing. He bellowed and managed to grab my ankle, and I went down. We both got up, and he was swinging at me. He didn't land, and he was yelling for his friends to help, but his friends were busy helping themselves. The entire place had turned into a battlefield. Except for groups of girls huddled at the sides, everyone was fighting. It looked like one of those silly movie scenes where a crowd splits into two equal sides to fight over something started by a few men. Only here the sides weren't equal; Carmine's friends were being ganged. They were the older, tougher boys, and maybe the others had been wanting to gang them for a long time. They were putting up a good fight, but it couldn't last long.

Tony was jumped by a lanky blond kid, and that gave me my chance. I broke for the back door, heard a whistle blow and turned to see cops coming in the front. There were at least four of them.

I reached the back door, opened it and saw the bulky shadow coming through another door to my left, a door that gave a glimpse of wet pavement, an alley door. The big man coming through it had a club in his hand.

If Louise hadn't been waiting for me I'd have stopped and submitted to the cop. But this was my last chance with her. I couldn't go to a police station, waste hours and maybe get locked up.

I bent low, sprinted at him and felt the laughter bubbling in my throat. What a night!

I heard him say, 'Hold – '

I shouted, 'Inside! God, they're killing those cops!' And then I was dodging around him. He swung his club and I took a glancing blow on the shoulder that made me cry out. But I was at the door, through it into a light rain, then looking down the alley to the street. There were headlights and people, and I couldn't go there. I turned and ran up the alley to a wooden fence. It was about eight feet high, and I climbed it without too much trouble. I came down in damp earth, landing on my feet and staggering forward a few steps. I stopped and listened. No one was following me; that cop hadn't been able to take the chance that I was lying about his buddies being in trouble.

I looked around and saw that I was in a large back yard. Ahead of me was a two-family house with lights showing on both first and second floors. I walked across earth, then grass, and then through a vegetable or flower garden. I reached the back of the house and saw the path running to the right, past a garage and into an alley. I went down the alley, moving quickly, and the rain began to come down harder. I turned left when I reached the street, ran toward New Lots Avenue, turned left on the rain-swept, deserted avenue, then ran to the corner of the block on which the cellar club was located, on which I'd parked my car.

I could see the patrol cars pulled up in ragged formation near the club. Directly across the street was my Dodge, and huddled miserably against the Dodge was a woman. Louise. The cops weren't bothering her. She'd been outside the club when they'd arrived, so they didn't bother her. They wouldn't bother me either if I walked casually to my car. They couldn't – unless that cop I'd ducked happened to spot me.

I ran a pocket comb through my wet hair, straightened my jacket, brushed at my pants. I adjusted my tie, then crossed the street and went toward my car. When I reached it Louise straightened and said, 'I thought they'd keep you in there! I didn't know what to do. The car's locked and – and – ' She seemed about to cry. 'Oh, Harry, let's go home!'

I opened the doors, and we got inside. Two cops standing near the cellar club turned and looked our way, but they didn't make a move as I swung out from the curb and drove by.

'God,' Louise said, 'I thought we were going to die! I thought they'd kill us! That knife – How's your arm?'

'Just a scratch,' I said. 'Don't even feel it now.' I looked at her. Her hair was wet, but it only made the black deeper, more attractive. Her dress didn't show dampness, but she moved her arms and legs and said, 'I'm soaked. How did you get out, Harry?'

I told her.

'My God,' she said. 'You took a terrible chance running from that officer! What made you do such a thing?'

'The same thing that made me fight Carmine.'

220

'I left my raincoat there,' she said quickly. 'I'm glad I didn't bring a purse.'

'I did it for *you*,' I said, refusing to drop the subject. 'I'd do anything for you.'

'I carried a lipstick and tissues and few dollars in my pocket,' she said, and her voice was shaking now. 'Bet you didn't notice it. See?' She touched her hip, traced what I had taken for a decorative line of stitching. 'It's a pocket.'

I reached out and dragged her across the seat until she was tight against me. I drove with one hand, stopped for a red light at Pennsylvania Avenue, and bent to kiss her. She raised her lips to mine. They were open, and she was shaking violently. The light changed and I drove toward the Belt, my arm curled around her shoulders, my hand cupping her breasts.

'Harry,' she said, but it wasn't a reprimand. She leaned against me, shivering. 'Harry.'

I kissed her again, slowing on the dark approach to the Belt, running my free hand from her breasts to her hip to her leg. It was pouring again, and the wipers slapped in rhythmic unison. I couldn't wait. There wasn't much traffic on the stretch of road running through filled-in, deserted swamp land, and I turned off into the blackness of a shabby, two-pump gas station, closed either for the night or for good. I saw the lot in back of the wooden shack, drove carefully past some unidentifiable hunks of metal and went through the opening in a tall wooden fence. The lot was spotted with wrecked jalopies. I pulled to the side and cut my lights and ignition.

'What – what are you doing?' Louise whispered. 'Harry, this place – '

I wondered if she'd fight the final step. I thought she

might, and I wouldn't be sorry. Because I wasn't going to let anything stop me.

That would make it rape, and she might destroy me by going to the cops. Which didn't seem to bother me; it seemed to make it all the more exciting.

Moe would have repeated his theory of my seeking self-destruction. And I wouldn't have argued the point. It was beginning to look as if he was right.

I took her in my arms, kissed her and told her of my need, my inability to wait any longer. She said, 'No,' but it was in a husky whisper, and when I kissed her again, she responded fiercely. My tongue probed her mouth as my hands explored her body. She made no attempt to stop me until I began to open the buttons of her white blouse. She said 'No' again, but weakly, softly, and the hand she placed on my wrist made no real effort to halt my progress. I put my mouth down hard on hers as I began to slide the blouse off her shoulder. She made a small whimpering sound, and straightened her arm to help me free her of the garment. My heart was beating wildly as I freed her other arm and reached round to unsnap her brassiere. Again she helped me, and I gazed down at her luscious breasts. I pressed my lips to them, feeling the nipples harden under my tongue and teeth. Louise put both hands on the back of my head, pressing my mouth hard against her as she repeated my name over and over again.

I moved my hand down to her hip, searching for the fastenings of her skirt. I found the hook and eye combination and tweaked the hook loose. I slid the zip down, almost expecting her to stop me, to look down at me and laugh, and tell me that was enough. If she did, I knew I would not stop. I would not be able to. It had gone too far now, and I had to have her, even if it was in rape. I was past thinking about the consequences, beyond any balancing of loss and gain. I didn't care what happened, so long as I had Louise now.

There was no laughter. Instead, she raised her hips and helped me as I slid the skirt down. She gasped something about not getting it dirty as I tossed it into the back of the car, then raised her hips again as I removed her half-slip and panties.

She was breathing hard now, her eyes huge and glazed with desire. She took my hand and pushed it down between her legs, crying out that she hated me, loved me, wanted me, despised me, had to have me or she'd die.

I was disappointed; I'd actually wanted her to fight. But the disappointment lasted only a second. Desire which had accumulated during all the frustrating dates, during the childish rejections, insults and arguments, was free to work, and it worked well. She was completely responsive, everything I could ask for.

She pulled my head down and kissed me hard as I began to touch her. She was very wet, stimulated no doubt by Carmine's approaches, and the fight in the club, now by my headlong desire. I felt her hands move between us, cupping my bulging crotch, squeezing. Now it was I who moaned, and Louise who undressed me. She put her arms around me and hugged me with surprising strength. I hugged her back, our mouths meeting again, tongues touching, caressing, probing. I ran my hand down the smooth plane of her back, along the curve of her hip, the firm smoothness of her thigh. I touched her breasts with my fingers and my lips, my teeth. I stroked the satin skin of her belly, the lush triangle of her pubic hair, the moist, waiting lips below. And as I touched her, her hands were on me, following the same erotic, exploratory

223

path. A path that lead always back to the throbbing column between my legs. Her fingers danced over the length of me, lightly, barely touching before withdrawing again, as though nervous, afraid. But always returning, becoming bolder, more positive, until she held me in her hand and began to stroke.

Briefly, I thought of that night on the couch, but it was a fleeting thought. Tonight was different. Tonight I knew I would have Louise, and knew that she wanted me to have her. There would be no cry of rape, only the total fulfillment of everything I had wanted for so long.

I withdrew my hand from between her legs and gently took hers from my penis. I began to lift her, and she understood immediately what I wanted, rising to a kneeling position on the seat, then lifting her right leg across until she straddled me. She raised herself as I placed my hands on the firm-soft globes of her buttocks, putting first one breast, and then the other to my lips. The tip of my penis was touching her vagina, and the contact set me on fire as she moved her hips, rubbing herself gently against me.

I could stand it no longer; I had waited too long already. I moved my hands from her buttocks to her hips and raised my mouth from her breasts. I looked up at her and saw her great golden eyes staring at me, burning with rampant, unhidden desire. Her face was slack, her lips parted and moist, her breathing harsh, fast. She said my name and brought her lips down against mine. At the same time, she drove her hips down, guided by my hands, and I sank deep inside her. A sobbing cry burst from her mouth, then she was kissing me again and my hands were under her buttocks, lifting her, lowering her, our timing adjusting so that we moved in perfect harmony, Louise driving down against me as I rose to meet her. She threw her head back, neck arching, and I pressed my lips to that sweet-tasting column, caressing, biting as she moaned and strained against me, drawing me steadily, exquisitely, towards a peak of ecstasy.

I don't know what I said at the time or what she was moaning, but we strained together, frantically, and every second was magnificent.

When it ended, everything drained away. I'd won the game. It was over. All over. Just as I'd known it would be. I didn't want her any more. I wouldn't want her ever again. I looked at her and saw a rather stupid, unpleasant girl.

A few minutes later I started the car, drove out of the lot and reached the Belt. I hit sixty, despite the rain, anxious to get her home. I was dead tired. I was drained and empty.

Then I felt guilty and slowed down. 'Want to turn off at Cross Bay Boulevard, Louise? We can get a bite to eat at one of the roadside – '

'Take me home, Harry.'

I looked at her, shocked at the sickness in her voice, the terrible sickness that shouldn't have been there. Resentment or anger or shame, yes, if that was her reaction. But not this sickness.

'It's finished,' she said in the same terrible voice. 'But don't feel too good about it. You're not the first. There were others. There were plenty of others. Or maybe you've guessed by now – ' She began to cry, bent over with hands to face, sobbing heavily.

I couldn't understand the depth of her misery. I tried to soothe her, saying comforting things, flattering things, then switched to a man-and-woman-of-the-world attitude when she continued to sob. 'After all, honey, what did it amount to?' She looked up at me. 'We made love,' I continued. 'So what? It was good, wasn't it? We enjoyed it, didn't we? I protected you, and nothing can happen, and we have a memory of some pretty special moments.'

'Yes,' she said, and her eyes were wide and sick. 'But is that enough?'

'Enough? That's about *all* there is to life.'

She shook her head vehemently. 'No. That's not true. It has to mean something. I know it has to mean something. Normal people have to be in love to enjoy it.'

I laughed and wanted to answer, but she cut me short.

'You can't be a judge, Harry. You're not normal. You run around. And – and I'm not normal, either.' The tears and sobs started again.

I tried once again to soothe her. 'You're a very attractive girl. You'll meet the right guy some day and marry, and then you'll have exactly what you want. There's no reason for this – this unhappiness and fear. You'll certainly marry.'

She looked at me, wiping the tears from her face with a tissue. 'And will marrying make me happy, Harry?'

That stumped me. 'But it's what you want. It's what stopped us at the beginning, what's been on your mind. You've always said – '

'I know what I've said,' she wailed. 'I say it because other girls say it, but do I *mean* it? Do I want to get married or do I want the men I can't ever get? I think that's it. I think I want the men I can't possibly get. I think I don't want marriage – I'm afraid of it – I'm afraid I'll hate it! My mother and father fight all the time. I hate their kind of marriage! And it's not just my mother and father. One man all my life – ' She pressed her hands together, moaned, shook her head. 'See? I'm no good. No good at all.'

I said something about her being distraught, but she went on.

'I'm sure I'll hate marriage. And I think that's why men like you seem to hunt me out. There's some sort of signal, some sort of advertisement in me. And it's getting worse! Worse, Harry!' She bent her head and cried, and I was convinced. I believed her.

It made her much more interesting than she'd ever been, but it also negated my conquest. I hadn't seduced a prim, self-sufficient believer in morals and good family background. I hadn't attained the near-unattainable. I'd had a girl more susceptible than any I knew, more of a tramp than Terry Drego.

I felt like laughing, and crying, and banging my head against a wall. I was tired of everything. My motives were twisted, and Louise was twisted, and we'd mated to no purpose.

I tried telling myself what I'd told Louise – that the pleasure we'd had was motive enough, reason enough for our affair. But it didn't help. It wasn't true.

When we reached Roslyn it was twelve-thirty, and we parted without so much as a good-night. I drove to Brooklyn and the apartment house. It had stopped raining by the time I parked and went upstairs. I took off my shirt and examined my left forearm. It was nothing; just a scratch that had bled a few minutes and then stopped.

I cleaned and bandaged the cut, drank two large glasses of wine and had a third while I smoked a pipe. I was pleasantly stewed when I climbed into bed, and still I couldn't sleep. I thought of Louise, and of what would happen now that I'd finished with her.

I knew what would happen. In a week, or two, or three, I'd meet someone else who impressed me as hard to make, and I'd get the hunger. I'd go on having affairs

227

with that kind of woman until I'd be discovered by family and friends and business acquaintances – until my life would be shattered.

I laughed aloud and said the hell with it, and fell asleep.

I slept until three Sunday afternoon. When I got up all I wanted to do was have a few quick shots and get back to bed. I just couldn't face being awake and sober; I couldn't face myself and my thoughts.

I went to a bar on 16th Avenue and paid seven bucks for a five-buck bottle of rye. I also bought four quarts of beer.

Back in the apartment, I made myself a few sandwiches and began washing them down with glasses of beer and whisky – half and half.

By the time it got dark I was roaring drunk. I undressed, dropping my clothes on the floor, and staggered into the bedroom, slamming into chairs and dressers and walls. I lay down and thought that I'd finally found a way to lick the blues.

Have a few drinks. Have a few drinks, man, and it's a beautiful world! Hell yes!

Something about that idea worried me; I knew there was danger in it. But then the room caved in and I was laughing because the darkness tickled, and then I wasn't anything any more. It was like being dead . . .

I had one beautiful hangover in the morning. It took four cups of black coffee, five minutes of retching, more coffee and a cold shower before I was able to shave, dress and get out of the apartment. And even then, I had to stop on 13th Avenue for a Bromo before being able to face the subway. Not that I had to contend with the rush hour. It was nine when I caught a West End Express, and there were plenty of seats.

228

Though the thought of liquor nauseated me, I knew I'd have to take a drink at noon. Maybe more than one. How the hell else could I get through this miserable day?

16

I got to my desk a few minutes after ten. Mary Braken took one look at my face and changed her mind about cracking wise. Francine Loes turned in her chair a few minutes later and saw me, then cocked her head on the side as if to ask what had happened to make me so late. I shrugged and took out my new layouts. Ramona and Curt Sawyer were busy, though Curt glanced up quickly, then down again. Moe Crown was still out.

At ten-thirty Mary asked if I wanted to have lunch with her. I shook my head, explaining that I wasn't up to snuff.

'That's obvious,' she said. 'Want me to bring you anything from downstairs later?'

I shook my head and walked around the partition to Ramona's desk. 'Hear anything from Moe?' I asked.

'No. He – his sister, I mean – didn't call in this morning. Gee, he's been sick a long time now, Harry. Six, seven days, right?'

I said yes, went back to my desk and lit a pipe. It tasted terrible, and I put it down. I wondered what was going on at Moe's place. I looked at my phone and wanted to call, and knew I wouldn't.

I got up and walked out the door, then stopped. Where was I going? I didn't want to see Louise. I wasn't ready for any other girl. I had no business to transact any place but at my own desk.

Vince. I'd go to the stockroom and talk to Vince if he was there, if he wasn't in the clink.

Vince was slipping western magazines into pre-addressed brown envelopes. He looked up as I came in, and he had one of the blackest black eyes I'd ever seen. He grinned at me. 'Some party, eh, kid?'

I nodded. 'I see someone got to you.'

'Yeah. That creep Sid. Landed one good sock and it had to be on my eye. You oughta see *him*. Only you can't. He's in jail. Him and Carmine and six or seven others.'

'Brief me.'

'Man, it was a riot.' He laughed. 'A riot, get it?'

I nodded.

'Well, the cops came in and everything stopped fast, and they lined us all up against the wall – not the girls. They made us lean there, hands first – you know, like they do in the movies. They shook us down, went over us with their hands, and you should've heard some of the guys laughing. Ticklish, and crocked too. Those cops weren't so nice, though. They slapped a few of the guys for no reason. Hell, they slapped Frank Greesham for no reason.'

'How'd they happen to come in just then?'

'Some old bitch next door heard the noise when you and Carmine rumbled. She called them. Four squad cars, Harry. Christ, you'd think we was public enemies or something.'

'So what happened after they shook you down?'

'They found things on Carmine and Sid and some of the other older guys. Carmine got rid of his knife, but he had reefers in an inside jacket pocket and couldn't dump them in time. Anyway, he got caught with one, and that was enough. The others had knives and dope and one guy – Hero they call him, from Wyona Street – had a zip gun.' Vince paused. 'And now I hear Carmine and Tony were in on some kind of caper a few months ago. They'll get a stretch.'

'Good,' I said. I stuck out my hand. 'I want to thank you for helping me out of that jam.'

He shook my hand self-consciously and looked embarrassed. 'Aw, it was nothing. I figured you were in the right. Anyway, you sure can use your fists, Harry. I couldn't take Carmine.'

'Think he'll make trouble for you when he gets out?'

'Hell no. He asked me to help him. I'm gonna be a witness at his trial. I'm gonna say some man came down the club earlier and handed out those reefers and told the guys they was plain butts. Carmine might get off the marijuana rap that way. And my story'll help some of the other rocks, too. They won't bother me. I know how to get along.' He winked his black eye, winced, said, 'You don't have a scratch, you lucky stiff.'

I could have told him I had bruises that didn't show – bruises of the mind, bruises that went deeper than any he could imagine, bruises that were killing me.

'You get home all right?' he asked.

'Yes.'

'Take Louise?'

'Sure.'

He laughed. 'I'll bet she'll never invite herself on a party again – not one of mine!'

I was about to answer when Louise came in the door. She looked at me and her eyes jumped away, and she said, 'I need carbon paper, Vince.'

He grinned. 'Some party, huh, honey?'

She didn't answer his grin. 'The carbon paper.'

'What's the matter?' Vince jibed. 'Didn't you have a good time? You wanted to dance with me, and my friends, and everybody. Didn't you have fun?'

232

'Are you going to give me that carbon paper or must I complain to Mr Henrich?'

'Take it easy,' Vince said. He looked at me. 'Saturday night she – '

Louise turned to leave.

'Okay, okay,' Vince said. 'I'm getting it.'

He went to the supply closet. Louise and I glanced at each other, and glanced away again. I wondered how I'd ever thought her desirable. From her expression, I gathered she felt the same way about me.

Vince brought her a sheaf of carbon paper, and she said, 'Thank you.'

He grinned nervously. 'Hey, Louise, you want to see a movie maybe? There's a good show at the Paramount. We can go after work.'

She stared at him, and then laughed. 'Really,' she said. She laughed again and walked out.

Vince went brick red. I felt sorry for him. 'Forget it,' I said. 'She's a screwball.'

'Saturday night she acted – ' He turned away, hurt and ashamed. 'Hell, she oughta get slugged!' He was crushed, humiliated.

'She's a sick girl,' I said.

He turned, his face reflecting relief. 'Yeah? You mean she's mixed up? Psycho?'

I nodded. I'd help him recover his pride. I owed him that much after Saturday night. 'Yes. Mixed up. Maybe not really psycho, but definitely mixed up. Had a bad love affair. Now she's afraid of being hurt. Better leave her alone, Vince. She's not ready for dates and fun. She's trouble for any guy.'

'That so?' He shook his head, smiling. 'I knew something was wrong. At the party she was so nice and all, and now she gets on her high horse. Yeah, I'll let her alone. Thanks for the tip, Harry.'

When I left, he was working happily, whistling through his teeth. I'd done my good deed for the day.

I went back to my desk. I couldn't work. I sat there, staring at the drawing board, and felt Curt Sawyer's eyes on me. I looked up, and he glanced quickly away. That was the second time this morning I'd caught him examining me. And it happened once more before he glued his eyes to his desk. He'd had a funny expression on his thin face – a tense, expectant, frightened expression. He looked like he was waiting for something to happen. I wondered what it could be, and what it had to do with me.

At eleven-thirty I found out. The phone rang. It was Ellie. She asked me how I was. I said fine. She talked about the baby, the lake and the weather, and then stopped talking and cleared her throat. She was terribly nervous.

'Well,' I said, 'guess that's about all, isn't it, honey?'

'I have – ' she began, and cleared her throat again. 'I – Well, a funny thing happened.' She laughed, and it was like a small scream. I looked up and Sawyer was watching me. His face was gray and his eyes wide, and he suddenly got up and turned his back and fiddled around with some papers on Moe's desk.

I knew he'd done something. He'd hated me since the day I'd humiliated him in front of everyone; he'd followed Louise and me once, and perhaps other times when I hadn't detected him. Now he was having his revenge; now he was afraid.

'I got a letter,' Ellie said.

I could've told her what kind.

'You wouldn't know about it, would you, Harry?' She

234

laughed weakly. 'I – I mean, you wouldn't know about anyone who'd want to kid me? Though it's no joke; not really.'

'No,' I said. 'I don't know anything about a letter. Tell me.'

'Well, I don't really – ' She paused, and I could hear her breathing heavily, irregularly. 'Oh, forget it. It's – it's nonsense. A dirty trick of some kind. A stupid joke.'

I wasn't afraid. I wasn't even excited. I felt a little ill, but I'd felt that way before she called. I did feel a touch of shame, and I was sorry for her. 'Okay,' I said. 'Then we'll forget it. How's Debbie?'

'Fine. Well – '

I watched Curt Sawyer. He kept bending over Moe's desk; he wouldn't turn and face me. I wasn't even angry at him. I guess I didn't really care. He was a pretty poor example of a man.

'Listen, Harry,' Ellie said quickly. 'Listen, I'm not saying I believe a word of this nonsense, but I got a letter with some crazy things in it.'

The poison pen had done its work. 'Like what?'

'You going out with a girl. You dating her, and – and it said you'd been – been sleeping with her since I left for the lake.' That laugh again, that laugh that was like a scream. And she said more, speaking so quickly that the words ran into each other, speaking with embarrassment, with an agony of shame, with a basic disbelief in the poison-pen material. But she had to hear me refute it. She read me the letter, laughing that terrible little laugh every few words. 'It's signed, "A Friend," Harry. Some friend! It's a joke, isn't it?'

All I had to do was answer 'Yes,' and then get angry about the 'prankster' who had sent it. Or else say I'd had trouble with someone in the office and this was his way of getting back at me.

But I couldn't.

'How was it written?' I asked. 'I mean, was it typed, or printed, or written in longhand?'

'Typed. But – but what about – this girl Louise – '

A few words, a little effort, and I could save my marriage. I said nothing.

'Harry! It's not true?'

'I'm sorry,' I said, and wondered at the dullness pervading my mind and body. It was almost like the time I'd had a spinal anesthetic in the Army hospital. I felt nothing, but I could see and hear and speak. 'I didn't mean to hurt you.'

'Harry! But – why – weren't you happy? I mean, our marriage – ' Her voice thickened, and I knew she was ready to cry.

'There's nothing to say,' I murmured.

'Nothing – to say! And you won't even – Debbie and I mean nothing?'

I kept quiet. Sawyer had finally turned and was going back to his desk. He had himself under tight control now. He would try to bluff it through. But he didn't look at me.

'Harry,' Ellie said thickly. 'Harry, if you – you feel that way – ' She began to cry, but kept talking. 'I won't take it! I won't! If you want other women – then – then you can have them – but not me and Debbie too!' She hung up.

My marriage was on the rocks. I wouldn't do anything to save it, so it was as good as finished right now.

I still couldn't feel anything. I remembered what Moe had said, and I knew he was right. I'd wanted this. I'd

236

done everything to accomplish this. Curt Sawyer had merely made things easy, quickened the process.

Soon, no more family to worry about. Maybe then I'd get out of New York. Maybe I'd go somewhere. Or I'd stop going anywhere. Either way, I'd change my life.

I looked at Sawyer. He was flipping pages of a manuscript as if he were scanning it before reading. But his hands trembled and he was flipping much too fast, and I knew he wasn't doing a thing except sweating. I got up and walked around the partition and came directly to his desk. I looked down and saw perspiration on the back of his neck.

'Interesting manuscript, Curt?'

His head came up in a series of jerky movements; his eyes swung to mine and then past me into nothing. He showed his teeth in a death's-head grin and nodded. 'Yeah,' he said. 'Yeah, damned competent writer.'

'Good,' I said, and I still wasn't angry. I felt nothing but contempt for him. 'I hear you've been doing some competent writing on your own.'

'What?' he said, and his face seemed to be coming apart. He leaned to the side, away from me, and kept showing his teeth. 'What?'

'Competent writing,' I said. 'Good story. Told in letter-form. Wasn't that you? Sure it was.' I smiled down at him, and he leaned as far away as he could and almost fell out of his chair. I grabbed his shoulder and steadied him. 'Careful, Curt. You might get hurt.' I kept smiling at him, and his lips moved, and I thought he was going to cry. 'What's the matter?' I asked, and began pressing home the veiled threats. 'You look ready for the hospital. I think that's where you're headed, Curt. I really do.'

'What's that?' he whispered. He was so terrified I wondered how he'd ever worked up the nerve to send that letter. Probably done it in the white heat of anger. Now he'd had two or three days to worry himself into a state approaching hysteria. 'What's that, Harry? I don't get you. I – '

I grinned, shook my head and walked away. I went back to my desk, sat down and looked at him through the glass. He retreated behind his manuscript. A minute later he got up, rushed around the partition and out the door.

So he'd had his revenge, and I'd had mine, and the hell with it. Whatever punishment he deserved he'd mete out to himself. Maybe I'd help things along with an occasional hard look, but he'd do the real work.

I thought of Ellie, Debbie and my mother, and what would happen when Ellie finally realized I wasn't going to give an inch. She'd divorce me. She'd have to. I'd leave no other course open.

The noon whistle blew and I went downstairs. I walked to a bar on Lexington and 40th, entered the cool dimness and climbed on a stool. I ordered a Martini, figuring I'd have a sandwich at a luncheonette a little later. I downed the Martini fast, ordered another and lit a cigar. I sipped and smoked, and soon the potent gin-wine mixture had me feeling reasonably human. I was going to leave after that second drink, but the place was so dim and cool and pleasant and the street so hot and crowded and noisy. I had a third.

Three Martinis was one above my limit, especially for a workday lunch hour. I left that bar wrapped in cotton, my head thick and fuzzy, my feet barely touching the ground. As I came into the street I almost bumped into a tall, middle-aged blonde with huge breasts. She swiveled aside, and I said, 'Sorry, we almost had fun.' She kept walking, but then turned her head and smiled back at me.

I crossed the street, heading for the office. That blonde would have made for a pleasant evening or two. And so would the dark girl who was walking ahead of me, and the short one waiting near the hotel entrance, and the others – all the others who were young enough and reasonably attractive – all the women all over the city. It would be nice to sample a little of each. At least that's how I felt now. Later, I'd want only the hard-to-get ones. But still, just a sample of the others – just an evening or two.

That made me a bastard. That made me a real bad guy, a villain of books, plays, movies, radio and television. Even worse, because characters in stories are generally given strong *reason* for being unfaithful. The male character who plays around, or wants to play around, is usually married to a *bad* woman – at least she's bad in some way. She doesn't love him, or she's old, or she's unwilling to go to bed with him, or she's sick in the way a drunkard or gambler is sick, or she's two-timing him, or something – something bad. But Ellie wasn't bad. She was good, a good wife, capable and loving and understanding and faithful. And yet I wanted other women – I wanted *all* women right now; a crazy, driving need that ripped through me. I wanted! God, how I wanted! And I'd never have enough while feeling this way. So I was bad.

I crossed Madison, sweating under the broiling sun, wilting in the gasoline-filled air, shrinking from the bedlam of cars and trucks and people. I was sure I would feel this way – want all women – more and more often.

But why did I want? Why want so much more than I could possibly get? Why want quantities of women, and love, and sex adventures – quantities obviously out of reach?

239

For purposes of self-destruction, Moe would say. And he was right. He'd been right all along.

But a pretty girl passed and I wanted her anyway. I wanted her, and more. More!

I walked toward the office, churning inside, no longer relaxed by the liquor. I wanted everything, and wanted nothing, and felt I wouldn't be able to get through this day. I passed several luncheonettes, but couldn't make myself step inside and sit down with people and eat. I couldn't eat, period.

I returned to the office. Everyone but Ramona was out to lunch, and she was eating a sandwich at her desk. She glanced up and smiled at me, and I wondered how a thin little thing like that would be in bed. Probably a lot better than she looked. Probably excellent.

I sat down and worked on the layouts. At least I went through the motion of working. Actually, I was just moving my hands, tossing away sheet after sheet of drawing paper.

Later, Francine Loes and Mary Braken returned from lunch. Much later, Curt Sawyer came in and walked quickly around the partition to his desk. I looked at him, and he buried himself behind a manuscript. The manuscript trembled. He'd built himself a sweet little hell. Cowards shouldn't write poison-pen letters; but then again, who else would do such a thing?

At three o'clock Francine Loes got a telephone call. I wouldn't have noticed except that she said, 'Oh no!' in loud, shocked tones. We all looked at her, and we knew something was wrong by the way she leaned forward and put her free hand to her face and bit her lip. When she hung up she was crying. She said something to Ramona and Curt Sawyer, and then Ramona came around the partition.

I'd heard Moe's name. I wasn't sure, but what could create that reaction besides death?

Ramona stopped at my desk, and Mary Braken got up and came over to join us, and I said, 'Moe's pretty sick, eh?'

'He's dead,' she said, face pale, eyes excited. 'I gotta tell – ' She ran out the door.

'Good Lord,' Mary said, and went back to her desk. She sat down and slumped in her chair.

I went around the partition to Francine's desk, and Curt Sawyer walked away and out of the bullpen. Francine was wiping her eyes.

'I can't believe it,' she said. 'He died a few hours ago. His sister called Mr Lobert, and Mr Lobert's secretary just called me. Heart attack. He had one right here in the office last Tuesday. He had one right here and we didn't know – ' She shook her head and looked at me. 'I forgot. You're to call his sister. At his house. That's what Mr Lobert's secretary said. Have Harry Admer call Moe's sister.'

I nodded. I was sick, and I didn't want to call anyone, especially Moe's sister. Moe was dead. Moe had been dying all week long and I hadn't even called him. Moe had been dying last Tuesday, and I'd treated him so badly. But I'd been right to reject his friendship. I'd been right, but too late. I'd known him, and liked him, and so I was hurt. I didn't want that. But it was too late – as with my father.

It wouldn't be that way with anyone else! The pain would never come again, because I'd cut loose from family and friends and I'd be free of love and free of pain. Yes! The hell with this crummy life! Pain, and more pain, and then more pain.

It was better to die oneself. That way the pain took place only once, and then everything was over.

I couldn't think straight. I wondered how to free myself completely, and wondered how to die easily, and wondered how to call Moe's sister when I was afraid to.

What did she want with me? I didn't know her. Why did I have to get closer to the pain?

'He liked you,' Francine said. 'He liked you very much, Harry. Call his sister. I'm sure it's important.'

'Yes,' I said, and stood there.

She sighed, blew her nose and said, 'I wonder who'll take his place. It's quite a job. I'll bet he made over ten thousand.' She took out a compact and began fixing her face. 'Wish my boy friend knew the publishing line. I'd call him right now, and he'd come over – ' She went on daydreaming aloud, and she'd forgotten Moe Crown. Moe Crown was gone, and soon everyone would forget him.

I went back to my desk and sat down. I picked up the phone and dialed and waited while the ring sounded at the other end.

Moe was gone. Death was always close. Everyone died. The years were short; everyone's years; my years. Waiting for death was too much to bear. Why wait?

When Ellie had that infected hand two years ago the doctor had given her twelve Nembutal capsules to get her through the long, pain-filled nights. But she'd been afraid of them. She'd used only three. The small green bottle was still on the top shelf of the medicine chest. The label warned that no more than one capsule should be taken in any ten-hour period. The doctor had stressed the fact that a large dosage could be fatal.

If I bought a fifth of the best Scotch and sat on

the couch listening to music, and then took all nine capsules –

Of course, I wouldn't do it – but it would be such an easy way. I wouldn't have to wait for heart attacks, hemorrhages, cancer, auto accidents or any other kind of horror. I would fall asleep.

The bullpen seemed to darken. It was such a grim room. Every room was grim, and every street, and every place on earth. So grim. So terribly grim and unhappy.

Moe's phone kept ringing – six, seven, eight times. On the ninth ring a woman answered. I identified myself, and she said she was Moe's sister Zelda. Her voice was hoarse.

'Yes, he made me promise to give you something if anything happened to him. He made me promise. I didn't even want to consider he could die, but he – ' She choked and wept, and I waited. 'It's a letter,' she finally said. 'It's in an envelope – private. I'd like you to come over and pick it up now. He wanted you to have it right away if anything happened. And – and it happened.'

I mumbled something about being sorry, and she thanked me.

I left the office and took the subway to West End Avenue and the big apartment house. I rode up in the elevator and walked to Moe's door, and I remembered how I'd come here only two weeks ago, how Moe had been so alive and interesting and amusing, so worried about *me*.

Now he wasn't anything. Now he was cold meat. And my mother would follow. And other people. And me.

Scotch and music and nine Nembutal capsules and then sleep, sleep.

A tall, heavy, elderly man opened the door. I asked for Moe's sister Zelda, and he introduced himself as

Moe's brother-in-law Nathan. We walked into the living room. There were at least twenty people there, and all the women had red eyes and all the men had grim faces. A nice-looking woman, slim and spry as Moe had been, came over, shook my hand and introduced herself as Moe's sister. She looked at the closed bedroom door to the left of Moe's son's room, and she said, 'He's in there. He's sleeping in there.'

For a minute I thought she meant the son, but then she sobbed and covered her face with both hands, and I knew she meant Moe.

I felt I couldn't stand it, and prayed that she'd give me the note and let me get out. She wiped her eyes and said, 'Would you like to see him?'

I looked at that closed door, and it was the last place in the world I wanted to go, but I nodded. I would see him. I would see Moe Crown stilled forever. I would hammer the lesson home to my brain, and then I would be a step closer to my Scotch and music and sleep.

She led me across the crowded living room to the door. People looked at us, and it was suddenly very quiet. She opened the door and stepped ahead of me. I hesitated. My heart was thudding wildly. I was afraid. But I would see him, and remember, and know there was only one way to end the pain and fear.

I followed her into the large bedroom.

17

Moe was lying on the bed, a white sheet covering him to the neck, outlining his thin, still body. His face was pale, waxlike, with eyes slitted open, mouth closed hard and flat. His sister had said he was sleeping in here, and I'd thought he would look like a sleeping man. But he didn't. He looked like a dead man. Dull white showed behind those slitted eyes, the mouth was a thin line drawn in dust and the skin was ancient, lifeless, horrible.

I looked long at him, and the vastness of the change that had taken place in my friend overwhelmed me. He *was* my friend. Despite my attempts to antagonize him, to rid myself of him, he was my friend. I felt the terrible loss.

'Here,' his sister said, pressing something into my hand. 'The letter. He said I should give it to you. He had an attack in the office last Tuesday, but when he got home he felt all right. Then he had another the next morning and called a doctor, and almost died right then. But he pulled out, and the doctor felt there was a chance. He was going to enter the hospital this week end. He was going to – ' She cried again. 'This morning he looked fine. I was staying here, taking care of him and David. I said, "Moe, you look better, thank God." He smiled but he asked me for a pen and paper and something to write on – a board. He wrote this letter and put it in an envelope, sealed it and made me promise to give it to you. "Just in case anything happens," he said. So he must've known. He must've felt it. My brother. My friend and my brother – ' She turned, weeping, and left the room. She closed the door behind her.

I stood there, alone with Moe, and looked down at the envelope in my hand. My name was on it, in Moe's handwriting, the same handwriting that had outlined so many illustrations for me in the past four years.

I opened the envelope, took out three sheets of paper and unfolded them. The handwriting was the same, but as I read I noticed how weak it was, how it trembled and grew spiderish in spots.

Dear Harry,

When you read this, I'll be dead. Dramatic, isn't it? A good opening for a detective story. And then the hero goes on and solves the murder of his old friend. Only I'm not being murdered. Unless you call dying of a bad heart being murdered by life. Franz Kafka felt that way. If you've read his book, *The Trial*, you know what I mean.

I'd rather talk about Kafka than about myself. I'd rather talk about all sorts of things. But I've got to talk about myself, because that's the only way I can talk about you.

First of all, I know we're friends. Whatever you've tried to do, I know we're friends. And as your friend, I want you to live a full life, a good life. You're in trouble now. You're rushing into all sorts of things. You don't really want to live any more.

So I'm a bad psychiatrist. But I *feel* this, Harry. Don't brush me aside. I'll be melodramatic and say, Don't brush a dead man aside. I tell you that life is good. I'm dying and I say this. Life is good for many reasons, but let's pick the biggest – the biggest for people like you and me. Life is good because it's the only alternative to death.

I wish I could give you God, Harry. Jehovah or Christ or a belief in a First Cause. But I can't. Even though I'm facing death I haven't found God. And if I haven't found Him at this point I doubt if you will. We're alike in lots of ways, and I'm patting myself on the back when I say that. You think deeply – very deeply. It shows up in your awareness of death. I thought at first it was a pure and simple obsession based on the loss of your father, but now I know it's much more than that. What you have is a sensitivity, a grasping of the human situation. Don't let this sensitivity warp you, destroy you. Learn to live with it.

If you can think so deeply of death your mind is strong enough to move back to life. It figures, doesn't it?

There's so much to say, and there are so many other things I'm supposed to do. You know, there are unpaid bills that need my attention, and I should dig up my insurance policies – God knows where they are! I should talk to my sister about the payments on my car and whether or not to keep my daughter in that expensive school, and so many other things. But the hell with it. I'm done with it. My son will live with my sister, and that's all I care about – except for you. So I've put it all behind me and I'm talking to you.

I've got to tell you this – I'm afraid, Harry. I'm so afraid to die that my hands shake, and I want to beg someone. I cried twice this morning. But that's the way it should be. When the time comes a man should be afraid.

I wasn't afraid a week ago, the way you are. I didn't think of it day and night, and when I did it didn't bother me much.

You'll have to excuse the way this letter jumps around. I really should organize it and draw conclusions and make my points sharp and clear, even if it means writing two or three drafts. But I haven't the strength. And anyway, I have a hunch that no one ever organizes his thoughts too well on this topic.

You've got a lot to live for, and you *should* live. That's what I want to say – you *should* live. Your mind will take hold again, and this overconcentration on death will pass. You'll see – your wife and baby will become important again. Movies and ball games and books and plays and friends will be entertaining. Everything, and that includes pretty women, will take its proper place in your life. If you'll want a pretty woman then it'll be a healthy thing, not a means to self-destruction.

You've got to believe me. You've got to stop thinking of death. Give that mind of yours a chance to move upward again.

I like you, Harry. Maybe because David isn't the son I wanted. But that doesn't change the fact that I like *you*. And you'll like people again.

That's a point. The liking people have for each other is enough, in itself, to make life worth-while.

I know that because it made me write this letter to you, made you important enough to push aside my fear for a little while. Right now I'm more afraid for you than for myself. Honest. You've got to go on. It's important that we go on. It has to be. What else is there?

I'm very tired now, Harry. And yet I want to say more. There's always more to say.

You've focused on death. And when a person does that he really wants justification for living. Read what I've written, Harry, and find that justification. Read between the lines when I haven't been clear enough, clever enough, convincing enough. Add things, help my arguments along. Please.

Just stop being afraid, dammit! What is this death you fear so much for the people close to you and for yourself? At worst, a sleep.

Good-by. I like that last thought. I'm sick, and I'm afraid of death, but how bad can it be? At worst, a sleep.

Your friend,
Moe Crown

I folded the sheets of paper, put them back in the envelope and put the envelope in my inside jacket pocket. If I'd had a safety pin I'd have pinned the pocket closed as if I were carrying a thousand bucks. I was stunned at the meaning of that letter. He'd thought enough of me to write me while he was dying!

Tremendous! Fantastic and tremendous!

And he'd said so much. He'd said so many things lingering beneath the surface of my own mind, things blocked out in the past months.

I moved close to the bed and looked down at his face. I wanted to thank him for his friendship, his unbelievable kindness. But he wasn't there, and I couldn't convince myself he was, so I turned away.

I walked through the crowded living room and left without anyone stopping me. I took the subway back to the office and worked the remaining forty-five minutes, worked mechanically. I wasn't thinking of anything. I was tired, very tired.

I took the subway home at five, walked to my car and drove to my mother's. She greeted me, asked how my week end had been. I satisfied her with, 'Fine, Mom.'

After dinner, I told her Moe had died and that he'd been my friend and that I hoped she wouldn't expect me to be bright and cheerful. She was shocked and expressed sympathy, and then the boarders came in. I said hello to them and went to my room. I stayed there, reading an old magazine, until it grew dark outside. Then I walked through the empty apartment, went downstairs and nodded at my mother and the boarders on the porch. I got into my car and drove to the Belt. I drove all the way out to Hempstead and back. I drove slowly, listening to music, smoking a cigar.

I returned to my mother's at eleven-thirty, and she was waiting in the kitchen. We had tea, and I asked for the boarders. She said they were in bed. I said they had the right idea, kissed my mother good-night, and went to wash up. In the bathroom I took out Moe's letter and read it again. I went to my room, undressed, got into bed.

I slept without dreaming.

I stayed with my mother the next day, and on Wednesday I went to the office and did my work. Moe's replacement was brought in Thursday morning. He was a tall, heavy, ruddy-faced man with thick gray hair. He looked like the Hollywood version of an editorial executive, but he knew his business and had things running smoothly in no time at all. I didn't have anything to do with him because I still had my last assignment, but I felt I liked him. Everyone liked him.

I ate well and slept well those three days following

249

Moe's death. I didn't think well because I seemed to be tired most of the time. But I was able to do my work, and I was able to read Moe's letter at least once a day.

On Friday I sat at my desk and looked into myself and wondered what was happening. At noon I went down to the lobby cigar-stand, bought a straight Havana and stood there smoking it. I began to feel something – as if I were waking from a heavy sleep. I felt all sorts of things, and nothing. It was strange as hell. There was no violent change, but I was thinking again – thinking of Ellie and wincing at the memory of what I'd said to her and what I'd failed to say to her.

And then I wanted to see her, and the baby, and my mother, and Mort and Laura Brenner. I wanted to talk to the people I loved, and my friends, and maybe even some old friends I hadn't seen in a long time.

I was waking up. And yet, nothing had changed in me, nothing that I could put my finger on. I was finished with Louise, but I would still get hungry for new women once in a while; I was sure of that. I still missed my father, and remembered the horror of seeing him in that police-station driveway. I still felt the sickness and horror of the other deaths I'd witnessed. I missed Moe, and the pain of losing him was fresh and sharp.

So nothing had changed.

But I looked across the lobby toward the doors, and the sun was bright outside, and there was that smell of summer even here in the heart of Manhattan. That hot, growing, sleepy, alive smell of summer.

I still knew that I would die. I'd reached the point in my life where I couldn't help but know it. I was aware of my own mortality.

So nothing had changed.

Only I wasn't worried about my mortality; and the

thought itself didn't mean anything. I was young. I had plenty of time. Accidents didn't happen to people who looked out for themselves. And I was going to do that from now on! No more drinking except on social occasions, and not too much even then. I'd get out in the fresh air more often. I'd exercise regularly . . .

I laughed at myself. The guy behind the cigar-stand looked at me, grinned and said, 'Think of something funny?'

I nodded, stepped into the phone booth nearby, put through a call to the lake. I talked to Ellie, found myself crying and heard her crying with me. I begged her to forgive me, to go on loving me. I said I'd be up at the cabin that evening and tell her everything. She didn't discuss it, just whispered that the baby missed me and wanted to talk to me, and would I say hello. I did, and Debbie asked me to bring her a present and I promised her a beautiful doll. Then Ellie was back on the line, and we said good-by and she added, 'Harry, take care of yourself. Don't – don't worry, honey. I – I always knew – ' She said good-by again and hung up.

I ate a pretty good lunch, returned to the office, sat at my desk and worked. I looked around a few times. I watched the new man at Moe's desk, and Francine Loes, and Ramona, and Mary Braken and Curt Sawyer. I saw Curt shrivel under my eyes, and felt sorry for him, and wondered how long he'd be able to take working here with me. His fear and shame would drive him out – at least the odds stacked up that way. Unless, of course, I found myself a better job. Which I might.

Mary Braken told me a sexy joke, and I laughed, worked again and thought what a crazy life it was. I thought how people had died a million years ago and been buried, and new people had been born and buried,

251

and on and on until now so many had died that the whole Earth was a cemetery and the living walked on the dead. We stepped on the dead no matter where we went, and it was a terrible thought, and it didn't mean a thing.

At worst, a sleep.

Those words, Moe's words, were with me. I felt they would always be with me. I felt he'd saved my life.

Maybe it wasn't just Moe and his letter. Maybe I'd reached the end of my mourning period – the natural point of turning toward hope and life.

Life is the only alternative to death.

That was a philosophy to live by . . .

Later, Louise came through and spoke to the new man. He raised his big, handsome face and she glowed. He said something, and she giggled. She walked away with hips swinging, and he turned in his chair to stare after her.

I wished him luck.

At four-thirty Vince delivered a bundle of proof to Francine Loes. As he passed my desk on his way back he said, 'Yanks just took a close one from Detroit – three-two. Man, they look like they're going all the way!'

It made me happy.